FIRE STORM

ANDREW LANE

MACMILLAN CHILDREN'S BOOKS

First published 2011 by Macmillan Children's Books

This edition published 2012 by Macmillan Children's Books
a division of Macmillan Publishers Limited
20 New Wharf Road, London N1 9RR
Basingstoke and Oxford
Associated companies throughout the world
www.panmacmillan.com

ISBN 978-0-330-53796-4

1 3 5 7 9 8 6 4 2

A CIP catalogue record for this book is available from
the British Library.

Typeset by Nigel Hazle
Printed and bound by CPI Group (UK) Ltd, Croydon CR0 4YY

www.youngsherlock.com

Dedicated to the memory of my father, Jack Lane,
who passed away while I was writing this book.
Rest in peace, Dad.

And with grateful acknowledgements to: the lovely
people from the Scottish Children's Book Trust
(who kind of gave me the idea of setting a book in
Edinburgh without ever actually saying so); the guys
from the Book Zone for Boys in Ireland (who probably
deserve to have a book set there as well); Helen Palmer
for mentioning Mary King's Close; Polly Nolan for
editing so comprehensively and sensitively; Nathan,
Jessica and Naomi Gay for being so interested; and to
Jessica Dean, who made sure that this series of books
got the highest level of visibility.

PROLOGUE

The small Chinaman held the needle in steady fingers and dipped the point in the bottle of ink that sat on the table in front of him. Next to the ink rested the forearm of the sailor who was sitting in a chair on the other side of the table. It was huge – like a ham on a butcher's slab.

'You sure you want blue anchor?' the Chinaman said. His name was Kai Lung. His face was lined with age and the plait of hair that hung down his back was the colour of ash.

'I told ya,' the sailor said, 'I want an anchor! Cos I live on a ship, an' I work on a ship, right?'

'I could do a fish,' Kai Lung said quietly. Anchors were easy. They were also boring. He seemed to spend half his life tattooing blue anchors on the muscular forearms of sailors, sometimes with the name of their sweetheart beneath, inside a nice scroll. The problem was that he seemed to spend the other half of his life turning the tattooed names of *former* sweethearts into other things – barbed wire, flowers, anything that might disguise the underlying letters. 'I could do you a nice fish, maybe a goldfish with scales all the colours of a rainbow. You like that idea? Fish tattoo good for sailor, yes?'

'I want an anchor,' the man said stubbornly.

1

'Fine. Yes. Anchor it is.' He sighed. 'You got any special type of anchor in mind, or just the usual?'

The sailor frowned. 'How many different types of anchor are there?'

'Usual anchor it is then.'

He prepared to make the first mark with the needle. The ink would flow into the small pinprick in the sailor's arm and stain the underlying tissue. The skin on the outside of the arm would fade, change and tan over the years, but the ink would always remain there, beneath the skin. With enough small pinpricks and enough different colours of ink he could draw anything – a fish, a dragon, a heart . . . or a blue anchor. Another blue anchor.

The door burst open, pushed hard from the other side. It hit the wall, the handle on the inside leaving a dent in the exposed brickwork. A man stood in the doorway. He was so tall and so wide that there wasn't much space on either side of him or above his shaven head. His clothes were rough and dirty. They looked as if he'd been travelling in them for some time, and possibly sleeping in them as well.

'You,' he growled in an American accent, looking at the sailor, 'out!' He jerked a thumb over his shoulder, just in case the instruction wasn't clear.

'Hey! I got an appointment!' The sailor stood up, clenching his fists ready for a fight. He took a step forward, towards the doorway. The man who had pushed the

2

door open stepped forward. The top of the sailor's head barely came up to his chin. Without looking away from the sailor's eyes, the man reached out with his left hand and took hold of the metal handle on the outside of the door. He squeezed. For a moment nothing happened, and then with a sad heart Kai Lung saw that the handle was bending and twisting under the pressure. Within a few seconds it looked more like crumpled paper than metal.

'Fair enough,' the sailor said. 'There's other tattoo parlours around.'

The newcomer stepped to one side and the sailor pushed past him without looking back.

'You lose me customer,' Kai Lung said. He wasn't scared of the newcomer. He was so old and he had seen so much in his long life that he wasn't scared of anything much. Death was an old friend by now. 'I hope you bring me other customer to replace him.'

The man stepped back, out of the way, and another man entered the tiny front room of Kai Lung's lodgings. This man was smaller and better dressed than his herald, and he was holding a walking stick. A wave of coldness seemed to enter the room with him. A feeling swept over Kai Lung, and it took him a moment to work out what it was.

Fear. It was fear.

'You want tattoo?' he said, trying to keep his voice from quavering.

'I would like a tattoo on my forehead,' the man said. His accent was American as well. 'It is a name, a woman's name.' His voice was calm and precise. The light from behind him put his face in shadow, but in the meagre illumination from Kai Lung's oil lamp the head of the walking stick gleamed. Kai Lung thought for a moment that it was a large, rough chunk of solid gold, and he drew his breath in, amazed, but he suddenly realized what it was. The head of the walking stick was carved in the shape of a human skull.

'You want sweetheart's name on *forehead*?' Kai Lung asked. 'Most people want sweetheart's name on arm, or maybe chest – near heart.'

'The girl is not my "sweetheart",' the man said. His voice was still calm, still precise, but there was a tone somewhere deep inside it that made Kai Lung shiver. 'And yes, I want her name tattooed on my forehead, near to my brain, so that I can remember it. Your work had better be accurate. I do not tolerate mistakes.'

'I am best tattooist in whole city!' Kai Lung said proudly.

'So I have heard. That is why I am here.'

Kai Lung sighed. 'What is name of girl?'

'I have written it down. Do you read English?'

'I read very well.'

The man reached out his left hand. He was holding a piece of paper. Kai Lung took it carefully, trying not to touch the man's skin. He looked at the name on the

4

scrap. It was printed in a careful hand, and he had no trouble deciphering it.

'Virginia Crowe,' he read. 'Is that right?'

'That is exactly right.'

'What colour you want?' Kai Lung asked. He was expecting the man to say 'blue', but he was surprised.

'Red,' the man said. 'I want it in red. The colour of blood.'

CHAPTER ONE

'Stop it!' Rufus Stone cried out. 'You're *killing* me!'

Sherlock lifted the bow from the violin strings. 'Don't be so melodramatic.'

'I'm not being melodramatic – another few seconds of that and my heart would have leaped out of my throat and strangled me just to ensure that it didn't have to experience that cat-squalling any more!'

Sherlock felt his confidence shrivel up like a dry autumn leaf. 'I didn't think it was that bad,' he protested.

'That's the problem,' Stone said. 'You don't know what the problem *is*. If you don't know what the problem is, you can't fix it.'

He rubbed the back of his neck and wandered away, obviously struggling to find a way to explain to Sherlock just what he was doing wrong. He was wearing a loose striped shirt with the sleeves roughly rolled up and a waistcoat that seemed to have come from a decent suit, but his trousers were rough corduroy and his boots were scuffed leather. He swung round to look at Sherlock for a moment, and there was a kind of wild bafflement in his face, along with what Sherlock realized with a sickening twist of his heart was *disappointment*.

Sherlock turned away, not wanting to see that expression in the face of a man he considered a friend as well as a kind of older brother.

He let his gaze roam around the room they were in – anywhere so that he didn't have to look at Stone. They were in the attic of an old building in Farnham. Stone rented a room on the floor below, but his landlady had taken a shine to him and let him rehearse and practise his violin – and teach the one music student he had so far taken on – in the expansive attic area.

The space was large and dusty, with beams of sunlight penetrating through gaps in the tiles and forming diagonal braces that seemed to be holding the triangular roof up just as well as the wooden ones. The acoustics, according to Stone, were marginally worse than a hay barn, but considerably better than his room. There were boxes and trunks stacked around the low walls, and a hatchway off to one side that led down, via a ladder, to the upper landing. Navigating the ladder with a violin and bow clutched in one hand was tricky, but Sherlock liked the isolation of the attic and the sense of space.

One day, he thought, I will have my own place to live – somewhere I can retreat from the world and not be bothered. And I won't let anyone else in.

Pigeons fluttered outside, blocking the sunlight momentarily as they roosted. Cold penetrated the attic from the street, fingers of frosty air finding their way through the spaces between the tiles.

He sighed. The violin felt heavy in his hand, and somehow clumsy, as if he had never picked one up before. The music stand in front of him held the score of a piece by Mozart – a violin transcription, according to Stone, of a famous aria called 'The Queen of the Night's Song' from an opera called *The Three Oranges*. The black notes captured between the lines of the staves were, as far as Sherlock was concerned, like a code, but it was a code he had quickly worked out – a simple substitution cipher. A black blob on *that* line always meant a note that sounded like *this* – unless there was a small hash in front of it that raised it slightly to a 'sharp', or a small angular letter 'b' that lowered it slightly to a 'flat'. A sharp or a flat was halfway towards the note either directly above or directly below the one he was playing. It was simple and easy to understand – so why couldn't he turn the written music into something that Rufus Stone could listen to without wincing?

Sherlock knew he wasn't progressing as quickly as Stone would have liked, and that irked him. He would have liked to have been able just to pick up the instrument and play it beautifully, first time and every time, but sadly life wasn't like that. It *should* be, he thought rebelliously. He remembered feeling the same way about the piano that sat in his family home. He'd spent hours sitting at it, trying to work out why he couldn't play it straight away. After all, the thing about a piano was its relentless logic: you pressed a key and a note came out.

The same key led to the same note every time. All you had to do, surely, was remember which key led to which note and you should be able to play. The trouble was, no matter how hard he had thought about it, he had never been able to sit down and play the piano like his sister could – flowing and beautiful, like a rippling stream.

Four strings! The violin only had four strings! How hard could it be?

'The problem,' Stone said suddenly, turning round and staring at Sherlock, 'is that you are playing the notes, not the tune.'

'That doesn't make any sense,' Sherlock responded defensively.

'It makes perfect sense.' Stone sighed. 'The trees are not the forest. The forest is all of the trees, taken together, plus the undergrowth, the animals, the birds and even the air. Take all that away and you just have a load of wood – no feeling, no *atmosphere*.'

'Then where does the *feeling* come from in music?' Sherlock asked plaintively.

'Not from the notes.'

'But the notes are all that's on the paper!' Sherlock protested.

'Then add something of your own. Add some emotion.'

'But *how*?'

Stone shook his head. 'It's the small gaps you put in – the hesitations, the subtle emphases, the slight speedings up and slowings down. *That's* where the feeling lives.'

Sherlock gestured at the music on the stand. 'But that's not written on there! If the composer wanted me to speed up or slow down then he would have written it on the music.'

'He did,' Stone pointed out, 'in Italian. But that's only a guide. You need to decide how *you* want to play the music.' He sighed. 'The problem is that you're treating this like an exercise in mathematics, or grammar. You want all the evidence set out for you, and you think that your job is to put it all together. Music isn't like that. Music requires interpretation. It requires you to put something of yourself in there.' He hesitated, trying to find the right words. 'Any performance is actually a duet between you and the composer. He's given you the bulk, but you have to add the final ten per cent. It's the difference between reading out a story and *acting* out a story.' Seeing the forlorn expression on Sherlock's face, he went on: 'Look, have you ever seen the writer Charles Dickens reading one of his own stories to an audience? Try it sometime – it's well worth the cost of a ticket. He does different voices for different characters, he throws himself around the stage, he speeds up at the exciting bits and he reads it as if he's never seen it before and he's just as keen as the audience to find out what happens. *That* is how you should play music – as if you've never heard it before.' He paused and winced. 'In a good way,

I mean. The trouble is that you play music as if you've never heard it before and you're trying to work it out as you're going along.'

That was pretty much the way it was, Sherlock thought.

'Should I give up?' he asked.

'Never give up,' Stone rejoined fiercely. '*Never*. Not in *anything*.' He ran a hand through his long hair again. 'Perhaps I've been going at this the wrong way. Let's take a different tack. All right, you approach music as if it's a problem in mathematics – well, let's look for musicians who write mathematics into their music.'

'Are there any?' Sherlock asked dubiously.

Stone considered for a moment. 'Let's think. Johann Sebastian Bach was well known for putting mathematical tricks and codes into his tunes. If you look at his *Musical Offering* there's pieces in there which are mirror images of themselves. The first note and the last note are the same; the second note and the second from last note are the same; and so on, right to the middle of the piece.'

'Wow.' Sherlock was amazed at the audacity of the idea. 'And it still works as music?'

'Oh yes. Bach was a consummate composer. His mathematical tricks don't detract from the music – they add to it.' Stone smiled, realizing that he'd finally snagged Sherlock's attention. 'I'm not an expert on Bach by any means, but I understand there's another piece by him which is built around some kind of mathematical sequence, where one number leads on to the next using some rule. It's got an Italian name. Now, let's try that Mozart again, but this time, as you're playing it, I want you to bring back those feelings. *Remember* them, and let them guide your fingers.'

Sherlock raised the violin to his shoulder again, tucking it into the gap between his neck and his chin. He let the fingers of his left hand find the strings at the end of the neck. He could feel how hard his fingertips had become under Stone's relentless tutelage. He brought the bow up and held it poised above the strings.

'Begin!' Stone said.

Sherlock gazed at the notes on the page, but rather than trying to *understand* them he let his gaze slide *through* them, looking at the page as a whole rather than each note as something individual. Looking at the wood, not the trees. He remembered from a few minutes before what the notes were, then took a deep breath and started to play.

The next few moments seemed to go past in a blur. His fingers moved from one string to the next, pressing them down to make the right notes, fractionally before his brain could send his fingers a signal to *tell* them what the right notes were. It was as if his body already knew what to do, freeing his mind to float above the music, looking for its meaning. He tried to think of the piece as if someone was singing it, and let his violin become the

12

voice, hesitating on some notes, coming down heavily on others as if to emphasize their importance.

He got to the end of the page without even realizing.

'Bravo!' Stone cried. 'Not perfect, but better. You actually persuaded me that you were feeling the music, not just playing it.' He gazed over at the slanted rays of sunlight that penetrated the loft. 'Let's stop it there: on a high note, as it were. Keep practising your scales, but also I want you to practise individual notes. Play a sustained note in different ways – with sadness, with happiness, with anger. Let the emotion seep through into the music, and see how it changes the note.'

'I'm . . . not good with emotion,' Sherlock admitted in a quiet voice.

'I am,' Stone said quietly. 'Which means I can help.' He placed a hand on Sherlock's shoulder for a moment and squeezed, then took it away. 'Now be off with you. Go and find that American girl and spend some time with her.'

'Virginia?' His heart quickened at the thought, but he wasn't sure if it was happiness or terror that made it speed up. 'But—'

'No buts. Just go and see her.'

'All right,' Sherlock said. 'Same time tomorrow?'

'Same time tomorrow.'

He threw the violin into its case and half climbed, half slid down the ladder to the upper landing, then thudded down the stairs to the ground floor. Stone's landlady – a woman of about Stone's own age, with black hair and green eyes – came out of the kitchen to say something as he ran past, but he didn't catch what it was. Within seconds he was out in the crisp, cold sunlight.

Farnham was as busy as it ever was: its cobbled or muddy streets filled with people heading every which way on various errands. Sherlock paused for a moment, taking in the scene – the clothes, the postures, the various packages, boxes and bags that people were carrying – and tried to make sense of it. That man over there – the one with the red rash across his forehead. He was clutching a piece of paper in his hand as if his life depended on it. Sherlock knew that there was a doctor's surgery a few minutes' walk behind him, and a pharmacy just ahead. He was almost certainly heading to pick up some medicine after his consultation. The man on the other side of the road – good clothes, but unshaven and bleary-eyed, and his shoes were scuffed and muddy. A tramp wearing a suit donated by a church parishioner, perhaps? And what of the woman who passed by right in front of him, hand held up to push the hair from her eyes? Her hands looked older than she did – white and wrinkled, as if they had spent a long time in water. A washerwoman, obviously.

Was this what Rufus Stone had meant about seeing the wood instead of the trees? He wasn't looking at the people as people, but seeing their histories and their possible futures all in one go.

14

For a moment Sherlock felt dizzy with the scale of what he was staring at, and then the moment was gone and the scene collapsed into a crowd of people heading in all directions.

'You all right?' a voice asked. 'I thought you were goin' to pass out there for a moment.'

Sherlock turned to find Matthew Arnatt – Matty – standing beside him. The boy was smaller than Sherlock, and a year or two younger, but for a second Sherlock didn't see him as a boy, as his friend, but as a collection of signs and indications. Just for a second, and then he was Matty again – solid, dependable Matty.

'Albert isn't well then,' he said, referring to the horse that Matty owned, and which pulled the narrowboat he lived on whenever he decided to change towns.

'What makes you think that?' Matty asked.

'There's hay in your sleeve,' Sherlock pointed out. 'You've been feeding him by hand. Usually you just let him crop the grass wherever he happens to be tied up. You wouldn't feed a horse by hand unless you were worried he wasn't eating properly.'

Matty raised an eyebrow. 'Just because I sometimes likes to give 'im 'is grub,' he said, 'there's no need to make a song an' dance about it. Albert's the closest thing to family I got.' He shrugged, embarrassed. 'So I likes to treat 'im sometimes wiv somethin' special.'

'Oh.' Sherlock filed that away for later consideration. 'How did you know I was here?' he asked eventually.

'I could hear you playing,' Matty replied laconically. 'The whole town could hear you playing. I think that's why Albert's off his food.'

'Funny,' Sherlock observed.

'You want to go get some lunch? There's plenty of stuff goin' spare in the market.'

Sherlock thought for a moment. Should he spend some time with Matty, or go and see Virginia?

'Can't,' he said, suddenly remembering. 'My uncle said he wanted me back for lunch. Something about getting me to catalogue and index a collection of old sermons he recently obtained at an auction.'

'Oh joy,' Matty said. 'Have fun with that.' He smiled. 'Maybe *I* could go and see Virginia instead.'

'And maybe I could hang you upside down from a bridge with your head under water up to your nose,' Sherlock replied.

Matty just gazed at him. 'I was only jokin',' he said.

'I wasn't.'

Sherlock noticed that Matty's gaze kept sliding away, down the road towards the market. 'Go on,' he said. 'Go and pick up some bruised fruit and broken pies. I might see you later. Or tomorrow.'

Matty flashed a quick smile of thanks and scooted away, ducking and diving through the crowd until he was lost from sight.

Sherlock walked for a while along the road that led out of Farnham and towards his aunt and uncle's house.

Every time a cart came past he turned to look at the driver, but most of them avoided his gaze. He didn't take it personally – he'd been doing this for long enough that he knew the success rate was around one in twenty carts. Eventually one of the drivers looked over at him and called: 'Where you going, sonny?'

'Holmes Manor,' he shouted back.

'They don't take on casual labour.'

'I know. I'm . . . visiting someone.'

'Climb aboard then. I'm going past the main gates.'

As Sherlock threw his violin up the side of the still-moving cart and clambered up after it, falling into a deep mass of hay, he wondered why it was that he still didn't like admitting where he lived. Perhaps he was worried that people might change their attitude if they knew that his family were part of the local land-owning gentry. It was so stupid, he thought, that something as simple as inheriting land and a house from your parents could set you apart from other people. When he grew up he would make sure that he never made social distinctions between people like that.

The cart clattered along the road for twenty minutes or so before Sherlock jumped off, calling a cheerful 'Thanks!' over his shoulder. He checked his watch. He had half an hour before luncheon: just enough time to wash and perhaps change his shirt.

Luncheon was, as usual, a quiet affair. Sherlock's uncle – Sherrinford Holmes – spent his time balancing eating with reading a book and trying to move his beard out of the way of both his food and the text, while his aunt – Anna – spoke in a continuous monologue that covered her plans for the garden, how pleased she was that the two sides of the Holmes family appeared to be on speaking terms again, various items of gossip about local landowners and her hope that the weather in the coming year would be better than the one that had just passed. Once or twice she asked Sherlock a question about what he was doing or how he was feeling, but when he tried to answer he found that she had just kept on talking regardless of what he might say. As usual.

He did notice that Mrs Eglantine – the manor's darkly glowering housekeeper – was conspicuous by her absence. The maids served the food with their customary quiet deference, but the black-clad presence who usually stood over by the window, half hidden by the light that streamed through, was missing. He wondered briefly where she was, and then realized with a flash of pleasure that he just didn't care.

Sherlock finished his food faster than his aunt and uncle and asked if he could be excused.

'Indeed you may,' his uncle said without looking up from his book. 'I have left a pile of old sermons on the desk in my library. I would be obliged, young man, if you could sort them into piles depending on their author, and then arrange the individual piles by date.

I am attempting,' he said, raising his eyes momentarily and gazing at Sherlock from beneath bushy brows, 'to catalogue the growth and development of schisms within the Christian church, with particular reference to the recent creation of the Church of Jesus Christ of Latter-day Saints in America. These sermons should prove very useful in that respect.'

'Thank you,' Sherlock said, and left the table.

Uncle Sherrinford's library smelled of old, dry books, mildew, leather bindings and pipe tobacco. Sherlock felt the quietness as something almost physical as the door closed behind him: an actual pressure against his ears.

Sherrinford's desk was piled high with loose papers of various sizes and thickness. Some were typed, some handwritten in various different styles; most were bound with ribbons or string. As he sat down, not without a tremor of nerves, in Sherrinford's creaking leather chair, Sherlock realized with a sinking feeling in his heart that the piles were taller than he was, and blocked his view of the rest of the library. This was going to be a long and tedious task.

He set to it. The process was simple on the face of it – take a manuscript from the nearest pile, find out who wrote it and when and then place it on one of a number of separate piles on the floor behind him – but of course it wasn't as straightforward as that. Some of the sermons didn't have an author named anywhere in them, some weren't dated, and some had neither date nor name. Sherlock realized quickly that he had to make his judgements based on other clues. Handwriting was one of them. Some of the sermons were obviously written by the same person, based on the jagged, spidery text, and Sherlock could happily place them all in one pile. Other sermons mentioned particular places – churches, usually – which meant he could place them in at least the same geographical area and thus probably assign them to the same person or group of people. After a while he realized that some of the typewritten sermons had the same characteristics – a faded n, a partially raised a – which suggested to him that they might have been typed on the same machine, so he put them together in a pile as well. He didn't actually read the sermons in any detail – that would have wasted a lot of time that he couldn't afford – but as he flicked through them looking for indications of ownership and date he still managed to pick up a smattering of details: the ebb and flow of life of the countryside, the unsatisfied yearning for the love of God, the detailed analysis of things that were, in the end, unknowable. He also thought he had an understanding of the characters of the men writing the sermons – one of them serious and dour, terrified of eternal hellfire, another wide-eyed at the beauty of God's creation, a third focused on details and minutiae and completely missing the wider context. At least one, he thought, was a woman writing sermons for her husband to deliver.

All in all, the work kept him busy for a good hour or two, during which he remained undisturbed.

After a while he decided to take a break and stretch his aching back. He stood up and wandered away from the desk, amazed at the way the piles of papers didn't seem to be any smaller despite the fact that he had some fourteen or fifteen other piles on the floor around the desk by now.

Sherlock found himself wandering along the shelves of his uncle's books, letting his eyes idly scan the titles. For a while he wasn't sure what he was looking for, or even if he was looking for anything at all, but then it occurred to him that he could check to see if his uncle had any books on Bach, or music in general. Maybe he could find out some details on the way composers used mathematics in their music. Although Sherrinford Holmes spent his time writing sermons and other religious tracts for vicars and bishops around the country, his library was more than just a repository of books on Christianity. He had a good selection of works on virtually every subject under the sun.

And, Sherlock reminded himself, Johann Sebastian Bach *was* a noted composer of religious music. He had certainly written a lot of material for the church organ, and Sherlock was fairly sure that he had seen the composer's name attached to various hymns in the church hymnals at Deepdene School for Boys, as well as in the local church. It would make sense for a religious author to have books about Bach in his collection.

Sherlock moved deeper into the shadowy lines of bookcases, looking for anything to do with music. He was out of sight of the door when he heard it open. He assumed it was his uncle, and moved back towards the light to tell him how far the work had progressed, but when he emerged from the aisle between two bookcases he was just in time to see the black bustle of a crinoline skirt vanishing behind a case on the far side of the room.

Mrs Eglantine? What was she doing here?

She seemed to know exactly where she was going. Confused, Sherlock edged closer, keeping as quiet as he could. He wasn't sure why, but he had a feeling that she was doing something covert, secretive, and didn't want anyone to know. She certainly wasn't dusting the bookshelves – that task was below her station, reserved for one of the parlour maids.

Sherlock looked around the edge of the bookcase, keeping most of his head and all of his body hidden. It *was* Mrs Eglantine. She was kneeling down about halfway along the row of shelves, her crinoline skirt spread out around her, pulling out whole handfuls of books and letting them fall to the carpet. A part of Sherlock's mind winced to see the books so carelessly treated, some of them lying open with their pages bent or their spines creased. Once she had cleared them out she bent even further down, head close to the carpet, and scanned the space she had created. Whatever she was looking for wasn't there. With a *huff* of disappointment she quickly stuffed the books back again, apparently not caring what order they had been in or whether she was putting them back upside down or back to front.

She gazed to her left, away from Sherlock. Alerted, he ducked back just as her head began to swing his way. He knew it was fanciful, but he could almost see the intensity of her gaze scorching the carpet and disturbing the dust.

He counted to twenty and looked back just as he heard an irregular thumping noise start up. Satisfied that she wasn't being observed, she was sweeping another row of books, higher up this time, off their shelf and letting them fall to the floor. Again she looked carefully into the space before grimacing in disappointment and shoving the books back pell-mell.

'How dare you enter my library!' a voice cried. 'Get out of here this instant!'

Sherlock looked up, shocked. There, at the other end of the line of bookcases, was Sherrinford Holmes. He must have come in quietly, without either Sherlock or Mrs Eglantine noticing.

Mrs Eglantine straightened up slowly. 'You are a fool,' she said, slowly and distinctly. 'You have no authority in this house – not any more. *I* am in charge here.'

CHAPTER TWO

Sherlock felt his breath catch in his throat. How *dare* she talk to his uncle like that! The feeling was followed by a sudden flash of joy: she could not survive this. She would be gone from the house within the hour, and never mourned.

Sherrinford Holmes's fist was clenched against his leg, but the expression on his face was not anger. It was more like a powerless frustration than the justified rage of a man who had found a servant riffling through his possessions. Sherlock waited for his uncle to explode with fury, to fire Mrs Eglantine immediately, banish her from the house with no references, but instead he just shook his head while his fist beat ineffectually against his thigh. 'You have no *right!*' he cried.

'I have every right,' Mrs Eglantine retorted. 'I have any right I want in this house, any right I wish to exercise, because you and that insufferable wife of yours know what will happen if you *ever* cross me.'

'Y-you are a wicked, evil woman,' Sherrinford Holmes stammered. He couldn't seem to meet Mrs Eglantine's gaze. Instead he stared down at the carpet, and Sherlock was stunned to see his eyes filling up with tears.

Mrs Eglantine stepped very slowly and precisely along

the aisle between the shelves until she was standing in front of Sherlock's uncle. She was smaller than him, but the way he stooped and the way she held herself made it seem as if she towered over him.

'You pathetic fool!' she spat. She reached up with a hand and took his chin between her thumb and fingers. Sherlock, watching appalled from the shadows, could see the indentations she caused in his cheeks. 'You sit here, day after day, writing meaningless words for equally pathetic and deluded fools around the country to repeat like parrots, and you think – you actually *think* – that you are doing something worthy of praise. It means nothing, old man. I should bring it all crashing down around you, just to show you how little the world would care if it all stopped. I could, you know. With what I know, I could ruin this family.'

'Then why do you hesitate?' Sherrinford asked, voice muffled by the fingers that were clenched across his face.

Mrs Eglantine paused and opened her mouth, but no answer came out.

'You cannot,' Sherrinford Holmes continued. 'If you were to reveal what you know then yes, my family would be ruined, but you would lose access to this house, and then where would you be? You have spent a year or more searching it, from top to bottom and side to side. I do not know what you are searching for, but I know how important it must be for you, and I know that you will never do anything that might imperil your search.'

'I think you do know what I am searching for,' she said scornfully, releasing him. 'And I think it's here, in this library. That's why you sit here, day after day, like some old hen brooding over a batch of eggs that will never hatch. But I've searched everywhere else, and I know it has to be here, in this room.'

'Get out,' Sherrinford said, 'or I *will* dismiss you, and God protect me from the consequences. I *will* dismiss you, just to end this nightmare, and to know that I have prevented you from finding whatever pathetic treasure you think might be here.'

Mrs Eglantine stalked past him, heading for the door. As she got to the end of the row, she turned to face him. Twin spots of bright colour burned like coals in the otherwise glacially white surface of her face. 'You cannot get rid of me without consequences,' she hissed. 'And I cannot dispose of you without consequences. The question is, who fears those consequences the most?' She turned to go, but then turned back. 'I require you to get rid of that pathetic nephew of yours,' she added. 'Get rid of him. Send him away.'

'Does he scare you?' Sherrinford asked. 'Are you worried that he will uncover your true position in this house and do something about it?'

'What *can* he do? He is only a boy. Worse than that, he is only a Holmes.' With that she turned and left. A few moments later Sherlock heard the door to the library open and shut.

'She *is* scared of you,' Sherrinford said quietly. It took a moment before Sherlock realized that his uncle was speaking to him. Somehow he knew that Sherlock was there.

'I don't understand,' he said, emerging into the aisle and the light.

'There is no reason why you should.' His uncle shook his head as if it had suddenly become very heavy. 'Forget what you have seen. Forget what you have heard. Put it from your mind. Pretend, as I will, that there is no trouble in this house and that everything is calm and serene in the sight of God. Pretend that the serpent that is Satan has not slithered into our midst.'

'But Uncle . . .'

Sherrinford frowned and held up a thin hand. 'No,' he said with finality, 'I will discuss this no longer. It will never be discussed again.' He sighed. 'I would ask you how far you have got with the cataloguing of sermons, but I find myself tired. I will rest for a while, here in the peace of my *sanctum sanctorum*.' He gazed at the disarrayed books on the shelves and on the floor. 'Later I will do some tidying up. I would normally ask a housekeeper to do that, but under the circumstances . . .'

Quietly Sherlock retreated from the library. He could

hear his uncle murmuring to himself as he closed the door behind him.

Mrs Eglantine was in the hall, and he stayed in the shadows, watching her. She was speaking to one of the maids.

'Tell Cook that I will be joining her shortly. The menus for the meals this week are totally unsuitable. They will need to be changed. Tell her that I will not be happy until they are completely revised.'

As the maid scurried off, and Mrs Eglantine stood motionless for a moment, lost in thought, Sherlock found his thoughts pulled in an audacious direction. Mrs Eglantine apparently felt free to search the entire house, looking for something. What if he was to search her room while she was occupied? Maybe he could find some clue as to what she was looking for. If he could find that, and then locate the hidden object before she did, then there would be no reason for her to stay at the house any longer. Even if he couldn't find out what she was looking for, he might be able to work out what power she had over his aunt and uncle. If he could free them from *that*, then he would have paid them back for all their hospitality.

Mrs Eglantine moved towards the back of the house, presumably to what was going to be a rather fraught meeting with Cook. Sherlock felt a twinge of sympathy. He liked Cook; she always had a slice of bread and jam or a scone and cream for him if he passed through the kitchen. She was the only one of the servants who could stand up to Mrs Eglantine.

With his uncle in the library and his aunt presumably in the sitting room sewing, as she normally did in the afternoons, Sherlock knew that he was unlikely to be disturbed by his immediate family. He also knew that the servants' schedule meant they would be cleaning out the fireplaces in the main bedrooms at that hour. Nobody would be up on the top floor, where the staff quarters and Sherlock's own bedroom were located.

He reached the top floor without seeing anybody. His bedroom was the first one leading off the landing. Next to that was an empty room that would normally be occupied by a butler, if the family could afford one. Around the corner was Mrs Eglantine's room and those occupied by the various maids and the lads who worked in the stables and the gardens, as well as the back staircase, which they used to move through the house without being seen. Only Sherlock and Mrs Eglantine were allowed to use the main stairs.

He turned the corner. The rest of the landing was empty, of course. Mrs Eglantine's door was closed, but not locked. That would have been a terrible breach of the unwritten contract between employee and employer. In theory the servants' rooms could be entered by Sherlock's aunt and uncle at any time, for any reason, and even though that right theoretically extended to Sherlock he still felt his heart accelerate and his palms become moist as he reached out for the doorknob.

He turned it quietly, pushed the door open and entered the room, closing the door quickly behind him.

The room smelled of lavender and talcum powder, and faintly of some heavier floral scent that brought to mind decaying orchids. A threadbare rug was set in the centre of the otherwise bare floorboards. The bed was neatly made, and any clothes had been hung in the narrow wardrobe or folded in the chest of drawers. Apart from a hairbrush on the windowsill, a framed print of a landscape hanging on the wall and a Bible on a shelf by the bed, the room was bare of ornamentation.

There was something so impersonal about the room that it was difficult to believe that anyone actually lived there, slept there, on a daily basis. Given Mrs Eglantine's aloofness, her almost inhuman stillness, Sherlock could imagine her walking into the room late at night, at the end of her working day, and just *standing* there, like a statue, unmoving until the sun rose and it was time to start working again. Switching off her fake humanity until she had to pretend again.

He shrugged the thought off. She wasn't a supernatural creature. She was as human as he was – just a lot nastier.

Sherlock pressed his back against the door. The thought crossed his mind that Mrs Eglantine might have stood just like this in *his* room before searching it, and it made him angry. If she'd searched the house, as she had said, then she *must* have searched his room. Damn the woman! What *was* it she was searching for, and what was it that made her invulnerable?

He quickly memorized the positions of everything he could see – the hairbrush, the Bible, even the way the framed print was hanging at a slight angle and the distance between the top sheet on the bed and the pillows. Given Mrs Eglantine's eye for detail, Sherlock had a feeling that she would notice if anything was disturbed. He had to make sure that everything was returned to its original position before he left.

He started with the chest of drawers, quickly sorting through the clothes in each drawer. He quelled the sense of guilt he felt by telling himself that Mrs Eglantine had almost certainly done the same to *his* clothes. When he found nothing, he ran his hand across the floorboards beneath the chest, just in case something had been slid underneath. Still nothing.

He turned away, and then turned back as a sudden thought struck him. Quickly he pulled each drawer completely out and felt underneath it for bits of paper or envelopes that might have been attached there, then looked into the hole left by the drawer for anything that might have been pushed inside, but apart from dust, spider webs and an old lace handkerchief he didn't find anything.

Leaving the chest of drawers, with a final check to

make sure it still looked as it had before he arrived, he turned to the wardrobe, but a noise from outside made him freeze. His heart thudded painfully. Had that been a creak of a floorboard? Was someone standing outside, listening for him in the same way he was listening for them? Had Mrs Eglantine finished her meeting with Cook and returned to her room for some reason?

The noise happened again: a scratching sound, difficult to place. Sherlock looked around wildly for somewhere to hide. Under the bed? In the wardrobe? He took a half-step, hesitant, fearing that a board would creak beneath his feet and give him away.

Before he could move again he heard the noise for a third time, and he recognized it with a rush of relief. It was the sound of ashes being scraped from one of the fireplace grates downstairs with a shovel, echoing through the chimneys. He relaxed, and let his hands unclench.

Now that his attention had been drawn to the fireplace, Sherlock moved across to it. He ran his hands through the cold coals in case anything had been hidden there, and even craned his neck to look up the chimney, but there was nothing to see.

He turned back to his search of the room, checking under the bed, but apart from an empty suitcase there was nothing there. The wardrobe was occupied by a number of dresses on hangers and two hats on a shelf –

all of them black, of course. Sherlock wasn't sure if it was just a housekeeper thing, or whether Mrs Eglantine spent her entire life wearing black. She *was* a 'Mrs', which meant that she was either married or widowed, but Sherlock could only imagine her walking up the aisle in church wearing a black wedding dress. He shivered and pushed the grotesque thought away.

He stood in the centre of the rug and looked around. He'd checked all the obvious places. The room was small enough and neat enough that he could see virtually every hiding place, and there was nothing unusual, nothing that he wouldn't have expected to see in a housekeeper's room.

If he was hiding something in *his* room, where would he put it?

On a sudden thought he stepped to one side and pulled the rug back. Nothing underneath but floorboards. He wasn't expecting there to be – Mrs Eglantine was nothing if not clever, and hiding something beneath the only rug in the room was too simple and too obvious – but he had to check anyway, just in case.

Looking at the floorboards prompted him to test them with his foot, looking for any looseness. Maybe she'd levered up one of the boards and hidden something underneath. If she had, then she'd fastened it back too well for Sherlock to detect. He'd need a crowbar to lever them up, and that would leave traces.

The picture on the wall kept attracting his attention.

For a minute or two he dismissed it, thinking that it was just the way it was hung at an angle that disturbed his ordered mind, but his thoughts kept circling back to it. It occurred to him that something might have been hidden behind the picture. Gently he eased it away from the wall and turned it so that he could see the back.

Only a pencilled price mark.

He sighed and put the picture back at exactly the same angle he had found it.

Hands on hips, he surveyed the room again. If there was a secret in the room, then it was particularly well kept.

If, in fact, the secret was *in* the room to start with.

On a whim he crossed over to the narrow window that looked out over the gardens to the back of the house. He couldn't see anybody, so he was safe from observation. The window was open a crack. He pushed it further open and leaned out.

Something was hanging from a piece of twine that had been wrapped around a nail stuck in the wood of the window frame – a package that dangled a couple of feet below the level of the windowsill. It was small enough that it would have been almost invisible from the garden below, unless someone knew exactly what they were looking for.

Sherlock hauled it in and rested it on the windowsill. The twine was tarred to make it weather-resistant, and the package was wrapped in oilcloth. It left a reddish powdery residue on the windowsill. It looked to Sherlock as if the oilcloth had been rubbed with brick dust to make it even more difficult to see from outside. Someone had gone to a lot of trouble to hide this package.

With a momentary hesitation, and a shiver of anticipation, he untied the twine and unwrapped the package.

Inside was a folded mass of paper. Sherlock wiped his hands on a handkerchief before unfolding it carefully, making a mental note of which layers were on the inside and which ones were on the outside. It was bad enough that he was in her room; he certainly didn't want Mrs Eglantine knowing that he had found her hidden papers and was riffling through them.

The papers unfolded into two large sheets. The top one was a set of plans of Holmes Manor – architect's drawings showing all the rooms on all the floors, all to scale. Many of the rooms had been crossed off in red ink. Most of them had scribbled notes written in them, or arrows pointing to particular features with question marks attached. One particularly thick wall between the dining room and the reception room had a note written beside it which said: 'Check for secret compartments in the wall. Could be accessed from either side.'

The second sheet was slightly smaller than the first. It was a set of words and phrases written in the same handwriting as the notes on the architectural plans.

They had boxes drawn around them, and the boxes were linked by lines and arrows in a kind of network. It looked as if Mrs Eglantine – assuming it was her – was trying to connect up a series of disparate elements, discoveries or thoughts into a coherent pattern – and failing. Sherlock scanned through some of the notes and found names of members of the Holmes family, as well as names that he didn't recognize, alongside places that he thought he'd heard of and words that just seemed to be randomly chosen but presumably meant something to Mrs Eglantine. In the centre, like a spider sitting in the middle of its web, the words *gold plates* had been circled twice in an emphatic hand.

Gold plates? Was *that* what she was looking for?

Reluctantly Sherlock folded the papers up again, careful to make sure that he used the same fold marks in the same order as he had unwrapped the package. He wished he could keep them for further study, but that would be risky. He couldn't even copy them – there was too much information there, and it would take too long. He knew more than he had earlier, but he wasn't sure he was any the wiser.

He wrapped the papers up in the oilcloth, retied them with the twine and carefully lowered them out of the window, first checking that the garden was still empty.

Finally, he closed the window, remembering to leave it open a crack.

 36

He took a last look around the room, partly for anything he might have missed and partly to see if he'd left any traces. To both questions, the answer was no.

After listening at the door for a few moments to check that the coast was clear, he left Mrs Eglantine's room and slipped along the corridor. For a moment he considered going into his own room, but there was nothing for him to do there apart from rest for a while, and think, and he had other things to do. He headed downstairs.

The heavy oak door leading out into the drive and the gardens thumped closed as he entered the hall. Someone had just left the house. Through a narrow window Sherlock could see a black-clad figure walking to a waiting cart. It was Mrs Eglantine. She had put on a coat, which meant that she was probably going into town. She must have finished her conference with Cook, and a shiver went through Sherlock as he realized how close a call he'd had. If she'd kept her coat upstairs instead of in the kitchen, then she might have found him.

The cart clattered away and vanished through the gates to the road. Sherlock turned and headed back towards the kitchens.

'Master Sherlock!' Cook called as he entered. She was a large woman, her cheery face usually red from the heat of the ovens and her hands covered in flour, but today she looked pale and the skin around her eyes was creased as if she was trying to stop herself from crying. 'I just got some bread in the oven. Come back in a while and you can 'ave a nice hot slice wiv butter fresh from the churn!'

'Thanks,' he said, 'but I was looking for Mrs Eglantine.'

Cook's face seemed to age five years in as many seconds. 'She's gone to town. And good riddance too! 'Parently the quality of the vegetables I've been preparin' for this household is not up to the standards she expects.' She sniffed. 'Anyone'd think she was the lady of the house, rather than Mrs 'Olmes, and this was some swanky 'otel rather than a country 'ouse.'

'She's certainly a difficult person to please,' Sherlock said cautiously. He'd learned from Amyus Crowe that general statements, left hanging like that, normally encouraged talkative people to talk even more, and Cook was one of the most talkative people he knew.

'She is that. I never known such a person to find fault, and 'er tongue's as sharp as a butcher's knife. I worked with 'undreds of 'ousekeepers over the years, but she's got to be the most hoity-toity and the most unpleasant.'

'What made my uncle and aunt employ her in the first place?' Sherlock asked. 'I presume she must have had a good set of references from her previous jobs.'

'If she did, then I never got to 'ear about them.'

'I keep seeing her around the house,' Sherlock said. 'Just standing there, not doing anything apart from watching and listening.'

'That's 'er all over,' Cook confirmed. 'Like a crow,

just standin' on a branch waitin' for a worm.' Colour was coming back into her cheeks now. She sniffed again. 'Soon as she arrived she turned this kitchen upside down. Moved everythin' out into the garden and 'ad the walls an' the tiles scrubbed. Give 'er credit – she did it herself. Shut the door an' worked for a whole day, she did. Said she'd 'ad experience of 'ouses wiv mice an' rats an' she wanted to make sure there weren't none 'ere. The nerve of the woman! As if I'd let a mouse in my kitchen!'

'She's a strange woman,' Sherlock confirmed.

'I got some biscuits I baked earlier,' Cook confided. 'Do you want a couple, to keep you goin' before tea?'

'I'd love some,' he said, smiling. 'In fact, I'd happily miss tea and just eat your biscuits.'

'It's nice to 'ave someone who appreciates my cookin',' Cook said, beaming. She seemed more cheerful now.

After wolfing down three of Cook's biscuits, Sherlock headed back into the house. He wasn't sure that he'd made much progress, but he seemed to have established that Mrs Eglantine had somehow blackmailed her way into the house and that she was searching for something. The gold plates that had been mentioned in her notes? He supposed it was possible, but it sounded a little unlikely. Why would there be gold plates, of all things, in his aunt and uncle's possession? What would they want such a thing for? He'd been living there for over a year now, and he'd never seen any plates apart from the porcelain ones that were used every day and the bone-china ones brought out on Sundays and when anyone visited. Neither of those sets of plates had any gold at all on them, not even gold-leaf edging.

Suddenly he couldn't face the prospect of staying in the house for the rest of the day. It seemed to be weighing down on him like a heavy coat. He had to get out. For a few seconds he thought about heading over to see Amyus Crowe – and Virginia – but he felt as if there was more that he could do concerning Mrs Eglantine. If she was in Farnham, sourcing fresher vegetables than Cook had got, then perhaps he could find her and watch her for a while from hiding. After all, perhaps the vegetables were just an excuse. Perhaps she had a different reason for going into town.

He left by the front door and headed for the stables, where his horse was kept. He thought of it as *his* horse, although he'd effectively stolen it from the evil Baron Maupertuis, back when he'd first arrived at Holmes Manor. Fortunately the Baron hadn't appeared to ask for it back, and the horse seemed perfectly happy to stay with someone who looked after it and rode it regularly. He'd named it Philadelphia, as a kind of joke. The horse didn't seem to mind.

Saddling Philadelphia up the way he'd been taught by the groom who worked for the Holmes family, he cantered out of the grounds and along the road that led to Farnham. He'd got pretty good at riding over the past few months, ever since getting back from

40

the eventful trip that he and his brother had made to Russia.

That trip, he reminded himself as the horse calmly trotted along past the tall trees of Alice Holt Forest, had involved the mysterious Paradol Chamber – the international gang of criminals who had also been involved with the colossal schemes of Baron Maupertuis. Nothing had been heard of them since their plan to discredit Sherlock's brother Mycroft and assassinate the head of the Russian Secret Service had fallen apart, but Sherlock knew that they were still out there, somewhere. He occasionally asked Mycroft about them, but Mycroft professed himself to be as mystified as Sherlock as to what they were up to. The only certainty was that somewhere in the world they were up to something.

The outskirts of Farnham crept up on Sherlock before he knew it: solid red brick buildings with tiled roofs replacing the thatched cottages that had been scattered along the road from Holmes Manor. Rather than ride into the town centre, and risk having Mrs Eglantine see him, he left the horse tied up at a stables he'd used before on the outskirts of town, tipping the ostler a few pence to feed and water it. He walked the rest of the way.

If Mrs Eglantine was telling the truth about vegetables, then she would be at the market. Sherlock headed over towards where it was held, in the shadow of a two-storey building with colonnades all the way around. The marketplace was filled to capacity with stalls selling all manner of foodstuffs, from fruit to fresh beans, from smoked meat to shellfish.

He couldn't see Mrs Eglantine anywhere, but he did see Matty standing by a vegetable stall. He looked as if he was waiting for something to roll off in his direction.

Matty caught sight of Sherlock and waved. Sherlock saw his friend's gaze flicker back to the stall, and a look of momentary indecision cross his face before he walked over.

'Waiting for lunch?' Sherlock asked.

'I don't really separate stuff out into "meals" as such,' Matty admitted. 'I just eat whenever I can.'

'Very wise. Have you seen Mrs Eglantine around?'

'That housekeeper?' Matty shuddered. 'I try to stay away from her. She's bad news.'

'Yes, but have you *seen* her?'

Matty nodded over towards a stall selling fresh trout laid on grass. 'She was over there a few minutes ago. Said the fish was too small.'

'Did you see which direction she went?'

He shrugged. 'Long as she was heading away from me, I didn't really care. Why? What's up?'

Sherlock debated whether to tell Matty about the confrontation between Mrs Eglantine and his uncle, but he decided to keep quiet. That was a private family matter – at least for the moment. 'I just need to know where she is,' he said. 'I think she's up to something.'

'Shouldn't be too hard to find her,' Matty said. 'She dresses like every day is a Sunday, an' someone's died to boot . . .'

As the two boys moved across the marketplace, pushing past the various vendors, customers and browsers who filled the place, Sherlock caught fragments of conversation from all directions.

'. . . an' I told 'im, if 'e comes back without it I'm leavin' . . .'

'. . . you gave me your word that the deal was already made, Bill . . .'

'. . . if I see you with that lad again, girl, I'll wallop you so hard your head will be spinning for a week . . .'

One voice in particular snagged his attention. It was accented, American. He recognized the accent from talking to Amyus Crowe, and from his time in New York. He turned his head, thinking that maybe it was Crowe who was speaking, but the face that he found himself looking at was younger: all sharp planes and hard edges. The man's hair was pulled back into a tight ponytail, and beneath the hair it looked to Sherlock as if his right ear was missing. All he could see there was a mass of dark scar tissue. His clothes were dusty and well-travelled, and he was speaking to a companion who had short blond hair and a face covered in circular scars, the kind you got from a bad case of smallpox.

'. . . will flay us alive and turn our skins into hats,' the man with the missing ear was saying.

'We need to find Crowe and his daughter. They're our only chance!'

'Well, we know what'll happen to us if we *don't* find them. Remember Abner?'

'Yeah.' The dark-haired man's face twisted with an unpleasant memory. 'Don't do nothing but stare at the wall now, after what the boss did to him. It's like there's nothing left inside his head, apart from what he needs to breathe and to eat . . .'

They were walking in one direction and Sherlock and Matty were walking in another, and that was all Sherlock heard before the two men were out of earshot. It sounded serious though. Sherlock decided to go and see Mr Crowe as soon as he could. Crowe needed to know that someone was looking for him.

By the time he had formulated the thought, he and Matty were across the other side of the marketplace.

'Wait here for a minute,' Matty said. He dashed away, towards the two-storey colonnaded building on the edge of the marketplace. Sherlock lost him as he vanished into the shadows. He was about to turn away and scan the crowd for signs of a black-clad woman when Matty's head appeared above the parapet, running along the roof of the building. He waved at Sherlock. Sherlock waved back, amazed at how quickly Matty had got through the building. The scruffy barge boy scanned the crowd with his keen gaze. Within moments he was pointing at something.

Mrs Eglantine? Sherlock mouthed, trusting to Matty's skill at lip-reading to pick up the words.

Pork pie! Matty replied. Sherlock couldn't tell if he was actually making any sound or not, but the movement of his mouth was clear enough. Matty grinned. *Only kidding!* he mouthed. *She's over there!*

Sherlock gave him a thumbs-up, and Matty's head disappeared from the parapet.

Sherlock plunged into the crowd of shoppers and market traders, heading in the direction that Matty had indicated. He scanned the heads of the people in front of him, looking out for Mrs Eglantine's distinctive scraped-back hairstyle. Within the space of a few moments he had seen virtually every variation of hair and headwear possible: black, red, blond, grey, white and bald; straight, curly, pig-tailed and close-shaven; bare-headed, bonneted, scarved, flat-capped, bowler-hatted . . . everything apart from a woman with black hair pulled back so that it looked like it was painted on her scalp. Finally he spotted her. She was standing right on the edge of the marketplace with her back to him. She was talking to a short man with hair that was long, oiled and brushed back to either side of his head, leaving a parting dead centre. His skin was blotchy, and his jacket was shiny with old dirt and grease at the shoulders, elbows and cuffs. He wasn't the kind of man with whom Sherlock would have thought Mrs Eglantine would associate.

Sherlock drifted closer, deliberately looking away from the two of them so that they wouldn't notice they had an eavesdropper.

As he got closer he heard the man say: 'Time's gettin' on, darlin', and there's still no sign of the thing turnin' up. You sure it's in the 'ouse?'

'There is nowhere else for it to be,' Mrs Eglantine said in her cold, precise voice. 'And you don't need to remind me how long I've been working in that *place*.'

'Anythin' I can do to speed things up?' the man asked.

''You can get rid of that brat Sherlock,' she snapped. 'He's always snooping around, and he's too clever for his own good.'

'You want him gone temporary, like, or permanent?'

'So permanently,' she hissed, 'that I want him cut up and scattered over such a large area that nobody will ever be able to find all the bits.'

CHAPTER THREE

Sherlock felt his mouth drop open in shock. He knew Mrs Eglantine disliked him to the point of hatred, but the fact that she hated him enough to want him *dead* – enough to actually ask someone to *kill* him – that was a shock. What had he ever done to her? Apart from question her position and challenge her authority, that was.

The man with the oily hair was saying something, and Sherlock concentrated on hearing what it was.

'I'll take that into consideration,' he said, 'I surely will, but the problem is that I could be seeing a nice return on what I know about that hoity-toity Holmes family, but I'm holdin' back. Rather than get them to pay me a guinea a week to keep their secret, I'm usin' that influence to keep you employed by them.' He sniggered. 'Let's face it, who would employ a sour-faced harridan like you if they didn't have to? I'm losing money on this deal while you get a nice little job and a wage.'

Mrs Eglantine started to speak, but the man held up a hand and she stopped.

'I know what you're going to say,' he said. 'You're going to tell me that when you find this treasure of yours that's hid in the house, you'll split it with me and we'll both

47

be rich. The trouble is, that treasure is what's known as "hypothetical" – I ain't seen it and I ain't convinced that it exists. On the other hand, the money the Holmes family could be paying me to keep their secret is real. Cash in hand, if you like – or beer in belly, in my case. So I got to ask myself, am I better off with a smaller amount of real money or a larger amount of hypothetical money?'

Mrs Eglantine sniffed. 'We had an arrangement, Mr Harkness,' she said. 'If you go back on that now, then nobody will ever trust you again.'

'I'm a blackmailer,' Harkness pointed out calmly. 'The only thing people trust me to do is reveal their secrets if I don't get paid regular.' He sighed. 'Look, we've had a good thing going over the years, darlin'. You ferret out family secrets wherever you work and bring them to me, and I use them to make a few quid on a regular basis, but since you got wind of this supposed treasure the whole thing's gone to pot. Why can't we go back to the way things were?'

'Firstly,' Mrs Eglantine said icily, 'I am *not* your "darling" and I never will be, and secondly, the trivial way you blackmail the local townspeople over their petty thefts and even pettier romances barely brings you in enough money to fund those big bets you like to place on the horses and the illegal boxing. If you ever want to make anything of yourself, I am your only chance.'

Harkness sighed. 'You've got a sharp but persuasive

tongue in your head, Betty. All right – I'll go along with it for another month. But just a month, you hear? After that I'm getting my hooks into the Holmes family and soaking them for whatever cash I can.'

'To you,' she replied, 'I am Mrs Eglantine. *Never* take the liberty of calling me by my first name.' She seemed to thaw slightly, reaching out to touch his arm. 'I'm near to finding it, Josh – I *know* I am. I just need a little more time.' She paused for a moment. 'And I need that interfering brat Sherlock out of my way. Can you do that for me?'

'I'll get some of my lads on it,' he promised. 'You got time for a bite to eat?'

She shook her head. 'That damned family are expecting their evening meal. I swear, Josh, there are times when I just feel like poisoning the lot of them and watching as they writhe in agony on the dining-room carpet. But not just yet. I need to get back.'

'Stay in touch.' He laughed. 'Let me know if you find them golden plates you keep on about.'

'I will.' She turned away, then turned back. 'Oh, I almost forgot. I found this in the room of one of the maids.' She reached into a hidden fold of her crinoline skirt and withdrew a letter. 'It is a note from a boy who claims to love her.'

'I ain't interested in tittle-tattle,' Harkness said.

'You would be if you knew that the boy in question is the eldest son of the Mayor of Farnham.'

Harkness cocked his head to one side in sudden interest. 'The Mayor's son, seeing some little hussy of a housemaid? That ought to be good for a few quid. The Mayor's very particular about the company he keeps. He tells everyone that his son is going to marry into the nobility. He'll want to keep this one *very* quiet.' He frowned. 'The letter's in the boy's own handwriting? And he's signed it?'

'With love and kisses.'

Harkness grinned. 'People never learn, do they? I never commit anything to writing, just in case.' He reached out and took the letter from Mrs Eglantine. 'Thanks for this. You want cash now, or shall I add it to the account?'

'Pay me later. Just make sure you remember.'

'Oh, I'll remember. My memory's razor sharp.'

They parted, Mrs Eglantine heading off in one direction and Josh Harkness in the other. Sherlock almost expected the man to try to kiss her on the cheek, based on that momentary final flash of friendship, but if the thought crossed his mind he didn't act on it.

Sherlock's gaze flickered uncertainly between the two of them. Should he follow Mrs Eglantine, or Josh Harkness? It occurred to him that he didn't have to follow *either* of them – he could just go and find Matty and spend the rest of the day in Farnham – but he knew that he couldn't let this thing go. There was more at stake here than he had realized – not just his own safety, but the future of his family. He *had* to find out what was going on, and stop it. If he could.

After a few seconds he decided that he should follow the greasy-haired man. Mrs Eglantine was heading back to the house – she had said so herself. He knew where she would be and pretty much what she was going to be doing. The man was the uncertain quantity here, and Sherlock needed to find out much more about him. That was the direction that any immediate threat to Sherlock would be coming from.

Harkness now had something incriminating on one of the housemaids in Holmes Manor. Sherlock wondered which one it was. He didn't know any of them by name, and rarely said anything to them, but they all seemed pleasant enough, and good at their jobs. If one of them had found happiness with a boy who was from a different social class, then what of it? Sherlock didn't see why either of them should be punished for the fact, let alone the boy's father.

Not for the first time, it occurred to him that the British system of working class, middle class and upper class people was not only pointless and archaic, but damaging to the very fabric of society.

Checking to see that Mrs Eglantine hadn't turned around to come back for some reason, Sherlock slipped through the crowd after her friend.

Sherlock stayed well back, just in case Harkness looked over his shoulder. He probably didn't know what Sherlock looked like, but he seemed like the kind of man who would be constantly checking for pursuit. As the two of them moved through the crowd Sherlock couldn't help but notice how some of the townsfolk – usually the better-dressed ones – moved out of his way and turned their heads to avoid looking at him. He seemed to be known to a lot of people – and not in a good way. Sherlock couldn't help but remember some of the older boys at Deepdene Academy who had bullied the younger ones. They had swaggered through the school halls in much the same way, and the kids had moved out of their path like minnows moving out of the way of a stickleback.

Sherlock sensed a presence by his side. He turned his head a fraction, not sure that he wanted to acknowledge whoever it was. Maybe Mrs Eglantine had turned back and seen him. But no – it was Matty. He grinned up at Sherlock, one hand holding a cauliflower which he was eating raw.

'Wha's goin' on?' he said through a mouthful of vegetable.

'We're following someone.'

'Who? That Mrs Eglantine?'

Sherlock shook his head. 'No. Some other man she was meeting. Harkness, I think his name is. Josh Harkness.'

Matty's face seemed to freeze. His eyes widened in concern. 'Josh Harkness? Small bloke with hair that looks like he washes it in lamp oil?'

'That's him.'

Matty shook his head. 'Best not to get involved with him, Sherlock. I heard things about him. The barge hands on the canal talk about him in whispers. He takes a cut from most of the thieves that work this town. Five per cent of their earnings, he takes, payable every week. If they don't pay him, he takes five per cent of their bodies – just cuts it off. Fingers, toes, ears, noses . . . whatever it takes until he has five per cent of their body weight. That's his rule, and he never varies it.' He shuddered. 'We had a talk, him and me, a little time after I arrived in Farnham. He took me by the shoulder in the marketplace and said quietly, "I notice that you're not averse to nabbing bits of food here and there, young 'un. That's all right – never let it be said that Josh Harkness begrudges a boy his fill. But take a note from a friend – if you ever graduate to taking money rather than fruit and pies, I get a cut. Ask anyone. And if I don't get a cut –"' he made a snipping motion with his fingers – '"well, one way or another, I get my cut, if you see what I mean." He's not a nice man, Sherlock. Even on a scale of people who are not nice, he ranks right near the top.'

Sherlock nodded thoughtfully as the two of them moved through the crowd. 'I understand. I got the impression that he had few scruples, but he's got something on my family – some kind of information that he's holding over their heads.'

'Yeah, he dabbles in blackmail as well. He collects

all the little secrets that people have, and he gets them to pay him every week according to their means for the privilege of keeping it all secret.' Matty shook his head. 'It's a few pence here, a couple of shillings there and a handful of pounds every week, but it all mounts up. He's making a fortune without working for it.'

'And he's cashing in on people's unhappiness,' Sherlock said grimly. He found that the thought was making him angry. 'He's a parasite on the human race, and someone ought to do something about it. Why don't they?'

'The people he's blackmailing are too scared to go to the police, because if they do their secrets will be revealed. Besides, he's probably blackmailing half the police in Farnham as well. The last thing they're going to do is expose him.'

'Then I suppose I'll have to do it myself,' Sherlock said. The words surprised him even as he heard himself saying them, but they sounded right.

Matty was about to say something else, but up ahead Josh Harkness turned a corner out of the marketplace. He was still clutching the stolen letter in his hand. Sherlock gestured to Matty to keep quiet. Together they exited the fringes of the crowd and moved towards the corner. Sherlock sidled up to the edge of the brick wall and looked around it carefully, half expecting to come face to face with the blackmailer, but the man was up ahead, walking along an empty street. Sherlock hung back until Harkness was almost at the far end. If he and

Matty started after him while he was still only halfway along, then if he turned, he would see them straight away. They would be the only two people on the street.

Harkness got to the end of the street and turned left. As soon as he vanished from sight, Sherlock pulled Matty into the street and started running.

It only took a few seconds for Sherlock and Matty to get to the end of the street. They did the same there as they had before, Matty hanging back while Sherlock peered around the corner. Harkness was perhaps twenty feet away, still striding along, ignoring everything around him. He was, Sherlock judged, very confident in himself.

A smell began to prick at Sherlock's nostrils: a sharp smell, like a combination of cleaning chemicals and something darker, like sewage. Sherlock felt his eyes watering as the vapour – whatever it was – began to irritate them.

At the end of the street, rather than turning into another street or an alley, Harkness came to a door and opened it with a key. He stared right and left suspiciously, the stolen letter still held in his hand. Sherlock pulled back so that he couldn't be seen, trying to suppress a sneeze that kept trying to explode out of his nose. By the time he felt confident enough to poke his head back out, the man had vanished.

'What's in there?' he asked Matty.

Matty poked his head around the corner as well,

underneath Sherlock's. He sniffed. 'Tannery,' he said firmly. 'They get the cow hides coming in from the farms and the abattoirs, and they cure them to turn them into leather.'

'"Cure" them?' Sherlock asked. He'd heard the term before, but he wasn't sure what it entailed.

'Yeah.' Matty glanced up scornfully. 'You ought to get out more. "Curing" is what they do to turn skin into leather. It makes it harder, makes it last longer and stops it from rotting.'

'And how do they do that?'

'They scrape as much flesh as they can off the skins with sharp knives, and then they wash them with some kind of chemical stuff.'

Sherlock sniffed again, feeling the bite of ammonia at the back of his nose and throat. 'Yes, I can smell the chemicals.'

Matty grimaced. 'You can smell them all over Farnham. The chemicals they use to cure the hides are made from some pretty horrible raw materials.'

Sherlock frowned. 'What do you mean?'

'Well, put it this way – some bloke told me that the chemical was called "urea".'

Sherlock thought for a moment. *Urea.* It sounded innocuous. It sounded like . . . oh. Yes. It sounded like 'urine'. He looked down at Matty, frowning. 'Are you telling me that they tan leather using *urine?*'

Matty nodded. 'That and other stuff, but you probably

don't want to even think about that. Just take my advice – hold your nose whenever you pass by that place.' He shook his head. 'I heard a story about one of the blokes who worked in there. He was trying to mix the skins around in the big tank they have, using a long stick, but he overbalanced and fell in.'

Sherlock felt his eyes widen. 'Fell into the . . . ?'

'Exactly.'

'What happened?'

'He drowned.'

'Drowned in . . . ?'

'Yeah.' He shuddered. 'When I die I want to die quietly, in my sleep. Not drowning in a bath of—'

'We've got to get in there,' Sherlock said decisively.

'*What?*'

'I said, we've got to get in there.'

'Are you *mad?*'

'Josh Harkness went in there.'

'Yes. I *know*. That was my point. Not only does that place smell worse than the wooden outhouse you rescued me from in that American railway station last year – which, by the way, smelled like someone had got stuck and died – but it's also got inside it the most dangerous man within a hundred miles. There are times when I wonder about you, Sherlock.'

Sherlock sighed. 'Look, I wish it wasn't necessary, but he's got some information about my family. He's blackmailing my aunt and uncle. They're nice people.

They've never done anybody any harm, and they've looked after me and fed me for over a year now. I owe it to them to do something.' He gazed down the street, feeling a grim expression settle across his face. 'I've decided that I don't like blackmailers.'

'All right.' Matty looked around. 'Going through that door would be a waste of time. Harkness probably locked it behind him, and even if he didn't we don't know where it opens out. Might be right into a room full of people. There's a broken window round the corner. We could probably get in that way.'

'How come you know there's a broken window round the corner?'

Matty looked at Sherlock with exasperation. 'I know where all the broken windows in Farnham are – just in case I need them. You wouldn't believe the stuff that people leave out on kitchen tables. Although in this case I decided never to use the window as soon as I found out what was in there and who owned it.'

Sherlock frowned. 'I wonder why Harkness doesn't get it repaired.'

Matty shrugged. 'Maybe he knows that nobody in their right mind would ever burgle the place, knowing who he is, an' all. Maybe it lets some fresh air inside. Lord knows, it needs a stiff breeze running through.'

Sherlock nodded, and led the way around the corner, walking along the street and past the closed door through which Harkness had entered the building. He deliberately didn't look sideways just in case the door was open a crack and Harkness was looking out, watching for people following him. The confidence with which he'd walked away from the market suggested that he didn't expect to be followed or didn't care if he was, but Sherlock couldn't take the chance. Maybe the man was trickier than he looked.

Sherlock's skin crawled as he passed the door. He half expected it to spring open. He breathed a silent sigh of relief as he left it behind him and reached the next corner.

Matty was right beside him. Together they turned into a deserted cobbled alley.

The wall of the tannery formed one side of the alley. Sherlock could see the window that Matty had mentioned. It was about eight feet off the ground, and the glass was cobwebby. The lower right-hand pane was missing.

The smell emanating from the hole in the window made Sherlock want to turn around and be sick. Instead, he deliberately clenched his stomach muscles and swallowed a couple of times. He couldn't afford to let his body betray him. He had work to do.

He glanced at the window: too high for him to pull himself up, and the plaster of the wall looked as if it would crumble under his feet if he tried to get purchase against it. He had to think of another way to get through.

'I'll boost you up on my shoulders,' he said to Matty.

'You open the window and get in, then you'll have to pull me up.'

'Not going to work,' Matty said firmly. 'Take it from an expert at getting into buildings. I can get up and in the window, no problem, but I can't take your weight for long enough to pull you in after me.' He grimaced. 'We'll have to do it the other way round. I'll bend over – you climb on my back, get in the window and pull *me* up and in.'

Sherlock's gaze moved between the high window and Matty's small form. He nodded reluctantly. 'You're right,' he said, 'but I don't want to hurt you.'

Matty shrugged. 'Stuff happens,' he said casually. 'But bruises and scratches heal. Frankly, if your boot in my face is the worst thing that happens to me today, I'll be as happy as Larry.'

'Who's Larry?' Sherlock asked.

Matty stared at him. 'It's just an expression,' he said. 'People say it all the time.'

'I've never heard it.'

'As I said, you should get out more. Mix with people.' He smiled. 'Now come on – you're wasting time.' He bent over, bracing his hands against his thighs. 'Get up there quickly. You're just as thin as you were when we first met, but I think you've put on some muscle in the meantime, and muscle is heavy.'

Before he could reconsider, Sherlock put his right knee on to Matty's back and then brought his left foot up, boosting himself until he was standing upright. Matty grunted, but his back remained steady. Quickly Sherlock reached in through the hole in the window and felt around for the catch. He undid it, then, pulling his hand back, slid the window open. He jumped for the opening, feeling Matty move beneath his feet as he did so. Sherlock's stomach caught against the window frame, and he wriggled inside. The wood scraped against his skin. Before he could fall to the floor, he caught himself and crouched, looking around.

He was in a small room that was empty of people but filled with boxes. Up against one wall was a wooden chute like a child's slide, set on its end. The floor was about five feet below the edge of the windowsill – obviously built up a couple of feet from where the ground was. That made things easier. He lowered himself to the floorboards, turned and leaned out of the window. Matty was looking upward expectantly. When he saw Sherlock he extended his hand. Sherlock reached down and pulled him up. His friend was surprisingly heavy, and Sherlock felt the muscles in his back protesting, but he managed to haul the boy in through the window without causing himself permanent damage.

Together they moved past the boxes to where a door interrupted the wall. It was closed. Sherlock turned the knob and edged it open an inch.

Through the gap he saw a large room that occupied the centre of the building. A raised walkway ran around the edge of the room, with several doors leading off and a gap on the right that presumably led to the door to the street, but most of it was at the same level as the ground outside. In the middle of the room were four wooden vats, like the bottom halves of enormous barrels. Inside each one was a liquid. In two of the barrels the liquid was discoloured and lumpy, like soup, with bubbles rising slowly to the surface, but in the other two it was clearer, more like water.

The smell rising from the vats was so strong that Sherlock could swear he saw the air itself rippling above them.

'I ain't going to eat for a week now,' Matty complained in a whisper.

'Breathe through your nose,' Sherlock suggested.

'I am. What I need to do is breathe through my *ears.*'

There was no sign of Josh Harkness, but there were two other men in the room. They were moving from vat to vat, using wooden poles as long as their bodies to swirl the contents around. Each time they did so, the smell got momentarily worse.

'I know those blokes,' Matty said. 'They go round town collecting cash for Harkness. They're bad news.'

Sherlock looked at the various closed doors. One of them presumably sheltered Josh Harkness. He didn't dare explore until he knew where the blackmailer was.

As the thought crossed his mind a door across the

other side of the room opened and Harkness emerged. He wasn't holding the letter any more.

'Keep stirring them leathers,' he yelled at the men by the vats. 'That last batch came out patchy and baggy. I ain't paying you to stand around doing nothing.'

'It ain't got nothin' to do wiv us stirrin' or not stirrin', boss,' one of the men yelled back. 'It's got to do with the quality of them skins. The cows you're usin' are's old as my gran. Their skins are just as baggy an' just as blotchy. You want better leathers, you get better skins for us.'

'Don't give me none of your lip!' Harkness shouted. 'If you think you can do it better, then you set up your own tannery! Until then, you work with whatever you're given!'

The men shrugged, looked at each other and got back to stirring. Harkness glowered at them for a few moments, then stomped along the raised walkway to where some steps led down into the centre. He walked over to one of the vats and looked inside, having to stand on his toes to do so. The smell didn't seem to bother him.

'There's not enough skins in here,' he shouted. 'Throw some more in.'

The two men headed over to an area hidden from Sherlock's view by the vats. Harkness stomped across to join them. For a moment the room seemed empty.

Sherlock took his chance. He quickly and quietly raced out on to the wooden walkway and ran along it to the door from which Harkness had emerged moments before. Matty followed silently.

He got to the door, quickly opened it and slipped inside, closing it behind him before the three men could re-emerge from behind the vats. Part of his mind, the emotional part, worried about how he was going to get out again, but the rest of it, the logical part, told him that if the men had disappeared once then the chances were that they would again. All he had to do was wait. For now, the important thing was to search the room for its secrets.

He looked around. One wall had a set of poles leaning against it. They had hooks on the end – presumably for pulling hides out of the vats. The other walls were lined with shelves, and each shelf had several cardboard boxes on it. Written on the boxes were letters: *A, B, C,* and so on. He went to the first box, pulled it from the shelf and took the lid off.

The box was filled with paper: newspaper clippings, letters, official-looking documents and the occasional daguerreotype photograph. He scanned a couple at random. The newspaper clippings were a strange mixture of reports on criminal activity – burglaries, stabbings and so on – and reports of a more social nature – births, marriages and deaths. The official documents were much the same – some court reports or witness statements, with a smattering of notarized statements on legal paper, and some certificates of birth or marriage. One or two

64

appeared to have been torn directly from church registers. The letters ranged from handwritten declarations of love or hatred to typed proposals of business, along with a couple of invitations to duels. Some of the photographs were simple, innocent portraits, usually with a note of the person's name on the back, while others were the kind of thing that made Sherlock suddenly turn them over in embarrassment. In total, the box was a complete cross section of human life.

He thought for a moment. Although most of the stuff in the box – with the exception of some of the photographs – was completely innocent, it presumably meant something more serious if taken in context. The letter to the housemaid at Holmes Manor from her boyfriend – which Sherlock assumed was now in another box somewhere in the room – was just a simple declaration of love on the surface, until you knew who had written it – the Mayor's son, a man out of the housemaid's class. The same must be true of everything else. A birth could be a simple birth – or not, if the mother was not married. That would be scandalous. A marriage could be quite innocent – unless the groom had been married before and his wife was still alive. That would be bigamous. Even a death – *especially* a death – could be suspicious if there were relatives who would inherit money in the will. That might be murder.

He looked around the room grimly. The contents of those boxes could destroy lives quickly if they were made public, but they would just destroy lives more slowly if they weren't. Josh Harkness would bleed money from the people he was threatening until they were destitute, living on the streets.

His eyes fixed on the box labelled *H*. Somewhere in there was the secret that Mrs Eglantine had discovered about the Holmes family. He could, if he wanted, quickly take a look. Find out what it was that she knew – a secret so powerful that his aunt and uncle would rather keep the poisonous viper that was Mrs Eglantine close to their bosom than get rid of her and risk its exposure.

Or he could destroy that box, along with all the rest of them, and free hundreds of people from misery.

Put that way, was there even a choice to make?

The only question was: how?

CHAPTER FOUR

Sherlock knew that he had to use the tools to hand to destroy the letters, the photographs and the other documents. There were too many boxes for him and Matty to remove from the tannery, and they'd be spotted quickly if they even tried. No, he had to destroy them on the premises.

But how? He supposed he could set a fire. That would destroy Harkness's treasure trove of blackmail material, sure enough, but it would also destroy the building, and probably spread to the ones on either side. There was a good chance that people might die, and Sherlock didn't want that weighing on his conscience. For a moment he felt paralysed, brain whirling as it sorted through the various things that he'd seen in the short time he and Matty had been inside the tannery. Then it struck him: the vats! He could dump the boxes into the vats! If the alkaline chemicals didn't bleach the ink off the pages or dissolve them into their constituent parts, then they would become sodden and disintegrate of their own accord. There was something poetic about using one part of Josh Harkness's little empire to destroy another.

'Right,' he said, 'let's go.'

'Thank God,' Matty responded. 'I'm on the verge of passing out, thanks to the smell.'

'No,' Sherlock clarified, 'I meant that it's time to destroy all this stuff.'

Matty just stared at him.

'We can't let Harkness get away with it,' Sherlock said insistently. 'He's slowly destroying people's lives.'

'And he'll destroy *our* lives a lot quicker than that if we do anything to cross him.' Matty shook his head in despair. 'The man's an animal! He's more dangerous than a rabid badger backed into a corner!'

Sherlock shook his head stubbornly. 'I don't care. I can't leave here and then walk around town knowing that every third or fourth person I see is paying him to keep their secrets quiet. People have a right to privacy.'

'Even if the secrets they're keeping might get them put into jail if they were known about?' Matty asked shrewdly.

'Even so,' Sherlock said. 'If a crime has been committed, then there's a process for that. It gets reported. The police investigate. Evidence gets collected. If there's enough evidence then people get arrested. Josh Harkness isn't punishing criminals because he thinks of himself as some unofficial part of the police force – he's preying on people's guilty consciences to make money.'

Matty grimaced. 'It's still evidence,' he said. 'And I think you've got a rosy view of the police. Like I told you earlier – the police around here are either taking money themselves or they're doing their own little petty thefts on the side. Give a criminal a uniform and he's still a criminal.'

Sherlock thought back to the time, some months before, when his brother Mycroft had been accused of murder. The police hadn't seemed too interested in collecting evidence then, he had to admit, but even so, the principle was sound.

'Look,' he said, 'I admit the system isn't ideal. I don't even know what an ideal system would look like. Maybe the police need to be paid more. Maybe people need to be checked out and tested before they're allowed to join the police. Maybe they need more training. Maybe they need consultants to help them out when they're investigating difficult crimes. I don't *know*. I just know that people like Josh Harkness aren't the answer. He's doing nothing to *stop* crimes – in fact, from his point of view, the more crimes the better.'

'I ain't going to convince you to give this up, am I?'

'No.'

'And you're going to do it whether I help or not.'

'Yes.'

'Then I suppose I'd better help out, if only to keep you alive. My life would be a lot more boring if you weren't around.'

'Thank you,' Sherlock said.

'I'm not saying that's a good thing or a bad thing,' Matty responded. 'I'm just saying, is all.' He sighed. 'All right – what's the plan?'

'We take all of these boxes and dump their contents in the vats outside.'

Matty shrugged. 'Somehow I knew it would mean getting closer to those vats. You know those workers aren't going to let us come back once, let alone twice?'

'Then we'll have to distract them.'

'With what?'

'I'm still working on that.' He thought for a moment. 'It's got to be something that will attract them all to one side of the building.'

'Fire?' Matty suggested.

'Too dangerous.'

'What if I let myself be seen, and they chase after me?'

'That leaves me having to shift twenty-six boxes by myself.'

'Oh.' Matty's expression brightened. 'What if we wait until it's dark, then we come back, break in and destroy them for good in peace: undisturbed, like?'

Sherlock shook his head. 'This place is so important that Harkness will have it guarded at night. We were only able to sneak in now because it's daylight, and there's a lot of activity in the tannery. At night, in the quiet, any guard will hear us or spot us straight away, so that rules out hiding here until the sun goes down. No, it's got to be now.' He thought for a moment, 'I suppose,' he said slowly, 'we could pull up some floorboards. This room is built up above ground level. Maybe we could hide the boxes beneath the floorboards. Harkness wouldn't know what had happened to them.' He frowned, thinking through the obvious problems. 'No, we couldn't lever the floorboards up without leaving splinters and marks. Harkness would guess straight away what we'd done.'

'Well, I'm stumped,' Matty said. 'Let's just call it a day, shall we?'

'Let's not. There has to be a solution.' He let his mind go blank, hoping that the various pieces of the puzzle that were whirling around his head would settle down into some meaningful pattern. Gradually they did. 'Right – here's what we'll do. You're going to sneak around the vats to the far side and make a hole in one of them.'

'With what?'

'Have you got a knife?'

Matty reached into a pocket and took one out. The blade was folded into the handle. 'I got this.'

'Use it to carve out a hole in the wooden slats that make up the side of the furthest vat, or put it between two of the slats and prise them apart. Do it without being seen.'

'All right. Assuming I'm not seen, what happens then?'

'The stuff inside the vat starts leaking out. When they spot it, they'll call everyone over to help seal the hole and mop up the stuff on the floor.'

'So they're all distracted for a while. That's when we take the boxes out and throw them in the nearest vat?'

'That's right. Except that we need to find a faster way of doing it. You remember when we came in, we saw a wooden chute leaning up against the wall?'

'Yeah,' Matty said dubiously.

'That's probably what they use to get the cow hides into the vats. I can't imagine they hoist them up on their shoulders and throw them in one by one – that would be hard, and very messy. I think they just slide them down the chute. While they're distracted, I'll get the chute and run it down from here to the nearest vat. We can slide the boxes down.'

'It's a plan,' Matty said. 'Not sure it's a good one, but I can't think of anything better.'

'Right – let's go.'

Sherlock moved to the door and opened it a crack. The eye-watering, nose-grating sewer smell of the tannery intensified. Gazing out, he noticed that the room was still deserted, although he could hear voices. Whatever Josh Harkness was doing with his workers, it was taking time.

He turned his head to see Matty. 'All right – go!' he hissed.

Matty squeezed past him and through the door. Moving quietly, he made his way along the raised wooden flooring to a set of steps that led down into the central area of the room, past another of the wooden chutes. He slipped across the room, moving from vat to vat, using each as cover, until he vanished from Sherlock's view.

The next few minutes were nerve-racking. Sherlock waited, hardly able to breathe, not knowing whether Matty was actually making a hole in the furthest vat. Maybe he was desperately trying to carve his way through wood that was too hard for his blade? Maybe he had been caught by Harkness or one of his men?

A movement off to one side attracted his attention. One of the men with the long hooked poles was coming around the side of a vat. He stopped and started to roll a cigarette one-handed. Sherlock's gaze flicked across to where he'd seen Matty vanish, but the boy wasn't visible. The worker didn't look as if an intruder had just been discovered, so Sherlock had to assume that he was still safe.

Just as he was about to look away, he saw a head peeping out from behind one of the vats. It was Matty. From his position, Matty couldn't see the man with the hooked pole, but if he moved forward a few feet he would be in the man's line of sight. Sherlock desperately willed Matty to look his way, but his friend seemed to be nerving himself up to run back to the steps.

Sherlock was preparing himself to make some noise that would attract Matty's attention when the boy looked up at him. Sherlock gestured to him to stay where he was. Matty shook his head. Sherlock nodded towards the place where the worker was standing and made a walking movement with his fingers. Matty nodded in understanding.

Sherlock stared over at the worker again. He had lit his cigarette and was strolling forward, hooked pole held over his shoulder like a rifle. Another few steps and, if he looked to his left, he would see Matty.

Sherlock didn't know what to do. If he attracted the man's attention away from Matty, then he would expose himself, but he couldn't let Matty be discovered.

Someone shouted from the other side of the vats. It sounded as if it might have been the worker who had argued with Josh Harkness. 'We got a leak!' he shouted. 'You know the drill! Marky – get some sheets to mop up the stuff. Nicholson – you and me need to caulk that hole with some hemp quick and then nail a patch across it!'

The man with the pole ran to help. Sherlock beckoned Matty, who raced across to the steps. Sherlock ran to join him.

'You start hauling the boxes out,' he said. 'I'll get the chute.'

Matty disappeared back into the storeroom and Sherlock quickly moved to where the wooden chute was leaning up against the railings. It was heavier than it looked, and it took all his strength to manhandle it back to the storeroom and then from the railing to the edge of the nearest vat.

By the time Sherlock was ready Matty had stacked four boxes. While he went back for more, Sherlock took the boxes one at a time and pushed them down the chute. The angle wasn't steep enough to allow the boxes to slide by themselves, but Sherlock found that he could use the second box to push the first, and then the third box to push the other two. In less than a minute he had all four boxes on the chute, and he was straining against the last one, trying to get all four to move.

The first box was teetering over the vat now. Sherlock took a step back and then ran forward, hitting the last box in the same way he'd tackled players on the rugby field at Deepdene School. The box jerked forward, transmitting its force down the line to the first one, which tumbled into the vat.

Too soon for congratulations. As Matty kept delivering the boxes, Sherlock kept stacking them on to the chute and ramming them forward. Box after box tumbled into the vat. Sherlock could see them floating in the poisonous, noxious mixture before it filled them up and they sank. Hopefully into oblivion.

On the other side of the vats he could hear raised voices and the sound of hammering.

The work fell into a repetitive routine. Pick up box. Put box on chute. Push box as hard as possible. Pick up another box. His muscles ached with the strain.

Eventually he became aware that Matty was standing beside him, helping push the boxes. 'Last ones,' Matty said. He looked exhausted. Dust coated his hair and his face.

'What the . . . ?' a voice shouted.

Sherlock looked down into the centre of the room.

Josh Harkness was staring up at the two boys. His face was a mask of outraged disbelief.

'Quick,' Sherlock said. 'Let's get the last boxes in there!'

'I saved the lightest for last,' Matty said. 'You can probably throw them.'

He was right. Sherlock picked up the box marked *Y* and, balancing himself like a shot-putter, launched it towards the vat.

'Oi!' Harkness yelled. 'Stop that!'

The box hit the edge, and for a moment Sherlock thought it was going to topple backwards, but fortunately its momentum carried it forward and over.

'Get them!' Harkness yelled. Two of the workers Sherlock had seen earlier ran from the far side of the room. They hesitated slightly when they saw the boys, but the vicious anger in Harkness's face propelled them forward. They swung their hooked poles forward like lances.

Sherlock grabbed Matty's shoulder and pulled him along the raised platform, towards the room where they had entered. Behind them he heard the clattering of feet on the wooden stairs.

Matty got to the door first. He turned to say something to Sherlock. Before he could, Sherlock pushed him backwards and ducked. A pole sliced the air above his head, and a sharp-edged hook embedded itself in the door frame.

'Get out!' Sherlock yelled. 'Quickly!'

Matty scooted backwards into the room on hands and feet. Sherlock swung around to confront the man who had attacked him. He was tugging at the pole, trying to free it from the door frame. His friend was about ten feet behind him, approaching with violence in his eyes. Harkness had grabbed a ladder from somewhere and was climbing up the side of the vat into which the boxes had been dumped, obviously hoping that he could rescue something from the mess that Sherlock had made of his raw blackmail material.

Sherlock offered up a rapid prayer that he would fall in, before quickly following Matty inside the storeroom. He slammed the door shut, knowing that it would only buy them a few seconds.

Matty was already over by the window. He turned, saw Sherlock and made a step with his hands: palms up and fingers interlaced. 'You get up,' he said. 'Pull me after you.'

The door behind Sherlock shuddered as something slammed into it.

Sherlock took three steps across the room, bent, grabbed Matty's legs and hoisted him up to the window. 'Get out!' he said. 'I'll follow.'

Matty looked as if he wanted to argue, but he was already half out into the street. Sensibly he struggled forward rather than backwards.

The door burst open. One man was framed in the

doorway, with the other man visible behind him.

'You little whelp!' the first man snarled. He stepped forward, pole upraised.

Sherlock grabbed another pole from the bundle that had been stacked against the wall. He stood, pole held diagonally across his body, feet planted apart, knowing that it was going to come down to a fight. It sometimes seemed to him that he could use all the logic in the world and things would often still come down to a fight.

The man was average height, with a paunch, but the battered nature of his ears, and the bend in his nose, suggested to Sherlock that he had a history of boxing – probably illegally, in rings set up in fields, rather than using Queensberry Rules. He stepped forward, holding his pole diagonally as well, but the other way. He smiled.

'I'll be Little John,' he said, 'and you can be Robin Hood.'

'This isn't a kids' game,' Sherlock said.

'Too right,' the man said. He suddenly struck out with his pole, trying to smash Sherlock's knee with the bottom end. Sherlock blocked with his own pole. The sudden shock as they clashed vibrated up his arm and made his teeth ache.

The man nodded, acknowledging Sherlock's un-expected manoeuvre. He lashed out again with the bottom end of his pole, but it was a feint. He reversed direction suddenly, bringing the top down towards

Sherlock's head. Sherlock raised his pole with both hands, preventing the man's weapon from knocking him out and probably splitting his skull, but before the poles could touch the man had reversed his strike again, bringing his pole up towards Sherlock's groin. Sherlock twisted to one side, but the pole struck his right hip. He fell to one knee just in time to see the pole scythe sideways an inch above his head.

Desperately Sherlock climbed back to his feet, ignoring the spasms of pain that shot from his hip down towards his knee. The man was off balance, and Sherlock reached out with his pole and caught the back of the man's shoe with the hook on the end. He pulled, and the man fell backwards, swearing. He hit the ground with a *thud* that sent a vibration through the wooden flooring.

The second man stepped over his fallen comrade. He was more cautious, weaving his pole from side to side in an attempt to deceive Sherlock as to the direction the first strike would come from. He feinted once, twice, then drew the pole back and lashed out at Sherlock as if he was holding a spear rather than a quarterstaff. As Sherlock jerked backwards he realized that the sharp hook on the end could be just as lethal as a spear point.

The man pulled his pole back again. Instead of attacking Sherlock he turned his head slightly and spoke to his companion. 'Get up, you moron! Go outside – get that other kid if he's still around, and stop this one getting out of the window if he's not.'

The man shook his head as he climbed to his feet. His expression was a mixture of sullen and furious. 'I want this one, Marky. I *really* want this one. You saw what he did.'

'I saw you fall over on your fat rump,' Marky snarled. 'Now get outside. This ain't a time for bruised muscles and bruised feelings. The boss will want to talk to this one, and knowing you like I do, you'll slit his throat for making you look stupid, and then the boss will take it out on both of us.'

The man – presumably Nicholson, based on the names Sherlock had heard earlier – backed away and turned towards the door to the outside. He cast a last, baleful glance at Sherlock before he left.

'You don't want to go through the window,' Marky said, smiling at Sherlock. 'If Nicholson catches you, then the chances are you'll be dead before your feet touch the ground, despite what I told him. He don't like being embarrassed. Really don't like it at all.'

'So what's my alternative?' Sherlock asked, keeping his eyes fixed on Marky's eyes, looking for some indication that the man was about to strike with his hook-tipped pole.

'The alternative is that you put that pole down and come with me. The boss wants to talk with you, is all. Just a little talk.'

Sherlock shook his head. 'Based on what I've done, I think I've got a better chance with your friend outside than with Josh Harkness. At least I'd die quickly.'

Marky shrugged. 'I see your point, I really do. It's a conundrum, isn't it? Go out of the window and you die straight away, but quickly. Come with me and you stay alive for a little longer, but your death is more painful and slower.' He dropped his voice, trying to lull Sherlock into relaxing. 'You know, kid, if I were you, I'd –'

Without warning he lashed out with the pole, trying to get the hook past Sherlock's shoulder so he could catch it in the flesh and muscle over Sherlock's shoulder blade and pull him forward, but Sherlock had noticed the slight widening of his eyes that meant he was about to do something physical. It was one of the things Amyus Crowe had taught him – how to predict from small movements what people were going to do. 'Body language', he had called it. Sherlock swept his pole left and right across his body, intercepting Marky's weapon as it flashed towards him and deflecting it sideways.

'So that's the way you want it then,' Marky said, pulling back again. 'A stand-off, right? Except that when the boss arrives it'll be two against one, and you won't stand a chance.'

'There's always a chance,' Sherlock said with as much bravado as he could muster.

'Two ways to escape,' Marky pointed out, 'both of them covered. Unless you can magically walk through walls or disappear through the floor, you ain't got a hope of escaping.'

'I do if –' Sherlock caught himself before he said Matty's name – 'if my friend escaped before Nicholson got to the window. He'll have gone straight to the police. They'll be here in a few minutes.'

Marky shook his head scornfully. 'The local peelers don't dare make a move against the boss. He knows too much about them.'

'But how's he going to prove it?' Sherlock asked. 'All his blackmail material has just been destroyed.'

Marky frowned, thinking.

'Once the police know that all the letters and documents Harkness was holding over their heads have vanished into the tanning vats, they'll know he can't blackmail them any more. What will they do then?' Noticing Marky's perturbed expression, he pressed on more urgently. 'Firstly they'll want to come out here and make sure it's true, and secondly they'll pay Harkness back for everything he's done to them. Once he's lost his power, he's just like any farmer or brewer in Farnham – with the exception that they hate him. He'll be lucky if he makes it to the cells in one piece.'

Sherlock could tell from the way Marky's shoulders slumped that his points had hit home.

'How's he going to pay you?' he asked. 'All the material he's been using to blackmail people has gone, one of his tanning vats is contaminated and another one is leaking. One of his businesses is finished and the other one is in trouble. If I were you, I'd be looking for other employment.' He paused for a moment. 'Unless he's got something on you as well, but if that's the case then the proof's in the vat along with everything else. All Josh Harkness has is word of mouth, but that's not going to get him very far. Nobody's going to believe a story with no proof.'

'You're a smart kid,' Marky acknowledged. He nodded thoughtfully. 'You're right – Harkness is finished. If the police don't get him, then some of the landowners around here who he's been blackmailing will soon take the law into their own hands. He'll end up as compost on someone's fields before long.' He relaxed, letting the pole drop. 'If anything happens – if I get caught – you'll put in a good word for me. Tell the peelers I let you go.' He nodded once, decisively. 'Time for a career change,' he said, and then he turned and vanished through the doorway.

Sherlock couldn't believe what had happened. He'd been expecting to have to fight his way out. He'd been talking in order to distract Marky, to give himself time to catch his breath and work out a plan of attack, but he seemed to have actually talked himself out of trouble.

He gazed at the window. It was tempting, but the other man – Nicholson – was probably underneath by now, and after what had happened earlier Sherlock didn't think that the man would be amenable to argument.

Reluctantly he headed for the door back into the tannery.

He looked around, alert for Josh Harkness's presence, but he couldn't see the blackmailer. The only sign that he'd been there was the pile of damp, stained paper and cardboard boxes that slumped beside the nearest vat in a puddle of brown liquid. The smell was worse than it had been earlier – probably because Harkness had been stirring the stuff in the vats around while he was trying to rescue his blackmail material. One look at the papers and Sherlock knew they were useless for anything. What little printed material was still visible through the stains was smearing into incoherence.

He headed around the wooden walkway towards where the main door had to be, hoping that Harkness had already left.

He was wrong.

The blackmailer stepped out from behind one of the vats. His hair was sticking up wildly, and his eyes were so wide they were nearly popping out of his head. He held a knife in each hand. The light reflected off the wickedly sharp curve of the blades.

'Flensing knives,' he said casually, although his expression was anything but casual. 'Used for cutting the skin off cow carcasses. Very sharp. Very sharp indeed. As you are about to find out.'

'There's no benefit in killing me,' Sherlock pointed out calmly, despite the sudden rapid thudding of his heart.

'No benefit at all,' Harkness agreed, 'apart from the

fact that it'll let me sleep a little better tonight. You've ruined me. You've stolen the food from my mouth and taken the roof from over my head.'

'I've saved a whole lot of people from ruin and despair,' Sherlock pointed out. 'It seems like a fair bargain to me.'

'Nobody asked you.' Harkness shifted position. 'Half an hour ago I was a man contented with his lot. Now I'm destitute. I'll have to start all over again.'

'If the people around here let you.' Sherlock walked casually down the few steps that led to the central part of the room. He was too exposed on the walkway. 'When they find out your power over them has gone, some of them will come looking for you. Best thing you can do is run.'

'You're right,' Harkness nodded. 'But I'm going to take as much of your skin with me as I can cut off, and when I find a place to settle I'm going to have it tanned and made into a waistcoat so that people will be able to look at me and know what happens if you cross Josh Harkness.'

Before Sherlock could say anything in response Harkness drew his right hand back over his shoulder and jerked it suddenly forward, throwing one of the flensing knives at Sherlock's head. The knife seemed to spin lazily in the air. Sherlock ducked, and the blade embedded itself in the wood of the nearest vat.

Harkness hefted the remaining knife, tossing it from

left hand to right. 'You can't run forever, son. But by all means try. It'll make things sweeter for me.'

Sherlock turned and tried to prise the knife out of the vat, but it was stuck fast. A sudden intuition made him jerk his head to one side, just as the second knife whistled past his face. This one hit the vat handle-first, bounced and clattered to the floor. Sherlock bent to pick it up, but Harkness was rushing towards him, arms outstretched, and Sherlock converted the duck to a spring and a forward roll to take him out of Harkness's way.

The blackmailer scooped one knife off the floor and pulled the other one from the vat with extraordinary strength. He turned to face Sherlock. 'The longer you fight,' he snarled, 'the better that waistcoat will look on me.'

'Dream on,' Sherlock said. 'The only new clothes you're going to get are a prison uniform.' He reached to one side, to the ladder that Harkness had used to get up to the rim of the vat. Grabbing it by the rungs at the top end, he swung it around until the other end pointed at Harkness. The man's eyes widened even further. He pulled his right hand back again, preparing to throw a knife, but Sherlock rushed at him, hitting him in the chest with the bottom rung, pushing him backwards. Caught by surprise, Harkness staggered backwards, arms flailing. Before he could catch his footing and push back, his right heel caught in the slushy papers and cardboard that he had pulled from the vat. His foot skidded, and he fell. His head hit the wooden floor with a solid *crack*. His eyes rolled up in his head.

Before Harkness could recover, Sherlock threw the ladder to one side and dropped on to the man's chest, his knees pinning the man's arms to the floor. He scooped the knives from Harkness's nerveless hands and held them up, poised, with the blades pointing at Harkness's face. Harkness was horrified. Before he could struggle free, Sherlock brought the knives flashing down, one on either side of the man's neck. The knives embedded themselves into the wood, pinning the material of his jacket to the floor.

Sherlock climbed to his feet and stared down at the man. 'This is where the police will find you,' he said. 'Remember that sometimes the rabbits fight back.'

He turned and ran towards the door.

CHAPTER FIVE

After leaving the police station, where he had given the police an edited version of what had happened, Sherlock stood breathing the fresh air. It was like diving into a sparkling river when you were covered in mud. He could feel the horrible smells of the tannery being flushed from his lungs. He knew the air outside wasn't particularly fresh, but compared to the stench inside the tannery it was as pure as could be.

He had a feeling that his clothes had become impregnated with the smell, and he decided that he needed to change as soon as possible.

He found Matty standing beneath the window of the tannery. His friend breathed a visible sigh of relief when he saw Sherlock.

'Wasn't sure what had happened to you,' he said. 'I thought Harkness might have got you.' He frowned. 'What happened to Harkness? You didn't . . . *kill* him, did you?'

Sherlock shook his head wearily. 'We had a little talk,' he said. 'I left him there and told the police where to find him.'

Matty shrugged. 'It won't make any difference. When the big fish in the pond gets caught,' he said, 'the next biggest one takes over. That's the way things go.'

'I know,' Sherlock said, 'but I can't do anything about that. Not right now. At least we've got Harkness out of the way, and destroyed his blackmail material. That'll make a lot of people happy.' He frowned, looking at the way Matty was casually standing in the middle of the alley. 'What happened to that man who got sent out – Nicholson?'

'The bloke with the beer belly? He came out and just stood here. Didn't look happy. Looked like he'd tear someone's head off as soon as talk to them, in fact.'

'Where were you?'

Matty indicated a pile of crates on the other side of the alley. 'When I heard him coming I hid there. He wasn't exactly keeping quiet. There was curse words he used that I'd never heard before.'

'So what happened?'

'He stood there for a few minutes, then his friend came out.'

'Marky,' Sherlock confirmed.

'Yeah, him. He grabbed the other bloke by the arm and said something to him. Next thing I knew they were both heading off down the alley.'

Sherlock nodded. 'I managed to persuade Marky that, with Harkness's blackmail material gone, the town was going to become a very unfriendly place for them to be. I think they've decided to try their fortunes elsewhere.'

'Where to now?'

'Let's go home,' Sherlock said.

'I ain't got a home, apart from the narrowboat.'

'I meant Holmes Manor.'

Matty shook his head forcefully. 'I don't like that housekeeper,' he said, 'and she don't like me. If you don't mind, I'd rather stay here.'

'I think,' Sherlock said, 'that you'll find Mrs Eglantine's influence over the Holmes household will diminish rapidly within the next hour or so. I'm sure you'll find yourself welcome at the manor from now on.' He glanced critically at his friend. 'Well, if you dust yourself off and comb your hair, you will.'

With Matty perched behind him on Philadelphia's back, Sherlock cantered along the familiar roads towards Holmes Manor.

'Do you think I could get something to eat when we get there?' Matty called over Sherlock's shoulder.

'I think that can be arranged,' Sherlock called back.

It took about half an hour to get to the manor house, and when they turned in through the main gate and headed up along the drive to the house Sherlock could feel Matty tensing behind him. Bypassing the front door, he trotted around to the stables and left the horse in the care of one of the grooms.

'Come on,' he said. 'I'm eager to see this matter closed.'

He entered through the main door, Matty behind him. The shadowy hallway seemed empty, but he knew that appearances were deceptive.

'Mrs Eglantine!' he called.

A part of the shadows detached itself and stepped forward. The temperature in the hall seemed to drop by ten degrees. 'Young Master Holmes,' said a voice in a tone so cold that icicles could have formed. 'As you seem so determined to use this house as a hotel, coming and going when you please, perhaps you ought to be paying for the privilege of staying here.'

'I would expect the quality of the housekeeping staff in a hotel to be considerably better than here,' he rejoined.

The expression on Mrs Eglantine's face didn't change, but Sherlock felt the atmosphere in the hallway become even colder.

'Make your quips, child,' she hissed. 'Enjoy them while you can. Your time in this house is limited.'

'If you are expecting your friend Josh Harkness to do something about me, you are going to be disappointed. Mr Harkness is in custody, and won't be getting out in a hurry.'

'You are lying,' she said through clenched teeth, but Sherlock could tell that she was suddenly on the defensive.

'I never lie,' he said simply. 'I leave that to people like you.' He paused for a moment, working out his next move. 'Please tell my aunt and uncle that I wish to talk to them in the dining room.'

'Tell them yourself,' she said. Her voice could have cut glass.

'You are the servant here, not me. Pass on my request. Do it now. Please be so good as to ask Cook for a plate of sandwiches and a jug of lemonade as well. My friend and I are hungry and thirsty.'

The housekeeper stared at him with an expression on her face that indicated that she was re-evaluating him, and didn't like what she was discovering. She turned and disappeared into the shadows.

'Come on,' he said to Matty. 'Let's get ready.'

He led the way across the hall to the dining room. It struck him that he could have chosen to have the confrontation in the reception room, where guests were entertained, but he wanted to do this somewhere more formal, less comfortable.

The table in the centre of the dining room was bare apart from two candlesticks and a bowl of fruit. Matty helped himself to a pear while Sherlock sat in a chair on the far side, with the light of the windows behind him. Matty followed him around the table and stood behind him eating the pear.

Sherlock tried to quiet his breathing. He knew what he wanted to achieve over the next few minutes, but he knew that he was dealing with people, not chess pieces, and people sometimes did what you least expected them to do. What if Mrs Eglantine had more influence over his uncle and aunt than just her possession of some incriminating material? Perhaps they would defend Mrs Eglantine, despite what had already gone on in the house. Perhaps the three of them would join forces against him.

The door opened and Sherrinford Holmes entered, with Aunt Anna close behind him.

'It is unusual for a man who is master in his own house to be summoned by his ward,' he said mildly.

'I apologize if Mrs Eglantine gave the impression that I was summoning you,' Sherlock replied quietly. 'I merely wanted to talk to you both about something serious.'

'Is this related to what happened in the library earlier today?' Sherrinford Holmes asked. 'If so, I distinctly remember saying that we would speak no more about it.'

'This concerns a man named Josh Harkness,' Sherlock said, 'and his influence on this family.' He felt that he should ask his aunt and uncle to sit down, but that would have been rude. It was their house and their dining room: he didn't want to be seen as being arrogant.

Before Sherrinford could reply, Mrs Eglantine entered the dining room. Two maids followed her; one carried a plate of sandwiches while the other held a tray with a jug and four glasses. They put them on the table.

'Please,' Sherlock said to Mrs Eglantine as the maids

left, 'stay for a few moments. This concerns you as much as it concerns my aunt and uncle.'

She opened her mouth as if to say something, but then closed it again. She seemed edgy, uncertain. Even scared.

'You haven't introduced me to your friend,' Sherrinford said. He pulled out a seat at the dining table for his wife. She sat, and he followed.

'This is Matthew Arnatt,' Sherlock said. 'He lives in Farnham.'

'A gypsy,' Mrs Eglantine said. 'Of no worth.'

'I told you before,' Matty said from behind Sherlock, 'I ain't no 'Gyptian.'

Sherrinford Holmes tapped the table briefly. 'Even if you were,' he said, 'not only are the Egyptians a noble and ancient race who are often mentioned in the Bible, but you are also named for one of Jesus Christ's disciples and the author of one of the four Gospels. You are welcome in my house, Matthew.'

'Cheers,' Matty said.

'Are you hungry?' Sherlock's aunt asked. 'Perhaps you would like a sandwich and a glass of lemonade.'

'Don't mind if I do,' the boy said, and reached over Sherlock's shoulder to grab a couple of sandwiches.

'So,' Sherrinford Holmes said, 'what is so important that you have convened a family conference, and what does this have to do with the man you mentioned – a man whose name I cannot bring my lips to form.'

94

Sherlock took a deep breath. 'Josh Harkness is a blackmailer,' he said. 'He collects facts about people – facts that they would rather did not become public – and he threatens to expose them if they don't pay him money on a regular basis.'

'Are you implying,' Sherrinford said, a quiet note of warning in his voice, 'that this criminal has somehow discovered a secret about this family? I am a respected biblical scholar, and my wife is a pillar of the local community. What secrets could we possibly have that would attract the attention of a villain of this calibre?'

Sherlock shook his head. 'It doesn't matter what he may or may not have discovered. The important thing is that all of his files – his entire collection of documents and letters – have been destroyed.'

Mrs Eglantine gasped, and brought a hand up to her mouth.

'Are you sure?' Sherrinford Holmes asked, leaning forward. ' "But the tongue can no man tame; it is an unruly evil, full of deadly poison." James, chapter three, verse eight.'

'Absolutely sure,' Matty interrupted through a mouthful of sandwich. 'We did it together.'

'You saw it?' Sherrinford asked. 'You saw it yourself?'

'I did. The contents of every box have been rendered unreadable.'

Sherrinford Holmes leaned back in his chair and ran his right hand across his brow. With his left hand he reached out and patted his wife's arm. 'Then the nightmare is . . . over.' He sighed.

There was silence in the room for a minute or so. No noise, no movement, but something changed. It was as if a cloud had moved away from the sun. The room seemed lighter and warmer than it had before.

'You have done this family, and many others, a great service,' Sherrinford Holmes said. 'I can see the same mark of character in you that I see in your brother, and also in your father – *my* brother. I am in your debt.' He turned to face Mrs Eglantine. 'And I am no longer in thrall to you, evil woman that you are. Whatever you were looking for in this house, you will never find it. Pack your bags. If you are not out of this house within the hour then your possessions will be placed in a pile and I will personally set light to them and then horsewhip you into the bargain. I wish never to see your face or hear your voice for as long as I live. You are *not* welcome here.'

'I still know what I know!' Mrs Eglantine proclaimed, stepping forward. 'You will not get rid of me so easily.'

'Nobody will believe you,' Aunt Anna said. She stood up, her diminutive form seemingly towering over the tall housekeeper. 'England is full of former housekeepers with a grudge. Nobody believes their stories, and for good reason. "Gossiping and lying go hand in hand," as they say.'

Sherrinford nodded. '"Thy voice shall be a rebuke unto the transgressor; and at thy rebuke let the tongue of the slanderer cease its perverseness,"' he quoted softly. 'Leave here now, woman, while you still can.'

Mrs Eglantine glared at the four of them – Sherlock, Matty, Uncle Sherrinford and Aunt Anna. Her mouth opened and closed a few times, as if she knew she wanted to say something but she didn't know what exactly. Then she turned and slipped out of the room like a shadow banished by the opening of a curtain.

'Can it be that simple?' Sherrinford asked. He reached out to take his wife's hand.

'You'll have to watch out for her,' Sherlock replied. 'She may try to take something. She may even try to slip back into the house when there's nobody around. There's something here she wants, and I can't see her giving it up easily. But it's going to be a lot more difficult for her now. Her power base has been taken away.'

'I almost can't believe it,' Aunt Anna said. 'She has been such a malign presence here for so long that I almost cannot imagine life without her.'

'Do you have any idea what she was looking for?' Matty asked.

Sherrinford shook his head. 'She never said. It was some time before I even realized she was searching for anything. She applied for the job of housekeeper three years ago, and since her references were impeccable I gladly gave her the job, but she was sullen and the staff did not take to her. Eventually I asked her to leave, but she revealed that she knew . . . certain facts about this family that I would not wish to be revealed. She forced us to let her stay, and she forced us to make payments to her that she transferred on to that odious man Joshua Harkness.' He sighed. 'One day I found her searching our bedroom. I demanded to know what she was doing. She told me to mind my own business. I told her that she was in my house and it was my business to know what she was doing. She laughed scornfully, and said that it was her house now.'

'We became aware that she was searching every room, one by one,' Aunt Anna said quietly when it became apparent that Sherrinford wasn't going to continue. 'But we never found out what she was looking for. It's not as if there are many valuables in the house.'

'She had blueprints of the house,' Sherlock remembered. 'They're in her room, hanging outside the window. You should get them back, before someone else finds them.'

Sherrinford shook his head, and smiled. Sherlock couldn't remember ever seeing his uncle smile before. 'I believe that I have a bottle of Madeira which I have been keeping for a special occasion,' he said. 'This is probably as close to a special occasion as I will get in my life. I appreciate that you are both barely more than children, but I feel that God and your families would forgive me if I offered you a glass. A small one, of course.'

Sherrinford Holmes peered sideways at his wife and raised an enquiring eyebrow. She nodded, and he went to the sideboard to get a bottle and some glasses.

'I feel that we owe you an explanation,' he said as he returned and sat down. 'Mrs Eglantine has made your life here unpleasant, to put it mildly, and after what you have done for us the least we can do for you is tell you what it was that she knew.'

'Sherlock shook his head. 'It's not necessary,' he said. 'All families deserve to have their secrets.'

'But this secret affects you,' Sherrinford said. 'We have kept it from you for long enough.' He squeezed his wife's arm, and she patted his hand in reassurance.

Sherlock felt as if the ground beneath his feet was sliding slowly sideways. A secret that involved *him*?

Sherrinford opened his mouth to say something, but hesitated. He gazed at Matty, frowning. 'Perhaps . . .' he ventured, 'this should wait until later. When we can discuss things between ourselves.'

Sherlock looked over at Matty. 'Whatever it is,' he said firmly, 'I don't want to keep it secret any more. Matty is my friend. There isn't anything I don't want him to know about me.'

Sherrinford looked unconvinced. 'Even so, Sherlock, this *is* a family matter. Is it appropriate that others find out? Perhaps your brother should be consulted before we speak in front of others.'

'Others have already found out.' Sherlock's gaze moved from his uncle to his aunt and back again. 'Look, I once heard Mycroft say that sunlight is the best cleaning agent. I thought he meant it literally at the time, that rooms with the curtains drawn get dusty and cobwebby, but I've come to realize that he was speaking figuratively. What he was trying to say was that hiding things away just makes the situation worse. Knowing the truth, letting *everyone* know the truth, is usually the best course of action.'

Sherrinford sighed. 'Very well,' he said slowly, pouring the Madeira into the glasses. 'This involves your father. It goes back to when we were children together. Siger – your father – was a strange child, even then. Some days he would be bright and full of energy, able to climb any tree and jump any fence, bolting his food and speaking faster than people could understand. Other days he would just lie in bed or mope around the house, listless and uninterested. Our father said that he would grow out of it. Our mother was less sure. She called in various doctors to give a diagnosis. The ones who came when he was running around and not stopping for breath said that he was naturally boisterous. The ones who saw him when he took no interest in anything around him said that he was sensitive and maudlin in nature – melancholic. When the melancholia or the mania became too much for our father and mother to manage, he was taken into an asylum and looked after there.'

'My father was . . . *is* . . . insane?' Sherlock whispered.

'I would never have used that word to describe him,'

Sherrinford said sternly. 'He was . . . *is* . . . my brother, and there were days when you could not tell there was anything wrong with him.' He paused. 'But on other days he would become so excited that he could be dangerous, or so maudlin that he talked of ending his own life. I say he was "looked after" at the asylum rather than "cared for", because I visited him once, and I will never forget the abject horror of his surroundings. They left their mark on him, I am sure.' He paused, staring at the table, but Sherlock suspected that, in his mind, he was seeing things from long ago. 'One physician in particular who saw him when he was living at home, in between visits to the asylum, was particularly well read. He had heard of a Frenchman who had described a disease which he called *folie à double forme*, or ' "dual-form insanity". Well, this particular physician tried various remedies – a tincture of black hellebore to induce vomiting, a decoction of foxglove, and hemlock juice. They had some effect, but not enough. The only thing that truly helped was morphine.'

Morphine! The word struck Sherlock like an icy dagger through the heart. He'd had his own experiences with morphine. Baron Maupertuis's men had drugged him with laudanum, which was morphine in alcohol, and the Paradol Chamber had later used a similar drug on Sherlock's brother, Mycroft. Was the whole family's history tied up with the horrible stuff?

'What exactly *is* morphine?' Matty asked.

'It is a substance which can be derived from opium,

which is itself the dried sap of the poppy plant. It is an evil chemical, of which I will say no more, except that it did stabilize Siger's extreme mood swings.' Sherrinford laughed humourlessly. 'It is named for the Greek god of dreams – Morpheus.'

Sherlock shook his head. 'I'm not sure I understand. My father was ill, and this drug made him better. What's the problem?'

'The problem,' Sherrinford answered, 'is that our society is not tolerant of those who have . . . problems of the mind. With his morphine treatment Siger grew up tall and strong, with nobody outside the family knowing that anything was wrong. He married into a good family, and joined the Army. If it was discovered that he was ill in the head, then he would be cashiered from the Army. His friends and neighbours would withdraw from him. Shame would be brought on the family – not that I care particularly about that, but he and your mother would lose *everything*. Not only that, but the stigma would attach itself to him, to her, and to you and your brother. You would be labelled as the sons of a madman. People would assume you were likely to go mad yourselves.'

'How did Mrs Eglantine find out about this?' Sherlock whispered.

'She was a maid at the asylum,' Aunt Anna said quietly. 'This was when she was young. She must have seen Siger one day, quite by accident, when he was older and wearing his Army uniform. She realized the scandal that would attach itself to the family if it were known that he had spent time in an asylum and was dependent on drugs for his sanity, and she started blackmailing us.'

Sherlock frowned. 'That's what I don't understand,' he said. 'Why blackmail *you*? Why not blackmail my father, or my mother, or Mycroft?'

'Perhaps she was,' Sherrinford said simply. 'We never asked.'

A thought occurred to Sherlock. He paused before saying anything, turning the thought over and over in his mind, examining it from all angles just in case he'd missed something. It was a big thought, and he wanted to make sure he'd got it right before he said something embarrassing.

'From what you've told us,' he said eventually, and carefully, 'the family secret that you were keeping concerned my father, and my father's side of the family. It occurs to me that if the secret got out, the family shame wouldn't reflect on *you*. It would be us – and in particular *him* – who would face problems.'

Sherlock's Aunt Anna smiled at him and reached out across the table to pat his hand. 'Bless you, Sherlock,' she said. 'We couldn't let that happen to Siger. He's family. He and Sherrinford grew up together. We couldn't stand by and let him be shamed in that way. I remember how proud he was when he got into the Army. It would be quite wrong to take that away from him.'

'But your lives have been affected badly by Mrs Eglantine's presence in this house.'

'The Good Lord puts us all through the fire at some time in our lives,' Sherrinford said. 'He tests us, and we must not be found wanting.'

'What else should we have done?' Aunt Anna asked, more practically. 'Should we have told that odious Mr Harkness that we were not going to pay, and then watched as our own kin was humiliated in public? That would not have been right.'

Sherlock glanced from his aunt to his uncle. He found himself thinking about them in a different way. They weren't fusty old relics of a bygone age to him now; they were living people, with feelings and cares and concerns. He tried to visualize Sherrinford and his father playing together as boys. He tried to visualize his aunt as a younger woman, in her finest dress, perhaps attending the wedding of Siger Holmes and Sherlock's mother. For a moment he found that he could.

'Thank you,' he said simply. 'On behalf of my mother and my father, neither of whom can say this themselves for different reasons, thank you.'

'It was the least we could do,' said Sherrinford.

'It wasn't,' Sherlock replied. 'That's why it was such a noble and self-sacrificing gesture.'

'Now,' Aunt Anna said, 'I must go and see to hiring another housekeeper. This place won't run itself, and the maids are so flighty that they need someone looking over their shoulder all the time, otherwise who knows what will happen.'

'And I have a library to tidy,' Uncle Sherrinford said. 'That could take some time.'

They both stood. With a final smile from Sherlock's aunt, and an absent wave of the hand from his uncle, they left the room.

'Nice people,' Matty observed.

'Nice doesn't anywhere near cover it,' Sherlock replied.

'So, what do you want to do now?'

Sherlock thought for a moment. 'I was thinking of going over to Amyus Crowe's cottage. I think he ought to hear what's happened. We should also probably let him know about those American men who were looking for him in the market earlier. They did mention his name.'

Matty shrugged. 'He might have some advice on what to do if Josh Harkness decides to hang around and take his lost money out of your hide,' he said. 'And I suppose it would be nice to see Virginia again.'

Sherlock stared at him, but Matty just gazed back innocently.

'You don't have to come,' Sherlock said evenly. 'I thought maybe Albert might need feeding.'

'He's a horse,' Matty said, shrugging. 'Where I left him, he's surrounded by food. It's like leaving me in a pie shop. He'll eat grass until he's full, and then he'll sleep.'

'Do you think horses get bored?' Sherlock asked him. 'I mean, just standing around in fields all the time.'

Matty raised an eyebrow. 'Never really thought about it. I don't suppose they mind. P'raps they spend their time thinking deep thoughts about the world and the things in it, or p'raps they can't think much beyond what's at the end of their nose.' He frowned at Sherlock. 'You think too much. Anybody ever told you that?'

They headed out into the late-afternoon sunshine. Sherlock managed to borrow another horse from the stables, and together they rode across the fields towards where Amyus Crowe and his daughter lived.

As they rode, Sherlock found his thoughts flipping between two extremes – a nervousness at the thought of seeing Virginia again and a confusion over what he felt about his father: a man who had always previously seemed like a force of nature to Sherlock, with his loud laugh and his love of the outdoors, but who he saw now as someone much more complicated.

He couldn't help but wonder if the *folie à double forme* that his father suffered from was hereditary, like a birthmark, or just a disease that could be caught, like influenza.

As they rode up to the small cottage, Sherlock noticed that Virginia's horse wasn't in its field. 'Sandia's missing,' he pointed out. 'Virginia's not here.'

'You want to go looking for her?' Matty called.

Sherlock glared at him. 'Let's go inside,' he said darkly.

'It's been half an hour since you ate – you're probably hungry again by now.'

'I probably am,' Matty agreed.

They dismounted and tied their horses to the fence outside the cottage. Something was bothering Sherlock as they approached, and it took him a moment to work out what it was. The usual clutter of objects outside the cottage – axes, muddy boots and so on – was gone.

The door, unusually, was closed. Sherlock knocked, feeling an unaccustomed premonition that something was badly wrong. His mind returned to the conversation he'd overheard in the market. He'd assumed the two Americans had wanted Mr Crowe's help. Had he been wrong?

There was no answer from inside.

He knocked again. Still no answer.

He looked at Matty, who was standing beside him. Matty stared back, a frown on his face.

Sherlock pushed the door open.

The room inside was empty of any personal possessions. Not only were Amyus and Virginia Crowe not there, but there was no sign that they ever had been.

CHAPTER SIX

Shocked, Sherlock pushed the door fully open and entered the room. The size, the layout, the furniture – everything was familiar to him, but at the same time everything was different. The absence of the usual clutter made the room look much larger than he remembered.

The amount of bare wall disturbed him – he was used to seeing it covered with sketches and maps. The plaster was marked with pinholes where things had been fastened, which was reassuring because it meant that he was actually in the right cottage, not one the same size and shape just down the road that he had mistaken for Amyus Crowe's residence.

'They must've upped and left in a hurry,' Matty said, following Sherlock inside.

'Perhaps they left a note.' Sherlock indicated the downstairs area. 'You look down here – I'll check upstairs.'

'There's nothing obvious here,' Matty said. 'If they'd left a note, they would have left it in plain sight.'

'They might not have wanted it to be found by anyone who wandered in. Maybe they've hidden it.'

Matty looked at him critically. 'You're clutching at straws,' he said. 'Face it – they've just upped and left.

Done it myself too many times to count. Someone's after you for the rent so you do a midnight flit. Pull up roots and plant yourself somewhere new where nobody knows you from Adam.' He frowned. 'Wouldn't 'ave figured Mr Crowe for a runner though. Whoever's after 'im must be pretty fearsome for 'im to up sticks just like that.'

'You're forgetting those two Americans in the market,' Sherlock pointed out. 'They said they wanted to warn Mr Crowe about something.'

'Maybe they was the ones he was runnin' away from.'

'But he wouldn't have *done* that,' Sherlock protested. 'Not without telling us.'

Matty shrugged. 'Maybe you thought they were better friends than they actually were,' he said callously. 'In my experience, stuff like friendship gets thrown away when times are tight and money is scarce.'

Sherlock just stared at him. 'Do you really mean that?'

Matty wouldn't meet his gaze. 'It's a hard world, Sherlock. You've always had it easy. Wait until you're cold and hungry and poor – see how much friendship is worth then.'

'You're my friend.' Sherlock felt as if the world he depended on was suddenly slipping away from him. 'I'll never forget that. I mean it – I'm not lying!'

'I know you mean it, but your stomach is full and you've got money in your pocket. Tell me that again when you've lost it all.' He shook his head. 'Look, I'll check for a note. Nobody will be happier than me if I find one.'

As Matty began to check in drawers and behind cushions Sherlock headed up the narrow wooden stairs, nearly bumping his head on the low ceiling. He felt sick, partly because of the disappearance of his friends but partly at Matty's words. Was friendship really that disposable? Did Matty think Sherlock would just drop him if things got tough?

Would he?

He felt a shiver run through him, and he pushed the thoughts to the back of his mind. He had more important things to worry about right at the moment.

Upstairs was as unoccupied as downstairs. Amyus Crowe's bed was neatly made, and his wardrobe was empty of clothes. The bathroom didn't contain so much as a toothbrush or a hairbrush.

Sherlock stood in the doorway of Virginia's room, shifting nervously from foot to foot. He'd never seen her bedroom before, and even though she was obviously not there, he felt as if he shouldn't go in. As if it was somehow forbidden territory.

No, this was stupid, he told himself. It was just a room.

He went in. Like her father's room, the bed was neatly made and the wardrobe was empty. No personal possessions sat on the dresser or the windowsill.

He thought he could detect a trace of her perfume in the air. Strange – he hadn't even known she wore perfume, didn't think she was the kind of girl who *would* wear perfume, but if he closed his eyes he could imagine she was standing just behind him.

Just as he was about to leave, he caught a flash of colour from her pillow. He turned, and bent towards the bed.

There, on the pillow, was a single strand of her copper-red hair.

Something caught at his heart and squeezed it, hard. He suddenly felt as if he couldn't breathe.

'Anything?' Matty called from downstairs.

'Nothing,' Sherlock called back, feeling the grip on his heart relax. His voice sounded high-pitched to his own ears. 'You?'

'Nothing. No food in the kitchen cupboards or the pantry. Washing-up's all done. That means they took the food wiv 'em. In my experience that definitely means they're not comin' back.'

Sherlock descended the staircase, having to duck to avoid hitting his head. As he re-entered the downstairs room his gaze focused again on the pinholes in the plaster of the opposite wall. He hadn't realized there had been that many things pinned to the wall.

'Not a trace,' Matty said. 'They're gone for good. Good riddance to them.'

Sherlock shook his head violently. 'Amyus Crowe

wouldn't just up and leave without saying goodbye. Even if something urgent happened and he had to go straight away, he would have left a message. And Virginia . . .' He stopped, not wanting to finish the sentence. He still wasn't sure what feelings Virginia had for him, although he was becoming increasingly aware of his feelings for her. 'Well,' he finished lamely, 'she would have said something as well. We need to keep looking.'

Before Sherlock could move, Matty articulated Sherlock's greatest worry. 'Yeah, it must have been those two blokes in the market. They must have come here and taken Mr Crowe and Virginia. Either that or Mr Crowe somehow got wind that they were on their way, and he and Virginia scarpered. But why would someone be after Mr Crowe?'

Sherlock thought for a moment, remembering the little snippets that Amyus Crowe had let slip about his past life in America – hunting down escaped criminals after the War Between the States. 'I think Mr Crowe made a lot of enemies in America. That might be why he came here with Virginia. Maybe something in his past has caught up with him.'

'Must be something really scary if he ran away rather than face up to it. You know how big and how fierce he is. I can't imagine Mr Crowe taking fright at anything less than a rampaging elephant.'

Sherlock gazed across at him. 'When have you ever seen an elephant?'

Matty scowled. 'I seen pictures, ain't I?'

'No, something is definitely wrong.' He slammed his balled fist into his thigh angrily. 'I just need to work out what it is.'

'Maybe outside?' Matty suggested.

'We could take a look,' Sherlock agreed. 'Let's restrict ourselves to the walls of the cottage and a couple of feet out, otherwise we'll end up searching the whole countryside.'

They headed out of the door, Sherlock automatically turning right and Matty turning left. Sherlock scanned the brick walls of the cottage and the straw roof, his gaze tracking up, down and up again as he walked. He passed two windows and a wisteria vine that was growing out of the ground and up the wall, but he couldn't see anything that looked out of place. He wondered if anything had been tucked into the straw of the roof, either from inside or outside, but he rejected the idea. If Amyus Crowe had left a message then he would have put it somewhere easier to access, somewhere he knew that Sherlock would look.

About halfway around the building he nearly tripped over something lying on the ground. For a moment he thought it was a snake, and he stepped back hurriedly, but it wasn't moving, and it was too dusty and brown to be a snake. He bent down to take a look. It was a tube, made of canvas but strengthened with hoops of something inside to stop it from collapsing. It ran from a hole in the cottage wall towards a clump of grass, and vanished. Some experiment that Amyus Crowe was conducting? It was the only thing he could think of, but it didn't give him any clues as to where Mr Crowe and Virginia had gone.

He and Matty met again on the far side of the cottage.

'Did you find anything unusual?' he asked.

'Nothing.' Matty frowned for a moment. 'Apart from a dead rabbit. Well, most of a dead rabbit. The head was missing.'

'Where was it? Just lying on the ground?'

Matty shook his head. 'It had been buried under a pile of logs. Looked like it was deliberately put there, but I can't imagine why.'

Sherlock let the thought chase itself around his head for a while. 'A dead rabbit without its head?' he said eventually. 'I have to confess, if it's a message then it's a very cryptic one.' He sighed. 'Come on, let's keep going. We'll meet again by the front door.'

'But you've already done this next bit,' Matty complained, 'and I've already done the bit you're about to do!'

'Two pairs of eyes are better than one. I might have missed something that you'll pick up, and vice versa. Come on – it'll only take a few more minutes.'

They separated and recommenced their search. Sherlock found nothing that Matty had missed. He stopped and stared at the dead rabbit for a while, as it lay sprawled on the grass by a pile of split logs that Amyus Crowe had probably intended for the stove, but it didn't tell him anything. Apart from the fact that its head was missing, it was just a dead rabbit. The countryside was full of them.

Matty was already waiting for him when he reached the front door. He raised his eyebrow enquiringly. Sherlock shook his head. Matty shrugged, indicating that he hadn't found anything that Sherlock had missed. 'Saw some kind of tube thing,' he said, 'but that was it.'

Disconsolately Sherlock led the way back inside. He looked around the bare room, hands on hips. 'I keep getting the feeling that I'm missing something,' he said in a frustrated tone.

'If *you*'re missing something, then there's no chance *I'll* get it,' Matty said.

'Don't belittle yourself. You've got a good eye for detail,' Sherlock said. He stared once again at the wall with the pinholes in it, trying not to look at the details – the individual holes – but the entire thing. 'Matty, I think there's some kind of message there.'

Matty stared at him, then at the wall. 'You're seeing things.'

'Yes, I am. Have you got a pen?'

'Do I look like the kind of bloke who goes around with a pen in his pocket?'

Sherlock sighed. 'A pencil then?'

'The same.'

'A knife?'

'That,' Matty said, 'I can help you with.' He reached into a pocket and brought out the knife he had used on the tanning vat earlier. 'Here. Don't break it.'

'I won't.' Sherlock walked over to the wall. He stared at it for a few moments, trying to recreate the things that had been pinned there in his mind. 'There was a big map over here, wasn't there?' He pointed with the blade at part of the wall.

'I s'pose.'

'All right.' Using the blade like a pen, scratching the surface of the plaster, Sherlock joined up four pinholes in a rectangle that was, as far as he could judge, the right size, shape and position. 'That's the map. There were two bits of paper over here, to the right.' Quickly gaining confidence, he selected two sets of four pinholes and joined them up as well. He now had three separate rectangles on the wall. 'I remember there being some things up here. Pictures, I think.'

'They were at an angle,' Matty pointed out. Sherlock picked out four pinholes that seemed to match his memory, but Matty shook his head. ''Bout an inch to the left,' he said. 'No, not there – down a bit . . . Yeah, that's it.'

Progressively, Sherlock connected up the various pinholes until he had a recreation of everything that had been fastened to the wall. Some items had been attached to the plaster with just one pin rather than four, and in those cases Sherlock put an *X* to show that he had taken the whole item into account.

He stood back to look at his handiwork. The plaster was now covered with a series of overlapping scratches and *X*s.

'You've missed some,' Matty pointed out.

'No,' Sherlock replied, 'I haven't. Those pinholes are new.'

'Are you sure?'

'I'm *very* sure. Look closely at them.'

Matty moved towards the wall, squinting.

'No, Sherlock said, 'move backwards. Try and look *past* the wall, and ignore the holes that I've marked.'

Matty shook his head, but he complied. His eyes suddenly widened in surprise. 'It's an arrow!' he cried.

'Precisely,' Sherlock said. He followed Matty's gaze. There, marked out in pinholes that had no connection with anything that had been pinned to the wall – *new* pinholes that had presumably been made especially – was an arrow pointing towards the window.

Both boys followed the direction of the arrow and stared through the window at the green landscape outside. 'Is that the way they went?' Matty asked dubiously. 'If so, I'm not sure it's much help.'

'Closer than that,' Sherlock said. 'That's the window leading out to the paddock where Virginia kept Sandia.

Mr Crowe is telling us to look out in the paddock. He's left a message for us there.'

Matty shrugged. 'Seems a lot of palaver to go to when he could have just left a note pinned the wall.'

'Like you said, if he'd left a note, then anyone could have found it,' Sherlock pointed out. 'He's left a clue pointing to a note.' He held out Matty's knife. 'Here, thanks.'

Matty shrugged. 'Keep it,' he said. 'The way things go, you'll probably need it more than I do.'

Together the two boys headed out of the cottage and into the open. Sherlock led the way to the fenced-off area of ground that had been visible through the window. They climbed over the gate.

'Where do we start?' Matty asked, looking around the grassy area. 'I don't see anything obvious.'

'It won't be obvious,' Sherlock pointed out. 'Mr Crowe would have hidden it so it wouldn't be found.' He thought for a moment. 'If I had some string we could mark off a grid of squares and search each square individually, so we knew we'd covered all the ground. Without that, there's a risk that we'll miss something by accident.'

'Tell you what,' Matty suggested, 'let's you and me start at opposite sides and walk forward, looking at the ground, until we meet. We take a step to the side, turn around and each walk towards the fence again. Then we turn around, take a step to the side, and do it again. That

118

way we'll work in strips across the field and we won't miss anything.'

'Sounds like a plan.' Sherlock nodded. 'Let's do it.'

So for the next half hour they progressively moved together and apart across the field, each one meticulously examining the ground as they walked, checking each clump of grass, each rabbit hole and each pile of manure that Virginia's horse had left behind. Sherlock's back began to ache after a few minutes, thanks to the uncomfortable position that he was forced to adopt: bent over and taking small steps. He imagined that from some distant vantage point he and Matty looked like chickens checking the field for corn.

'I've got something!' Matty exclaimed.

'What is it?'

Matty lifted something from the ground and held it up. It was made of a grey metal.

'It's a fork,' Sherlock pointed out.

'I know it's a fork. Could it be important?'

Sherlock shrugged. 'Leave it where you found it. We may have to dig if we can't find anything else.'

Five minutes later it was Sherlock's turn to make a discovery. 'Matty – over here!'

Matty stuck the fork into the ground, and then ran over to where Sherlock was crouching. 'What is it?'

Sherlock indicated a root-edged hole that led away at an angle into the earth. 'I think it's a rabbit hole.'

'Congratulations. I've already found five of them.'

'But this one has something in it.' Sherlock reached into the hole, to the object he'd caught sight of in the shadows. His fingers encountered something that was simultaneously furry and sticky. Taking a grip, he pulled it out.

It was a rabbit's head, the severed neck covered in blood.

'A rabbit's head in a rabbit hole,' Matty commented drily. 'Ain't that an unexpected turn of events? Are you trying to tell me that a fox took Mr Crowe and Virginia away?'

'You see,' Sherlock replied, 'but you do not understand. Look at the neck.'

Matty considered it, then nodded in understanding. 'It's been sliced off with a sharp blade, not bitten through or ripped off.' He thought for a moment. 'This must be the head that goes with the body we found back at the cottage. Even so – it could have been taken off a kitchen table by a fox or a stoat and just . . . left here.'

'I don't think so. An animal, if it had stolen this thing, would have eaten some of it. There would be teeth marks. As it is, it looks like someone has just cut it off and put it straight in this hole.'

Matty turned his attention from Sherlock back to the rabbit's head. 'Pretty fresh,' he admitted. 'Probably less than a day old.'

'It's a message,' Sherlock said thoughtfully, 'but the

question is, what kind of message is it?' He paused for a moment. 'No,' he went on, 'the real question is, are there any more messages apart from this one?'

Matty looked around and sighed. 'You mean we have to finish searching the field?'

'We do. Just because we find one thing, it doesn't mean there aren't other things to find.'

'I was afraid you might say that.'

Leaving the bloodied head where it was, Sherlock and Matty continued their search, combing through the grass for anything that might have been left or dropped. It was another three-quarters of an hour before they found themselves searching along the far fence.

'Nothing?' Matty asked as they walked back to the cottage.

'Nothing,' Sherlock agreed. 'Either it's the rabbit head, or there's nothing here.'

Matty looked over to where they'd left the head. 'I can't see how there can be a message there, unless Mr Crowe's written it on a small piece of paper and shoved it in the thing's mouth. That would just be sick.'

'It's not the head itself,' Sherlock replied, 'or, at least, I don't think it is. It's more likely to be something to do with its placement, or just its existence. I don't think Mr Crowe had time to do anything complicated, like write a note. He just had time to make some pinholes in the wall pointing out here, and then throw the head into a hole.'

'He had time to catch and kill a rabbit,' Matty pointed out.

'I think it was already there. I think he probably caught it earlier and was preparing it for a meal – taking the head off, gutting it and skinning it. I think that something happened to make him want to leave, and after clearing out the cottage of everything he and Virginia owned he only had a few moments to come up with a message.'

Matty sighed in frustration. 'Yeah, but what *is* it? I think he had more faith in us than was warranted.'

'A rabbit's head in a hole,' Sherlock mused, trying to provoke some movement in his head, some sudden revelation that might only occur if he kept on repeating the obvious.

'Burrow,' Matty murmured as they entered the cottage.

'Sorry?'

'It's a burrow, not a hole. Rabbits have burrows, foxes have dens and badgers have setts. You're normally the one who likes to get words right – you need to learn these things.'

'A rabbit's head in a *burrow*,' Sherlock corrected. That elusive thought in his head finally started running. 'A *head* in a *burrow*. Matty, you're a genius!'

'I am?' the boy said, surprised.

'Well, technically you're not a genius, but you have an amazing ability to bring out the genius in others. It's so obvious!'

'It is?'

'Remember when you'd been kidnapped by Duke Balthassar's men and taken to New York, and we tracked you down?'

Matty nodded, mystified.

'Do you remember when I found you in that building? You tried to get me to understand that they were taking you on the train line to Pennsylvania?'

Matty smiled. 'Yeah, that was clever, wasn't it?'

'You mimed using a pen, then touched the windowsill, then pointed to a weather vane on a nearby building. It took me a while to put it together, but I did.'

'Yeah, I remember, but so what?'

Sherlock sighed in exasperation. 'Don't you see? That's what Amyus Crowe is doing here. A head in a burrow. He and Virginia are going to *Edinburgh*!'

Matty frowned. 'That's a bit of a coincidence,' he said dubiously. 'Him having a rabbit's head and a nearby burrow to put it in, and knowing he was going to Edinburgh.'

'I think it happened the other way around,' Sherlock said. He could feel the pure, cold flame of triumph flashing through his body, burning away the tiredness and the aching muscles. He'd done it! He'd cracked the code! He *knew* he was right! 'I'm not saying it's the best clue in the world, but Mr Crowe had to work with whatever he had to hand. He could use the pinholes in the wall to point us out here, he had the rabbit's body lying around and he knew there were burrows out here in the paddock. He used the ingredients to hand to make a clue, and then he took Virginia to Edinburgh because that was the only destination he could build a clue for!'

'But why has he let us know that he's going to Edinburgh?' Matty asked.

'He must want us to go after him. There's no other reason. If he didn't want to leave without saying goodbye, he could have left a note saying just that: "Goodbye". It wouldn't matter who found that. But it clearly does matter that nobody knows he has gone to Edinburgh. I think he's in danger. I think he wants our help.'

'We're goin' to follow him, aren't we?' Matty said gleefully.

'Well,' Sherlock answered cautiously, 'there are other options. Perhaps we should tell my brother.'

'How long will that take? And what's he going to do? Knowing your brother, I doubt he'll be getting the next train to Scotland. He'll just send lots of telegrams out, getting people to search for Mr Crowe, but they won't know what he or Virginia look like.'

Sherlock shook his head. 'We've never been to Edinburgh,' he said. 'We won't know anything about the place. How can we help them if we'll be practically lost there ourselves?'

'I've been there,' Matty said cheerfully. 'My dad took

me and me mum there on the barge. Took weeks, it did. We stayed there for a month or more while he looked for work.'

'Even so – the two of us, just kids, alone in Scotland?'

'You went to America. And Russia.'

'I had Mr Crowe with me in America.'

'Until you ran off with Virginia.'

'That was an accident,' Sherlock protested. 'The train left the station before we could get off. I also had Mycroft with me in Russia.'

'Before he was arrested.'

'But that wasn't part of our plan. Anyway, Rufus Stone was with us. He helped.' A bright light seemed to go on in his head. 'What if we asked Rufus Stone to come with us?'

'Would he?' Matty asked dubiously. 'I didn't think he and Mr Crowe got on.'

'They don't,' Sherlock admitted. 'They're like a cat and a dog locked in the same room, but . . .' He thought for a minute. 'But I'm pretty sure that my brother is paying Rufus Stone to hang around Farnham and make sure I don't get into trouble. Mycroft still thinks that the Paradol Chamber are going to take some kind of action against me. If I tell Rufus that you and I are going to Edinburgh, then he'll have to come with us, won't he? If he's supposed to stop me getting into trouble, then he won't have any choice.'

'Won't he just stop you from getting on a train?'

Sherlock smiled. 'You know Rufus Stone. You know what he's like. Given a choice between stopping me going to Scotland or coming with me and having an adventure, what do *you* think he'll do?'

'Fair point,' Matty admitted. 'When do we tell him?'

'Let's collect a bit more information first. I want to check the station in Farnham. If Mr Crowe and Virginia are heading for Scotland, then they're not doing it on horseback, or in a cart. They'd be too vulnerable. No, they'll go by train.'

Matty frowned, carefully thinking through what Sherlock had said. Watching him, Sherlock felt a sudden flash of kinship. Matty had become a part of his life in a way he had never expected. The boy was his opposite in so many ways – instinctive where Sherlock was logical, emotional where Sherlock was cold, impulsive where Sherlock would always think through his options – but he had a quick mind, and he was fantastically loyal. He was the closest thing Sherlock had to a best friend. Sherlock wondered if he always would be.

'If Mr Crowe bought two tickets to Edinburgh from the ticket office at Farnham Station,' he said slowly, 'then he'd be leaving a trail. If the Americans are chasing him they could just check at the ticket office and find out where he went. It's not as if he's inconspicuous.'

'No,' Sherlock agreed. 'So what would he do?'

Matty shrugged. 'I dunno.'

'He'd probably buy two tickets to an intermediate station – say, Guildford, but he and Virginia could get off earlier – maybe at Ash Wharf. He could then buy two tickets through to Edinburgh from there. If anyone was following then they'd go from Farnham direct to Guildford, and there they would lose the trail, because nobody at the ticket office in Guildford would remember him.'

'Clever,' said Matty approvingly.

'In fact,' Sherlock went on, 'if I were him, I would buy two tickets for Guildford, get off at Ash Wharf, buy two tickets for London, then when I got to London I'd buy two tickets for Edinburgh. That confuses the trail even more.'

'You're sure that's what he'd do?'

Sherlock nodded. 'He's a hunter. He knows the kinds of trail that prey can leave, and he'll be careful not to do the same thing.'

'So what now?'

'Now we go to Farnham.'

The two of them rode from the cottage towards the centre of Farnham, not without a twinge of guilt in Sherlock's mind. He hated leaving the cottage empty and unguarded. Who knew what might happen to it before Amyus Crowe and Virginia came back? They *would* come back, he was sure of it. He would *make* sure of it.

The ticket-office clerk at Farnham – a tall elderly man with fluffy white sideburns – confirmed that a big man in a white suit and hat, accompanied by a girl dressed like a boy, had bought two tickets the day before. Sherlock was pleased to note that the tickets had been bought with Guildford as the destination. So far his deductions were bang on target.

'Look,' Matty said, pointing across the road. In a small triangle of field next to a barn a horse was cropping the grass. It was tied by a long halter to a fence.

'That's Sandia,' Matty said.

'Are you sure?' Sherlock asked.

'Very sure.'

'At least we know he's all right. Virginia has probably paid someone at the station to keep an eye on him. If she had time to do that, they can't have been taken forcibly. They must have found out that somebody was after them. If I know Mr Crowe, he will have managed to keep one step ahead of them.' Suddenly Sherlock felt an awful lot better.

'Are we going on to Ash Wharf now?'

Sherlock thought for a moment. There was a point at which extra evidence did nothing more than confirm what you already knew. He was confident enough in his deductions. 'No, let's go and find Rufus Stone. We need to tell him what we're going to do, and then we need to talk to my aunt and uncle.' He remembered the events of earlier that day. 'I think there's enough residual goodwill there that they won't raise any objections to me going away for a few days, especially if they know that Rufus Stone is going with me.

Matty turned to go, but Sherlock reached out a hand and stopped him. Matty turned back enquiringly.

'What?'

Sherlock hesitated, wondering how to ask the question. Wondering if he *should* ask the question. 'That stuff you said earlier, about friendship getting thrown away when times are tight and money is scarce – did you really mean it?'

Matty looked away. His lips tightened for a moment before he answered. 'I've had friends before,' he said quietly. 'I don't have them now. They left, one by one, when it suited them. So I learned that's the way things work.'

'Not with me,' Sherlock said. 'And not with Amyus Crowe or Virginia.'

Matty nodded reluctantly. 'At least you've convinced me they didn't *want* to go. That's a start. Now come on. Time's slipping away.'

They found Stone where Sherlock had expected him to be – in his lodgings, practising by himself up in the attic space. The two boys could hear him faintly from the street, playing what sounded like a wild dance. As they climbed the stairs the music got louder and louder, until they entered the attic where it seemed to fill the entire space, whirling and spinning with the lanky figure of Rufus Stone sawing madly with the bow in the centre. If he heard them enter then he gave no sign. Eyes closed, he pulled wilder and wilder notes from his instrument until, with a final flourish, he finished. The air appeared to quiver like a jelly for a split second before collapsing back to normal.

'That's a hell of a tune,' Matty said approvingly.

'Very kind,' Stone said, turning and grinning at the two of them. 'Although I have to say, it sounds even better played by the light of a campfire in the middle of a forest at midnight. The trouble is that the older I get, the more I find I prefer the comfort of a warm, dry house.' He gazed from one boy to the other. 'Something has happened, hasn't it? Tell me.'

Between them, with Sherlock sketching in the facts and Matty filling the gaps with vivid descriptions, they told Rufus Stone the story. His face grew grimmer and grimmer as they spoke. When Sherlock finished by telling him exactly what the two of them planned to do, he stood for a moment, thinking.

'You really both intend going to Edinburgh?' he asked finally.

'Yes,' Sherlock answered.

'And there's nothing I can say to change your minds?'

'No,' Matty replied.

He sighed. 'Then it's a good thing I keep a bag packed

and ready by the door. It won't be the first time I've had to leave a place at a moment's notice.'

'The difference is,' Sherlock said quietly, 'that we'll all be coming back. With two extra people.'

CHAPTER SEVEN

It was the next day before the three of them could set out for Edinburgh.

After talking Rufus Stone into accompanying them as a responsible adult – a task that was surprisingly easy, Sherlock thought, all things considered – Matty had headed off to make arrangements for Albert to be looked after while Sherlock rode back to Holmes Manor to talk to his aunt and uncle. As he expected, they were still dazed and distracted from Mrs Eglantine's fall from grace, and the personal freedom they had suddenly gained as a result. He presented the trip to them as a fait accompli and, as he expected, they went along with it. After all, they had previously agreed to him travelling to America and Russia. Compared to that, Edinburgh was just down the road. Or up it.

Uncle Sherrinford did nearly throw the whole plan into chaos when he asked to be introduced to Rufus Stone. 'I cannot,' he proclaimed, 'in all conscience, let my nephew travel to the far end of the country with a man I have never even met. I know nothing about him.'

Remembering Rufus Stone's bohemian taste in clothes, his earring and his gold tooth, Sherlock suppressed a grimace of concern. If Uncle Sherrinford ever met Rufus Stone in person he would probably forbid Sherlock from ever associating with him again in Farnham, let alone travelling with him to Scotland. Sherlock had developed a lot of respect for his aunt and uncle – a respect that bordered on familial love – but they weren't exactly the most understanding of people. Grasping at straws, he said, 'If it helps, Mycroft has known Mr Stone for several years, and is currently employing him to be my violin tutor.'

'Ah,' Sherrinford said, nodding his head. 'In that case, I waive my requirement. Your brother is a perspicacious man, and I trust his judgement when it comes to character.' He peered sideways at his wife. 'You know, I recall that Mycroft said that there was something wrong with Mrs Eglantine the first time he met her. Perhaps I should have told him what she was doing to us. He might have been able to help.'

'What's done is done,' Anna said, patting his hand. 'The Good Lord does not place a burden on our shoulders that is too heavy to carry, and each burden makes us stronger.'

Sherlock dined with his aunt and uncle that night. The food wasn't up to the usual standard – the shock waves from Mrs Eglantine's disappearance seemed to have echoed down to the kitchen staff – and there was little conversation. Uncle Sherrinford and Aunt Anna seemed subdued by the magnitude of what had happened. Even Aunt Anna's usual constant stream of opinion, gossip and commentary on the day's events was absent. As soon as the meal was over, Sherlock excused himself and headed for bed. He'd had a busy day, and he needed to regain his strength for what lay ahead.

Sherlock, Matty and Rufus Stone met up at Farnham Station early the next morning. Each of them had a bag of clothes, toiletries and other travelling necessities.

'This,' Rufus Stone said with a grim face, 'is a remarkably bad idea. My initial flush of enthusiasm has dissipated like a rain puddle soaking into the earth. Edinburgh is a big city, with a lot of people in it. What you intend doing is a bit like searching an ant's nest for one particular ant. It won't be easy.'

'Nothing easy is worthwhile,' Sherlock pointed out.

'*Touché.*' Stone smiled.

Rufus Stone paid for the tickets. He bought them from Farnham to London, on the basis that they could buy the next set of tickets, from London to Edinburgh, once they had arrived, and because it would be embarrassing and potentially dangerous to leave a trail behind them when Amyus Crowe hadn't. Sherlock offered to use some of the money that Mycroft had sent him, but Stone shrugged. 'Your brother pays me a regular salary for teaching you the violin,' he pointed out. 'One way or the other, it's his money which is buying the tickets. It doesn't really matter which one of us hands it over.'

There wasn't a train for another hour, so Rufus

suggested having a cup of tea and a bacon sandwich before they left. The boys agreed enthusiastically. The nearest tea shop was just across the road, but while the three of them were eating Sherlock stared through the shop window and noticed two men standing in front of the station and looking around. One of them had black hair pulled back into a ponytail; the other had smallpox scars across his cheeks and forehead.

'Are those the two you think are looking for Amyus Crowe?' Rufus asked, following the direction of Sherlock's gaze.

Matty nodded.

They watched as the men approached the ticket office and asked the clerk a question. He shook his head. One of the men asked him something else, and slid some money across the counter. The clerk tore two tickets from a strip and passed them over.

'They've bought tickets,' Rufus pointed out. 'That means they'll probably be on the same train as us. Either they know about Edinburgh or they are moving the search to Guildford. Whatever the reason, we need to stay out of their way.'

Finishing their sandwiches and tea, they headed back across the road to the station. A few minutes later the train heaved itself alongside the platform: a behemoth of black iron shrouded in steam and hissing like some biblical demon. The three of them found a compartment to themselves. Sherlock kept an eye out for the two

Americans, but he couldn't see where on the train they got on – if they had got on at all.

Sherlock was used to train journeys by now. For a while he let himself become entranced by the scenery flashing past, but when that grew too boring he waited until they arrived at the next large station – which turned out to be Guildford – and quickly left the train to buy a newspaper from a seller on the platform. It was a London edition of *The Times*, presumably brought down as part of a large bundle on an early train.

The train was venting steam in a white cloud across the platform when he turned away from the newsvendor's stall. As he moved back towards the long wooden wall of the train carriages, an errant breeze pushed the steam away and he spotted one of the Americans walking across the platform. It was the taller man, the one with the black hair shot through with grey and the gnarled scar tissue where his right ear should have been. He was coming from the direction of the ticket office. His companion – the man with the pockmarks across his cheeks – was standing by the carriage door, holding it open so that the train couldn't leave before his friend was back on board. As the black-haired man approached his companion he shook his head. Whatever he'd been looking for – which Sherlock suspected was some news on Amyus Crowe's movements – he was disappointed.

As they got back on to the train, and as Sherlock headed for his own carriage, he wondered whether the men knew about him and Matty and Rufus Stone. Rufus hadn't spent much time with Mr Crowe, but Sherlock and Matty were regular companions of his. Most people in Farnham would have seen Sherlock and Mr Crowe together at one time or another, and people in small towns were inveterate gossips – something that Josh Harkness had traded on. It would only take a few pence changing hands, or the purchase of a pint of beer, for them to find out that Amyus Crowe spent time with people other than just his daughter. If they had descriptions of Sherlock and Matty, then they might recognize them on the train. The three of them would have to be careful.

Sherlock got back to his carriage just as the guard on the platform blew his whistle, warning passengers that the train was about to leave. He settled himself back into his seat. Matty was apparently asleep, and Rufus Stone was busy memorizing a musical score, the fingers of his left hand automatically making the shapes of the notes in the air as he read. Not wanting to interrupt them, Sherlock settled back into his seat with the newspaper.

The pages were filled with politics and reports of international events. Having heard his brother Mycroft speak disparagingly about newspaper journalists, and how little they really knew about the real reasons for things happening, he only skim-read the articles. Mycroft had once said that reading a newspaper piece about politics was like reading a book review written by a man who had never read the book, but had been told about it by a couple of people that he had bumped into in the street.

Sherlock did scan the pages for reports of the British Army's presence in India, but there was nothing. He hadn't heard from his father for a while now. He knew that things were busy out there, but he worried. He couldn't help himself.

The front page was filled with personal advertisements and he was about to skip over them when his eye was caught by something unusual and he found himself drawn into reading them. They were small pieces, usually ten or twenty words – written by readers of the newspaper who paid for them to be printed – but Sherlock found that they opened little windows on to a world he would probably never know anything else about. 'Dog missing, Chelsea area, answers to the name of Abendigo. Will pay handsomely for return, dead or alive.' Sherlock supposed that he could understand someone loving a pet enough to pay money to get it back if it went missing, but what kind of person would name their dog after an obscure biblical character, and would want it back even if it was dead? It didn't make any sense. And what about 'Footman required urgently, good references essential. Must be able to play ocarina'? People needed good staff, obviously, but why would they need a footman with musical ability, and with such an unusual instrument to boot? Each personal advertisement was a slice of life, and he wanted to know more about the circumstances behind them. Some were obviously in code – apparently random collections of letters and numbers – and he tried to use the skills that his brother and Amyus Crowe had taught him to unlock their secrets. With some of them he was actually successful. Most were arrangements for furtive meetings, probably of people who loved each other but couldn't, for whatever reason, meet in public, but others were stranger. One in particular made his blood run cold. After he had decoded it, the words said simply: 'Joseph Lamner, you will die tomorrow. Set your affairs in order. Prepare to meet your Maker.'

Sherlock turned reluctantly away from the personal advertisements before he became too obsessed with them and skim-read the rest of the newspaper. Two pages contained little snippets of news from around the country, and Sherlock found his gaze snagged by one report in particular, which involved the city to which they were travelling.

EDINBURGH. Prominent businessman Sir Benedict Ventham was found dead last night at his house on the outskirts of the city. Police have stated that murder by poisoning is a distinct possibility, considering the contorted expression on his face and the colour of his tongue, and have said that they are close to an arrest. Sir Benedict had made a number of enemies through his aggressive business techniques over the years. He had lived recently in a state of fear for his life and only ever ate food prepared by his faithful and trusted cook, who had served him for almost two decades.

Frustrated at the lack of detail, Sherlock wondered how he might find out more about this murder in Edinburgh. He didn't think it had anything to do with Amyus Crowe's disappearance – it would have been a coincidence too far if an article in a newspaper he'd happened to pick up at a passing station was directly related to the reason he was on the train in the first place – but he wanted to get a feeling for the place he was going to – a sense of what Edinburgh was like, and what kinds of things happened there. One of the things that Amyus Crowe had drummed into him on their regular walks through the woods and forests around Farnham was that the more you knew about your environment, the more you could control it. Most people, if they got lost in a forest, would be hungry and thirsty within an hour or two and would have no idea of the way out. Thanks to Mr Crowe, Sherlock now knew which plants to eat and which to avoid, knew how to follow animal tracks to find water, and also knew how to work out which way was north.

Thinking of survival in unfamiliar environments provoked a memory of New York, and his arrival in that city a year or so before. He'd been amazed then at the number of newspapers that had been on sale on street corners. Thinking about it now, he wondered how many different newspapers there were in London, and whether they all printed the same story. Presumably not – each must have its own style and its own bias. If he really wanted to know more about the background and the details of this murder in Edinburgh, then it might be a good idea if he bought as many different papers as he could, cut the relevant stories out and compared them against one another, looking for differences and for things that one report mentioned that the other ones ignored.

The train was some distance beyond Guildford now, and he had lost the opportunity to dive back out and pick up some more newspapers. He made a mental note to do it at Waterloo when they arrived.

Finishing the newspaper, he made sure that he carefully tore out the report of the Edinburgh murder and folded it several times before putting it in his pocket. If nothing else, comparing the various reports would be an interesting exercise.

Matty was curled up on a seat, head against the window, fast asleep. Rufus Stone had his eyes closed as well, but judging by the way his hands were twitching he was mentally rehearsing the violin part of the music score.

Sherlock glanced out of the window again, but the countryside flashing past held little to interest him.

He opened the bag that he had brought with him and pulled out a book. It was all about theatrical make-up – how to make it, and how to apply it to produce various effects.

He buried himself in the book, memorizing the details of how to make your own theatrical putty and make-up, and how to apply it so that nobody could tell unless they were within a few inches of you. The book also talked about changing posture – the way you stood – to make yourself look taller or shorter. He forgot about the train, and the journey, until they clattered over a particularly noisy set of points, and he looked up to find that Rufus Stone was staring at him.

'Thinking of a career in the theatre?' Stone asked, indicating the book. 'I advise against it, the way I would advise against sticking your hand inside a dog's mouth and pulling on its tongue. The pay is bad, the hours are long and unsociable and society does not value those who entertain it. I should know – I've spent more time than I care to think about in darkened theatres playing for small, unappreciative audiences.'

'I don't know what I want to do when I grow up,' Sherlock said honestly, 'but I like the idea of being able to change my appearance so that nobody knows that it's me.'

'To be honest,' Stone admitted, 'there are times when I've been grateful for the ability to slip past an irate landlord or a former girlfriend without them realizing.'

'You know about theatrical make-up?' Sherlock asked, intrigued.

'I've picked things up, over the years, working in theatres – or, more accurately, spending time in dressing rooms with young and beautiful actresses. Working for your brother, as well. There are some striking similarities between acting and spying.' He smiled, but there was little humour in his expression. 'Of course, dying on stage in front of an unappreciative audience is nowhere near as painful as dying in a back alley of a foreign city with a knife between your ribs.'

'Can you teach me?' Sherlock asked.

Stone shrugged. 'I could give it a go. You'll need a certain amount of raw artistic talent, and a lot of practice – not a million miles away from what you need to play the violin properly, in fact. Tell me what you already know, and I'll see what I can add.'

They spent the rest of the journey with Stone giving Sherlock tips on the art of theatrical make-up. He brought the dry facts in Sherlock's book to life with funny anecdotes of times when he'd seen false moustaches slide off actors' faces or watched their make-up streak as they perspired until they looked like some bizarre striped animal. Sherlock found himself laughing, but also learning at the same time, and the rest of the journey seemed to flash past in moments.

Arrival at Waterloo was becoming a regular occurrence for Sherlock by now. The station, with its soaring iron arches and its glass panels, was a familiar sight, as were the crowds of people in all kinds of clothes, from black tailcoats to bright red-and-yellow checked jackets.

Rufus Stone led the way outside. 'We need to get to King's Cross,' he said over his shoulder. 'It's on the other side of London. Trains leave there for the north of the country.'

Sherlock looked back over his shoulder, wondering if he would see the two Americans, but if they had been on the train then they were hanging back, keeping out of sight. Perhaps they had stayed at Guildford to ask questions about a big American and a girl who would have been travelling a day or two before.

A cab was waiting directly outside the station, ignoring the traffic that was struggling to get past. Its driver kept shaking his head at the various people who tried to hail it or climb in. Sherlock assumed that it was waiting for someone important, and he was prepared to walk right past it, but Rufus Stone walked straight up and opened the door. Instead of waving him away or shouting at him, the driver jumped down and took his bag, then looked at Sherlock and Matty expectantly, obviously wanting to take their bags as well.

Sherlock had been encouraged by his brother Mycroft never to hail the first cab that he saw – just in case it was a trap or a trick of some kind – so Stone's behaviour surprised him. The violinist was so confident,

144

however, that Sherlock found himself leaving his bag on the pavement and following him inside. Matty did the same.

Everything became clear when Sherlock found that he was settling himself opposite the impressive bulk of Mycroft Holmes.

'Ah, Sherlock,' Mycroft said. 'Welcome. Please make yourself comfortable. And young Mr Arnatt – perhaps you could squeeze yourself in beside me. I believe there is enough room, if you don't mind pressing yourself up against the far side. Do be careful of my top hat.'

'You sent a telegram to Mycroft,' Sherlock said accusingly to Rufus Stone as they sat. From outside he could hear the driver throwing their bags on to the back of the carriage.

Stone's face was impassive. 'I had to,' he said. 'I work for your brother, and if he found out that I had let you go to Edinburgh without notifying him, there would be hell to pay.'

'There would indeed,' Mycroft confirmed. 'I pride myself on knowing everything that goes on around me. If I discovered that my brother had slipped unnoticed through the city, I would be mortified.'

'I'm still going to Edinburgh,' Sherlock said levelly.

Mycroft nodded. 'Of course you are.' He reached up and rapped with his cane on the carriage roof. 'King's Cross!' he called.

'What?'

The carriage jerked and began to move away from the kerb.

'Do you think that the disappearance of Amyus Crowe is of no interest to me?' Mycroft shook his head. 'He is, apart from being the closest thing I have to a personal friend, a man of exceptional abilities, for whom I have a great deal of professional respect. If he has disappeared suddenly, then there must be a reason, and I wish to know what that reason is. The presence of these two Americans is unsettling as well, given that we do not know whether they are friends or foes. Like you, Sherlock, I am puzzled, and that is a state of mind that I find particularly painful.'

'What about you?' Sherlock asked. 'Will you be coming with us?'

'I fear my days of travelling are past,' Mycroft replied. 'Our Russian expedition convinced me that I am better staying in London, where I am comfortable, and letting others actually seek out evidence and answers. But I shall be doing my part – while you are looking for Mr Crowe and his daughter, I shall be making enquiries about these two American visitors.'

Sherlock felt his heart sink. He wasn't surprised at Mycroft's decision, but he would have felt more confident with his brother at his side.

'Oh,' Mycroft continued, 'I almost forgot. Congratulations on your deduction concerning exactly where Mr Crowe was headed. I cannot fault your logic, although I can fault Mr Crowe's use of a rabbit's head. There must have been something less offensive to hand and something less likely to have been stolen by a passing carnivore.' He peered around the inside of the cab. 'Do you think,' he mused, taking the conversation off at a tangent, 'I could have a carriage panelled, upholstered and carpeted to look like my office? Or like the Diogenes Club? That way I could travel in perfect comfort without the nausea that usually comes with a change of location.'

'But who would bring your morning cup of tea or your afternoon sherry?' Rufus Stone asked with a smile.

'Those things can be arranged,' Mycroft said. 'The cab could stop outside certain establishments at pre-planned times, and waiters could pass trays through the window. I could have entire meals delivered for me to consume on the move. Think of the time saved!'

'If you were allowed to eat and drink in here,' Sherlock pointed out, 'then you would grow so fat that you would never be able to get out again, which would undermine the entire point of having your own carriage in the first place. You would be like a snail in its shell.'

Mycroft nodded. 'A fair point,' he conceded.

'If you're not going to stop us going to Edinburgh,' Matty piped up, 'then why are you here, Mr Holmes?'

'An excellent question, young man, and one that cuts right to the heart of the matter. I am here to see my younger brother, of course – something that hasn't happened for a while now – and I am also here to warn the three of you to be careful. It has presumably occurred to you that anything which could cause Amyus Crowe to run rather than fight is likely to be bigger and more dangerous than you expect. I have always regarded Mr Crowe as a man entirely without fear. To find out that there is something that scares him is like finding out that the moon is entirely hollow at the back, like a dish, rather than a ball, like the Earth.' He sighed. 'I am also led to understand that Edinburgh is an unusually dark and violent city. The Scots themselves are a Celtic race, which means that they are prone to moods that range from maudlin depression to sudden anger. Do not think Scotland will be like Farnham, or London. Although you will not cross water – apart from the River Tyne, of course – and although the people you meet will speak English – of a sort – you should treat Scotland as you would a foreign country.' He handed across an envelope. 'I have taken the liberty of making your travel arrangements. Here are your tickets, and the address of a hotel into which you have been booked. Keep me informed as to what you discover. I regret to say that I have no agents of my own in Edinburgh, otherwise I would ask them to be on the lookout for Amyus Crowe and his daughter, and to keep the three of you from harm as well.'

'Thank you,' Sherlock said, taking the envelope. 'Mycroft . . .'

'Yes, Sherlock.'

He paused before going on. 'I think you should know that Mrs Eglantine has left the employ of Uncle Sherrinford and Aunt Anna.'

Mycroft stared at Sherlock for a long moment. 'Has she indeed?' he murmured eventually. 'Do I take it that this sudden reversal of fortune for that remarkably unpleasant woman has something to do with you?'

'It has a lot to do with him,' Matty said proudly. 'And me!'

'You must tell me the story when you get back.' Mycroft kept staring at Sherlock. There was a strange look in his eyes, as if he was simultaneously seeing someone very familiar and someone who was a complete stranger. 'You have my gift of being able to see a seed and extrapolate the flower,' he said eventually, 'but you also have something I lack – a regard for flowers, and a dislike of weeds. I admire you, Sherlock. I admire you greatly.'

Sherlock looked away, suddenly feeling a lump in his throat. He watched the buildings flow past the windows until he had his feelings under control.

'I shall write to our mother,' Mycroft announced suddenly. 'I shall ask her to invite our aunt and uncle to stay with her for a few days. This family feud has long passed the point where it should have been forgotten. By the time our father returns from India I want it forgotten.'

'Mother is . . . all right?' Sherlock asked hesitantly.

Mycroft's lips tightened almost imperceptibly. 'She has good days and bad, but I think she is on the mend.'

'And Emma?'

'Our sister is . . . well, she is what she is,' Mycroft said cryptically. 'Let us leave it there.'

The carriage suddenly swerved sideways, towards the kerb, and stopped. Sherlock heard a scrabbling sound as the driver climbed down from his perch. Moments later the door opened.

'King's Cross,' Mycroft announced. 'If I remember my *Bradshaw's Railway Time Tables*, then I believe you will find a train leaving for Edinburgh within the hour.'

'Thank you for meeting us,' Stone said. 'And for the tickets and the hotel arrangements.'

'Look after my brother,' Mycroft replied. He stared at Matty, and raised an eyebrow. 'If it isn't too much trouble, look after this one too. I find him curiously entertaining, and my brother obviously likes him.'

'You're a funny geezer,' Matty said chirpily, 'but thanks for the lift.'

Mycroft switched his glance back to Sherlock and stuck out a hand. 'Send me a telegram whenever convenient,' he said. 'You can reach me care of the Diogenes Club. Let me know how your search is going. And take care. Take great care. I have a bad feeling in my bones, and I do not think it is the gout from which I worry that I am beginning to suffer.'

The three of them – Sherlock, Matty and Rufus

Stone – climbed out of the carriage. The driver shut the door and climbed nimbly back to his seat. Sherlock heard the rap of Mycroft's cane hitting the roof, and his muffled voice calling, 'Admiralty Arch, my good man!' And then the carriage was pulling away from the station.

'We're on our own,' Matty said.

CHAPTER EIGHT

King's Cross Station was just like Waterloo – a large space filled with people waiting on the concourse and pigeons roosting in the cast-iron girders that held up the glass roof – except that it was smaller. Smoke drifted through the air, and the sulphurous smell of burning coal hung over everything. The walls and girders were coated with a thin film of black dust.

Sherlock looked around, wondering if it was worth asking someone if they had seen a big man in a white suit and hat with a younger girl in tow at some stage in the past day or two. Asking the people who were catching trains wouldn't do any good – the chance that they might have also been there at the same time as Amyus and Virginia Crowe was slim – but it might be worth talking to the ticket-office clerks or the station guards. Or, he thought, as his gaze scanned the walls of the arrivals and departures hall, he could talk to the beggars and pickpockets who moved like ghosts through the crowd, invisible and unnoticed apart from the occasional cries of 'I told you – I haven't *got* sixpence, and even if I did I wouldn't give it to you!' and 'My wallet! Where's my wallet?' that marked their progress. The beggars and pickpockets would always be there, he suspected – day and night. This was their place of work and their home as well.

He stopped himself before he could walk across to the nearest beggar and offer him sixpence for some information. Amyus Crowe had tried to explain to him a while back about the problem of trying to confirm something you already knew. Sherlock was as certain as he could be that Crowe and Virginia were making for Edinburgh and had gone through King's Cross on the way. Having a beggar tell him that yes, a big man in a white suit and hat had been there, with a girl, wouldn't change his certainty – it would just be extra information. On the other hand, having a beggar say that no, he hadn't seen a man or a girl fitting that description wouldn't mean that they *hadn't* been there. The beggar couldn't be expected to remember every single person who had been through the station concourse. 'The sensible man,' Crowe had said, 'don't look to confirm what he already knows – he looks to deny it. Finding evidence that backs up your theories ain't useful, but finding evidence that your theories are wrong is priceless. Never try to prove yourself right – always try to prove yourself wrong instead.'

The trouble was, in this case, if Sherlock's theory was that Amyus Crowe and Virginia had travelled through King's Cross, the only way to prove that theory wrong was to discover that they had travelled from a different London terminus – and that would mean a day wasted while they checked Paddington, Euston, Liverpool Street and the other major stations. They didn't have time to do that.

'You look pensive,' Rufus Stone said, clapping him on the shoulder.

'Just thinking through a problem,' Sherlock replied. 'I was wondering whether it was worth asking after Mr Crowe, but I think it would just be confusing.'

Stone nodded in agreement. 'Even if he bought a ticket here, it wouldn't have been for Edinburgh. He would have disguised his trail the same way he would have done leaving Farnham.' He looked around. 'We've got a while before the train, and my stomach is thinking my throat has been cut while it wasn't looking. Let's grab some food before we board the train – my treat.'

Stone was as good as his word. He found a chestnut seller on the fringes of the waiting crowd and bought three bags of hot nuts. He and Sherlock had to blow on them before they were cool enough to eat, but Matty seemed to have a throat lined with brick. He just swallowed them straight down, one after the other, smiling all the time.

After they had eaten their fill, Stone led Sherlock and Matty across the concourse towards the platforms. He showed their tickets to the guard, and they boarded the train. It was, in all respects that Sherlock could see, identical to the one that had taken them from Farnham to Waterloo.

'It's going to be a long journey,' Stone said, settling down in a small compartment. 'Make yourselves comfortable. Get some sleep, if you can. There's two things a man should grab whenever he can – sleep and food. You never know when your next chance will come along.' He glanced at Sherlock. 'If I'd have thought, I'd have brought along a violin. We could have continued our lessons.'

'In that case,' Matty muttered, just loud enough to hear, 'I would have taken a different train.'

Rufus glared at him. 'I suppose,' he said, 'your musical tastes run just as far as a tin whistle and a rattle, and no further.'

'Don't knock tin whistles.' Matty shook his head. 'There's plenty of good tunes come out of a tin whistle. That and a rattle is enough to dance to, and dancing's what music's all about.' He glanced truculently at Stone. 'Ain't it?'

Stone just shook his head in mock sadness and kept quiet.

'Actually,' Sherlock said, 'I wanted to talk a bit more about the theatre – about make-up and disguises, and things like that.'

Stone nodded. 'I can happily do that. I love reminiscing about the times I've trodden the boards myself, carrying a spear in the back of someone else's big scene, or played in the orchestra pit while the actors were on stage showing their craft.' He raised a quizzical eyebrow. 'You seem to have a strong liking for the art and craft of acting. What's brought this on, may I ask?'

Sherlock shrugged, uneasy at talking about his own hopes and likings. 'I suppose I just find it interesting,' he said. Stone kept looking at him expectantly, and to break the silence Sherlock added testily, 'If you really have to know, it goes back to Moscow, and that cafe we were in. I was sitting there with seven or eight people with whom I'd spent the past three days, and I didn't *recognize* them. Not *one* of them.' He felt his cheeks burning with a sudden rush of emotion that seemed to be a curdled mixture of embarrassment and anger. He hadn't realized until he'd said the words how much that incident had bothered him. 'I'm meant to be a good observer,' he continued. 'Amyus Crowe always says that I've got a talent for picking up on small details, and yet they fooled me. They fooled *me*!'

'They were better than you,' Stone said calmly. 'There's no shame in that. I'm not the best violinist in the world. I never *will* be the best violinist in the world. But I'm good, and I'm getting better.'

'I want to be the best,' Sherlock said quietly. 'I want to be the best violinist, and the best animal tracker, and the best at disguising myself. If I can't be the best, then what's the point of even trying?'

'You're going to find life very disappointing, my friend.' Stone shook his head. 'Very disappointing indeed.'

There was a tense silence in the carriage for a while, and then Rufus Stone, seemingly apologetic, broke it by telling Sherlock stories of his time working in the theatre, and of particular actors who could inhabit a part so well that they seemed to submerge their own personality in the performance. 'The thing is,' Stone said, 'that if *you* don't believe that you are an old man, or a woman, or a tramp, then how can you expect anyone else to believe you? Looking the part is just the surface; *being* the part is the true disguise.'

'But how do I *do* that?' Sherlock asked.

'If you're pretending to be sad, try and remember something in your life that made you cry. If you're meant to be happy, remember something that made you laugh. If you're meant to be a beggar, then remember being hungry and dirty and tired – if you can.' He smiled slyly. 'If you're pretending to be in love, remember the face of someone you care for. That way your face and your body will naturally fall into the right shapes, without your having to exaggerate for effect. Oh, and always trade on people's inattention.'

Sherlock frowned. 'What do you mean?'

'I mean that people usually see only what they expect to see. They don't look in detail at every person on the street.' He closed his eyes for a moment and ran a hand through his hair. 'How do I put this? It's like a theatrical backcloth. If you want the audience to believe that a play is set in China, you don't spend weeks painting a detailed backcloth showing a Chinese palace or a village so realistic that people think they're actually looking through a big window at the real thing – you sketch out some details, like a curved roof, or some bamboo, and let their minds fill in the rest. Minds are very good at deciding quickly what they're seeing out of the corner of their eye, based on a couple of things that snag their attention, and then taking a picture from their memory and putting that picture in place of the thing itself. If you want to look like a beggar, then what you *don't* want to do is to painstakingly recreate every detail of a beggar's clothes and hair and face. That will make you stand out. Concentrate on a couple of key things, and then blend into the background. Do you understand what I mean?'

'I think so.'

Stone gave some more examples, and they talked for a while, but the conversation trailed off into silence and Sherlock found himself gazing out of the compartment window. Towns came and went, fields flashed past, and gradually the landscape began to change from the neatness that Sherlock associated with the south of England to a more rugged, overgrown look. Even the cows began to look different – shaggy and brown, with horns that curved out in front of their heads, rather than black and white and short-haired. Once or twice they crossed bridges over large rivers, and Sherlock found himself remembering the wooden trestle bridge that he and Virginia and Matty had walked across when they were in America, escaping from Duke Balthassar.

Virginia. Even just thinking about her name sent a spasm through his heart. He couldn't deny that he felt something strong about her that he didn't feel for anyone else, but he couldn't characterize it. He didn't know what the feeling was, or what it meant, and its intensity scared him. He wasn't used to the idea of someone else being part of his life. He had always been a loner, at school and at home. He hated feeling *dependent* on someone, but that was the way he was feeling now. He couldn't imagine a life without Virginia in it, in some way.

The train stopped in Newcastle to take on fresh coal and water. The three of them took the opportunity to stretch their legs on the platform and buy some more food that they could eat from paper bags. This time it was apples wrapped in pastry and cooked until they were piping hot. Steam rose from them just like miniature versions of the steam rising from the train's engine.

After a while Sherlock headed back to the compartment, even though the train wouldn't be leaving for a few minutes. There was only so much walking up and down the platform that he could manage. The idea of exercise just for the sake of exercise had never appealed to him. He slumped in the upholstered seat, staring at the opposite wall. Train journeys, he decided, were excruciatingly boring. Sea journeys took longer, but there was more to look at, more to do. Ships had libraries, games rooms, restaurants and the whole entertaining routine of shipboard life. Trains had nothing.

Staring at the wall, counting off the minutes before they left Newcastle, he gradually became aware that he was being watched. It wasn't anything supernatural that led to that conclusion, no prickling of the neck or shivers down the spine. It was something simpler, more prosaic: a pink and red patch at the edge of his vision that refused to move. A face. Two blue eyes aimed unblinkingly at Sherlock.

Without giving away the fact that he had noticed the watcher by moving his head suddenly, he tried to pick up whatever details he could, but the person's body was partially hidden behind a pile of crates on a trolley.

When he'd squeezed about as much information out of the scene as he could without making it obvious that he had spotted the watcher, he decided to look properly. With no warning he quickly glanced to his right. Straight into the eyes of a man he thought he recognized.

Sherlock's heart skipped a beat.

He was the image of Mr Kyte, a man who had been introduced to Sherlock as the actor–manager of a theatre company in Whitechapel but had turned out to be an agent of the Paradol Chamber, and part of a plot to assassinate a Russian prince who was a friend of Mycroft's. He was a big, bear-like man with a chest the size and shape of a barrel, a mane of red hair that flowed down over his collar and a bushy red beard that hid his throat and fell halfway down his chest like a waterfall of rust. The last time Sherlock had seen Mr Kyte, the man had been engaged in a desperate struggle with Rufus Stone in a carriage in a Moscow street. He had escaped, leaving Rufus bleeding, furious and swearing vengeance.

The skin around Mr Kyte's eyes and on his cheeks, Sherlock remembered, had been covered with hundreds of small scratches. They had looked strangely like shaving cuts, but in areas where hair did not normally grow. Despite the smeary window between them, Sherlock was close enough that he could see those cuts now. There was no doubt – it *was* Mr Kyte.

Kyte stared Sherlock in the eye for a long moment. He didn't smile, or nod, or acknowledge in any way that he had been seen. After a few seconds he slowly drew back, into the shadow cast by a structure in the centre of the platform – a storage area of some kind. Sherlock's heart was racing, and the air seemed to catch on an obstruction in his chest every time he tried to take a breath.

He had to tell Rufus Stone! He had to tell Mycroft! He didn't know whether Mr Kyte's presence indicated that the Paradol Chamber were involved in Amyus Crowe's disappearance, whether they were following Sherlock because they blamed him for upsetting their plans or whether the whole thing was a complete coincidence, but the fact was that Mr Kyte was *there*, watching him, watching *them*, and that meant that things had changed. The situation was not the same as it had been just ten minutes earlier.

A blast from a steam whistle jerked Sherlock's thoughts back on track. The train was about to go. He started to get up out of his seat, aware that neither Rufus Stone nor Matty had returned, but just then the door to the compartment slid back and Matty entered. He was holding a pork pie in one hand.

'What's the matter?' he asked. 'You look like you've seen a ghost.'

'Close enough. Where's Rufus?'

Matty frowned. 'I thought he'd be back here by now. He was a minute or so ahead of me.' He tossed the pie in the air and caught it again. 'Saw a pile of these on a market stall just outside the station. The bloke who was selling them got distracted by some woman walking past. Just gave me enough time to swipe one.'

'But –' Sherlock started, then stopped. This was no time for talking. He pushed past Matty and headed out of the compartment, into the corridor that ran the length of the carriage. There were doors at either end leading to the platform. He ran to the nearest one and looked out of the window.

All along the platform passengers were getting back on board, but there was no sign of Rufus Stone.

The train whistle blasted again. Within moments the

platform was clear apart from the station guard, who was glancing back and forth along the length of the train, waiting to wave his flag.

Sherlock stared left and right. Rufus Stone wasn't in sight. Sherlock wanted to jump off and search the station for his friend, but the train was moments from leaving. What if Rufus had got on another carriage and was walking through the train at that moment? If that was what had happened, and Sherlock got off, then *he* would be the one who was missing. Stranded on a station where the Paradol Chamber were watching him.

But what if the Paradol Chamber had caught Rufus Stone? There was certainly unfinished business between Stone and Mr Kyte.

The train jerked into life. The engine pulled away from the platform, dragging its carriages behind it. Within moments the station was receding behind them, and they were heading out of the city and into the countryside.

Sherlock made his way back to the compartment and stood outside, looking left and right along the corridor, hoping against hope that Rufus Stone would appear, casually sauntering along in that infuriating way of his. After five minutes he had to admit to himself that Stone wasn't going to appear. He was still at Newcastle Station, probably the prisoner of the Paradol Chamber.

'What's the story?' Matty asked as Sherlock re-entered

the compartment. His lap was covered with pie-crust crumbs. 'Where's Mr Stone?'

'I think he got left behind,' Sherlock said grimly.

'What happened? Did he meet some girl? Typical if he did. He's got a roving eye, that one.'

Sherlock shook his head. 'No, I think he met the Paradol Chamber.'

Matty's face screwed up in disbelief. 'What, the people that the French Baron bloke was working for?'

'And the ones who framed Mycroft for murder and tried to kill his friend in Moscow.'

'What were they doing at the station?'

'They must have been following us,' Sherlock replied. He felt powerless, unsure what to do. 'There's no way of knowing from here. We can only make guesses, and guesses are worse than having no information because they pull you the wrong way.'

'So what are we going to do?'

Pausing only slightly to think, Sherlock said, 'We're going to keep on for Edinburgh. If a train guard comes along, we can tell him that our friend got left behind at Newcastle and we're worried that he might have had an accident. He might be able to get a message sent from one of the stations we stop at along the way. When we get to Edinburgh we'll head for the hotel Mycroft booked for us. If Rufus manages to get away from the Paradol Chamber or whoever has taken him, or if there's an innocent explanation for his missing the train, then he knows that's where we'll be.'

He settled back in his seat, folding his arms and resting his chin on his chest. Matty just stared at him for a while, then turned and looked out of the window. Despite his friend's presence, Sherlock had never felt so desperately alone.

'We could just go home,' Matty said after a while. His voice sounded very small.

The thought had already occurred to Sherlock, but he had rejected it. 'We could,' he replied, 'but that doesn't help Mr Crowe, or Virginia, or even Rufus. Besides, the Paradol Chamber know where we live. Our best bet is to hide out in Edinburgh until we can get this whole mess sorted. Go to ground.'

'Like Mr Crowe and Virginia,' Matty pointed out. 'They ran away and hid as well.'

'I know.' Sherlock didn't look over at Matty. 'I know. But I wish I knew *why.* I can't imagine what would frighten Mr Crowe enough to make him run rather than stand and fight his ground.'

At some point the train passed from England to Scotland, but if there was a sign to mark the moment then Sherlock missed it.

The stations slipped past more rapidly now and the names looked different to those on the platform signs in England. The landscape was rougher, wilder – craggy, dark hills in place of rolling fields. Even the sky seemed more overcast.

A ticket collector eventually appeared, and Sherlock explained about their friend not having made it back on to the train. The man *tutt*ed several times, and said he'd have a word with the stationmaster when they next stopped to see if a message was waiting, or whether one could be sent back to Newcastle. It was, Sherlock knew, too little too late. It was unlikely to produce a result.

Time seemed to slide slowly past. The ticket collector returned later to say that there was no news of Rufus Stone, and Sherlock felt his mood become blacker. Eventually, looking out of the window, he noticed that they were heading through more houses than he'd seen in one place for a while. Rather than being made out of brick, they were constructed from large blocks of grey stone. It gave them a serious, permanent look. The sun, which was balanced on the horizon, cast an orange light over them. The train began to slow down, wheezing to a halt just as it came alongside a platform that seemed to go on for miles. The signs on the platform read *Edinburgh*.

'We're here,' Matty said simply.

They left the train, clutching their bags. They took Rufus's too. Sherlock pulled Matty to one side and stopped. He wanted to watch the rest of the passengers leaving, just in case he recognized someone – like Mr Kyte or, hopefully, Rufus Stone.

The station was a teeming mass of people in different varieties of clothes, from top hat and tails to hairy tweed jackets and patched trousers. There were even – and

Sherlock had to suppress a gasp at this – men wearing skirts.

Matty noticed Sherlock's reaction. 'Yeah,' he said, 'sorry – I probably should have mentioned that. Took me by surprise when I was here a few years back.'

'Men with skirts? Well, maybe you thought I wouldn't notice.'

'They're not skirts,' Matty said firmly. 'They're *kilts*.'

'Kilts.' Sherlock sampled the unfamiliar word.

'They're a traditional piece of clothing worn by the Scottish clans.' He sniffed. 'A "clan" being a posh name for a family, as far as I can tell. Anyway, the clans used to be perpetually at war with each other until they all decided to get together and hate the English, and apparently the kilt makes it easier to fight. Or something. Anyway, they're coloured in different ways depending on which family you come from.'

'Presumably,' Sherlock said, 'so you can make sure that the man you're fighting is from another clan and not your second cousin twice removed.'

'Probably,' Matty replied.

Sherlock filed the information away in his brain. Different coloured kilts for different families – that would bear some further investigation. You could look at a man in a street in London and not have any way of finding out his name short of asking him, but if you could look at a man in a street in Edinburgh and know straight away that his name was MacDonald, well, that was a useful thing to know.

'Anything else I should know?' he asked.

'That purse-like thing that hangs down in front of the kilt is called a "sporran", and it's used to store things like money and such. Oh, and if a Scotsman's wearing a kilt then there's an odds-on chance that he's got a small knife tucked into his sock. It's called a "dirk".'

'Got it. Thanks.' Sherlock continued to look around, and to listen. Many conversations were going on within earshot, but the words were accented, difficult to understand. Sherlock was used to local accents of course – people in Farnham talked differently from people in London, and the various Americans he'd met talked differently from anybody in England, but he hadn't expected there to be an accent within a train ride of London that was so thick it was almost incomprehensible. He listened for a minute or so, analysing the passing conversations with Matty standing patiently by his side, until he had the basics sorted out. Once your ear was attuned to it, the accent seemed to fade into the background, letting the words come to the front.

'Right,' he said as the last passengers walked through the barrier and he stared along the empty platform, 'I think I've acclimatized myself. Let's go and find the hotel.'

They went outside and took the second cab they could find. The driver seemed to be in two minds whether he should risk taking two boys by themselves, but Sherlock showed him a handful of shillings from his pocket and the man nodded. As long as they could pay, he didn't care what age they were.

Sherlock had already looked inside the envelope that Mycroft had given them, and he called out the hotel's name to the driver.

The journey took about twenty minutes, passing terraces of tall buildings all made of the same grey stone blocks, and larger halls and mansions set back in acres of grass behind metal railings. Close up, Sherlock noticed that the grey stone contained hints of other colours – orange, yellow, blue, green – and that even the stone that was really grey often had ripples of darker hues running through.

The cab took them along the side of a park, and then jinked left and right into a wide thoroughfare lined with shops and hotels. It was the match of anything Sherlock had seen in London, New York or Moscow. Edinburgh, he could tell already, was an old and proud city.

The cab took a sudden right and drew to a stop. Sherlock and Matty got out just as the driver threw their bags down from where they had been stored behind him. He obviously felt that he shouldn't dismount for kids. Sherlock resisted the temptation to throw the money at his feet. Instead he just held it up, slightly out of reach, so that the driver had to lean forward precariously to get it.

They had stopped before a tall terraced building with a sign saying 'The Fraser Hotel'. The cab pulled away into a turn, back towards the main thoroughfare, and Sherlock noticed with part of his mind that the road sloped downward ahead of them. The rest of his mind was taken up with marvelling at the castle that had been revealed as the cab pulled away. It was enormous and dark, but the fact that it was built on a hill that was partly hidden by mist made the castle look as if it was a vast storm cloud hanging over the town.

'What now?' Matty asked.

Sherlock felt the absence of Rufus Stone weighing heavily on his mind. With Rufus gone he felt vulnerable, uncertain. Two kids, alone in Edinburgh. What *could* they do?

'I don't know,' he said.

CHAPTER NINE

After dumping their bags Sherlock and Matty headed down the hotel's staircase and out into the town. The sun had dropped beneath the horizon, and the darkness of the night was leavened by gas lamps and by flaming torches attached to brackets on the stone buildings. People were already thronging the streets, crossing from one tavern to another apparently in search of a better time than they were already having. Avoiding all of the activity as far as they could, the two of them found a relatively civilized tavern where they could sit in a corner and eat a gammon pie each, washed down with a watery beer which the barman seemed to have no problem serving them. However, when Sherlock asked for a pitcher of water the man just looked at him with a scowl on his face.

Every few minutes a different person tried to sit down beside them and engage them in conversation. Sometimes it was a woman with more make-up than was necessary and wearing clothes that looked as if they hadn't been washed in a while, but more often it was an unshaven man in a stained suit or a grey collarless shirt and braces. Matty always said the same thing – 'Our dad will be here in a minute, and he wouldn't like it if he found you here' – and they quickly left with a muttered apology or a curse. The first time it happened Sherlock just shrugged it off, but after the third time he stared at Matty with a question in his eyes. Matty avoided his gaze. 'There's some strange people around,' he muttered. 'Don't matter what town you're in, they always try and make friends with you if you're a kid alone. You learn early on not to have anything to do with them.'

Sherlock didn't ask any questions. It was obvious that Matty didn't want to go into details, but once again he was glad to have his friend with him.

For a while they discussed what to do about Rufus Stone. It was clear that they had both secretly hoped that they would find him, or at least a message from him, at the hotel. The fact that there was nothing had rattled them more than they wanted to admit.

'We could go to the police,' Matty suggested. 'Tell them that he's gone missing.'

'The trouble is that we don't actually know what has happened to him, so there's not much the police can do. It's not like we saw him being abducted. They'll say he just missed the train and he'll turn up tomorrow. Worse than that: they'll worry about two kids alone in Edinburgh. They'll assign a guardian to us, or place us in some philanthropist's home until Rufus arrives. That's the last thing we want.'

Matty nodded. 'I can see that. What about your

brother, though? We could send him a telegram, tell him what's happened.'

'And within an hour he'll send a telegram back telling us that we have to return to London until he knows what's happened to Rufus. If he does that, then I won't be able to disobey him – I've tried that before, and it never works out well. No, we need to be here. It's best that we don't tell *anyone* what's happened.'

'What do you think's happening to Rufus?' Matty asked quietly, not looking at Sherlock.

Sherlock sighed. He'd been trying not to think too hard about that. 'I don't know for sure. Maybe those two Americans have taken him, and they're asking him what he knows. Given that he doesn't know anything that they don't already know, they'll probably release him.' *Or kill him*, Sherlock thought, but he didn't put his fear into words. Although Matty was streetwise in a way that Sherlock would never be, he was younger than Sherlock, and there were some things he needed protecting from.

'He knows about Edinburgh,' Matty pointed out.

'If they were on the train with us, then they know about Edinburgh as well. That secret is out of the bag, I suspect.' He paused for a moment. 'On the other hand, if it's the Paradol Chamber, then I don't know *what* they want with him.'

Sherlock found that the conversation had blunted the sharp edge of his appetite. Thinking of what might be happening to Rufus while they were relaxing in a warm bar and eating well made his stomach lurch.

'I don't want to worry you,' Matty whispered after a while, 'but have you seen the bloke over there?' He nodded his head at the opposite wall. 'In the booth, sitting by himself.'

Sherlock glanced over, trying not to be too obvious about it. He was worried that Matty might have spotted Mr Kyte, but when he saw the unfamiliar thin man sitting alone in the booth he breathed a sigh of relief. A moment more and he started to feel uneasy, however. The man didn't show any signs of being interested in the two of them, but there was something odd about him, something Sherlock couldn't quite work out. He was *painfully* thin, for a start, as if he'd been starved for weeks, and his skin was so white it was almost translucent. His eyes seemed invisible in the dark shadows of his eye sockets, and the bones of his cheeks and his chin pushed out against the tautness of his face so much that Sherlock thought the skin might suddenly split as he watched. There was something strange about the man's clothes as well: they looked like they might have been his Sunday best, but they were coated in dirt, and there was a green tinge to his shoulders and sleeves. He was staring straight ahead, but he didn't appear to be looking at anything in particular. Nobody was sitting near him, and although he didn't have a drink in front of him, the barman didn't seem to want to go across and either take an order or throw him out. The man just sat there doing nothing.

The crowd in the tavern grew larger, and eventually the view of the strange pale-skinned man was blocked by people. Sherlock and Matty finished eating their pies and got ready to leave. As they stood up a gap opened in the crowd. Sherlock looked across. The man had gone.

'You ever heard of the Resurrectionists?' Matty asked as they left the tavern. He seemed edgy.

'I don't recognize the name,' Sherlock said.

'It was two blokes named Burke an' Hare. Both called William. They was notorious up in this neck of the woods a few years back. I heard about them when me dad was up here, working. Lookin' at that bloke back there reminded me of 'em. Edinburgh is one of the places doctors come to train, cos of the Edinburgh Medical College, but they've got a problem: how do they find out about the 'uman body if they can't examine 'em, cut 'em up, like, when they're dead – see where all the organs is, an' where the blood goes?'

'I thought medical schools were allowed to use the bodies of executed criminals,' Sherlock said, frowning.

'In theory, yeah,' Matty responded, 'but there's always less bodies available than there's student doctors wantin' to take a look at 'em. An' the number of things you can be hanged for has gone down a lot, which means there's a lot less bodies available for use. Sixty years ago there was over two 'undred different crimes that led to an 'anging.

Now there's only five. So only about two bodies a year came up for use by the College. Which is where Burke an' Hare came in.'

'I have a feeling I know where this is going,' Sherlock said quietly, feeling a shiver down his spine. 'They dug up corpses and sold them, didn't they?'

Matty stared at him. 'Not quite,' he said, 'although a lot of that did go on. "Bodysnatching", it was called. There was so much of it happening that friends and relatives of anyone who had just died used to keep watch over the grave to stop it being dug up. Some people – rich people – used to have cages built around graves of their relatives to stop anyone getting in. Before they realized what was going on, people used to visit the graves of their loved ones and find them disturbed, as if the bodies had come back to life an' just crawled out of their own accord.' He and Sherlock were pushing their way through the crowded streets towards their hotel. 'Course, once people got to know about the bodysnatchers, they had to change how they went about things. They was quite inventive, the bodysnatchers. They used wooden spades, cos they made less noise than metal ones, an' they used to dig down at an angle, so that any disturbance to the grave would be a way away, not directly over it. They'd uncover the end of the coffin, smash it open an' drag the body out with a rope.'

'All right, but you said this Burke and Hare weren't bodysnatchers. What were they then?'

'They was both Irish, for a start,' Matty replied, 'an' they moved to Edinburgh to work as labourers on the Union Canal. Burke ended up stayin' at a boarding 'ouse run by Hare's missus. They got to be drinkin' buddies, an' they got talkin' one night about ways of makin' some money. One of 'em suggested that they could steal the body of someone who 'ad died locally of natural causes an' 'ad no family, like, an' sell it to someone at the College who could use it to demonstrate 'uman anatomy to students. It weren't long before some old pensioner who owed Hare four quid died of natural causes. Burke an' Hare made sure the coffin that was buried was filled with tree bark, 'an they flogged the body to a Dr Knox 'ere in the city for seven quid.'

'Very enterprising,' Sherlock said drily.

'Problem was that people weren't dyin' of natural causes fast enough for 'em, so they decided to 'elp 'em along a bit. First one they actually killed was a local miller. They got 'im drunk on whisky an' then suffocated 'im. Second one was another pensioner, a woman this time, named Abigail Simpson. After that . . .' He shrugged. 'Well, they was off an' runnin'. Dr Knox would pay 'em a guaranteed sum for every dead body they delivered to 'im, no questions asked – ten quid if the body was in good nick, eight if there was anything wrong with it. They preferred women and kids, of course, cos they was easier to subdue an' to suffocate.'

Sherlock found he was feeling sick. It was the casual

nature of what Burke and Hare had done that offended him. The murders weren't crimes of passion, or 'spur of the moment' incidents – they were a series of what were effectively business decisions. Business decisions that left people dead.

'How many people did they end up killing?' he asked quietly as they turned the corner and headed towards the hotel's front door.

'Best guess is seventeen,' Matty answered, 'over the course of a year.'

'And didn't anyone suspect? I mean, the doctor they were selling the bodies to must have realized that they weren't executed criminals. Hanging must leave a distinct mark on the neck, and those corpses wouldn't have had that mark.'

'Dr Knox? Yeah, he knew, all right, although Burke later swore otherwise. He just didn't want to disrupt the supply of bodies. He was getting a reputation as being the best anatomy teacher around, an' students were flocking to his lectures, and payin' for the privilege. He wasn't going to give all that up.' He snorted. 'Story is that there was one bloke that Burke and Hare killed, name of Daft Jamie, who was well known around the town. When Dr Knox uncovered the body in the lecture theatre, ready to cut into it, some of the students recognized it. Knox said that it must be someone else, but he started the dissection on the face first, to make it unrecognizable quickly.'

'What happened in the end?' Sherlock asked, as he pushed open the front door. 'I presume they were found out, otherwise you wouldn't know all this.'

'Burke and Hare killed a woman in their lodging house named Marjory Docherty, but until they could get rid of the body they hid it under a bed. There was lodgers there, an' they got suspicious. When Burke was out of the way they checked his room, an' they found her. So they called the peelers. Burke and Hare got the body out of the house before the peelers turned up, but they took it to Dr Knox's place, where the peelers found it later. Hare turned Queen's evidence and testified against Burke in exchange for immunity from prosecution. Burke was hanged, an' his body was publicly dissected at the Edinburgh Medical College – perfectly legally, of course.'

'And what happened to Hare?'

'Vanished. Never heard of again.'

'So he might still be here, in the city?'

Matty nodded as he opened his bedroom door. 'Might well be, although it's more likely that he went back to Ireland.'

The next morning there was still no word from Rufus Stone. Disconsolate, Sherlock and Matty ate a breakfast of oat porridge served by a silent maid. It was so thick that Sherlock could have cut it into slices with a knife, and it looked like pigswill, but it was surprisingly tasty, and filling as well.

'What's the plan?' Matty asked.

'I'm going to find a bookshop or a library,' Sherlock replied. 'I need a map of the city, and I need to find out more about the place. I feel lost here. I can't find my bearings. Why don't you go and check the places you used to know, see if there's anyone who remembers you and can help us. We're going to need all the help we can get.' He paused for a second, thinking. 'That park, up the street from the hotel – let's meet just inside the front gates at midday.'

'I ain't got a watch,' Matty pointed out.

'Then ask someone.'

Having finished their porridge, they said their goodbyes and went out into the street.

Sherlock found a library a little way along the main thoroughfare. Inside, the dry smell of the books was comforting. It reminded him of Uncle Sherrinford's library. He always felt at home with books. Moving to the section devoted to Scotland, he pulled an armful of volumes off the shelf and settled at a nearby table to read.

Within an hour he had a much better idea of the geography and the history of Edinburgh, and its place within the wider history of Scotland. The town was built on seven hills, he discovered, which he supposed would explain the fact that every direction seemed to be either uphill or down.

After a while the close black print started blurring

as he tried to read it. He closed the book and shut his eyes for a moment. The problem was, he thought, that the kind of information he wanted wasn't the kind that went in reference books. Where did people go in Edinburgh when they were on the run? How did they avoid detection when someone was looking for them? Who was in charge of the local criminal fraternity, and were they more likely to help a person on the run or the people chasing them? These were the kind of things that Matty was more likely to find out from his contacts, but unless it was written down and kept up to date then it was the kind of information that would just slip away. Sherlock decided that he needed to write down all the little snippets and facts that he or Matty unearthed along the way. Maybe if he kept them on file cards then he could access them the next time he needed them.

A sudden, disturbing thought struck him, and he shivered. What he was proposing wasn't that different from what Josh Harkness had done – collect information on dubious and illegal activity and keep it. The only real distinction was that Sherlock wouldn't be using it for profit.

He checked the watch that usually hung from a chain on his waistcoat. It was half past eleven. Time to start thinking about meeting Matty.

As he returned the books to their shelves he noticed that there were maps of Edinburgh for sale at the front desk for sixpence. He bought one and took it back to the table where he had been reading to open it. His gaze scanned quickly across the details: the shape of the city and in which directions the main roads ran. He located the main railway line coming in from London, and traced the route the cab had taken. It had gone along a road named Princes Street – clearly the main road through the city. That enabled him to work out where their hotel was, and where he was now.

Folding the map up and putting it in his pocket, he set off for the park. He felt more confident that he could navigate his way around now.

The sun was shining through the clouds, casting beams of light diagonally across the mottled blue and grey as if girders of light were holding up the entire sky. Glancing down side roads as he strolled along Princes Street he caught glimpses of the castle. It no longer looked like a solid grey cloud hanging above the city, but there was something about it that defied geometry and perspective. It looked as if it just shouldn't be possible that the castle was up *there* while the town was down *here*.

As he passed one particular alley, something in the shadows made a scuffling noise. He stopped, intrigued, and looked sideways. He made no move to get any closer to the alley – that would have been stupid – but if anyone was following him then he wanted to know who it was.

For a moment he could only see a pool of shadow, like liquid darkness, where the sun could never penetrate, but after a few moments his eyes got used to the contrast and he could make out something that seemed to be floating in mid-air, like a pale balloon. It took a moment of concentration before his brain realized what he was looking at – the face of someone dressed entirely in black who was standing there, in the alley, staring out.

Sherlock took an involuntary step backwards. The face was bone-white, with eyes set so deep that the sockets were just black holes in the face. The cheekbones stuck out sharply, and the lips – if the figure had any lips – were pulled back from teeth that seemed to grin at Sherlock as if the figure was enjoying some private joke. For a long moment Sherlock was convinced that a rotting human body, something close to a skeleton, was standing there, in the alley, looking at him. Had it been ripped from the ground and left there, propped up against a piece of wood, as a warning? And who would do such a macabre thing?

The figure raised a hand to the side of its face and waved, then drew back into the darkness until Sherlock couldn't see it any more. Only after it had gone, leaving him cold and shaking, did he remember the man in the tavern, the one who had been sitting alone. Had it been him? This figure had looked even more skeletal, even less alive, but that might have been a trick of the poor light.

What was going on? He thought back to what his aunt and uncle had told him. Was he going mad, like his father?

For a few seconds Sherlock wanted to go further into the alley, looking for the figure – looking for the truth about what he'd seen – but he pulled back. Logically, the most likely explanation was that this was a trap, and the figure was bait to lure him in. But was it random, or did someone know that his curiosity often outweighed his good sense? Rattled, Sherlock walked away from the mouth of the alley and he didn't look back.

The park was only a few minutes further. When he got there, Matty was already waiting.

'Are you all right?' his friend asked. 'You look like you've seen a ghost.'

'Don't be stupid,' Sherlock replied sharply. 'There's no such thing as ghosts.'

'All right – keep your hair on.'

'Did you find anything out?' Sherlock asked.

Matty shook his head. 'Most of the blokes and kids I knew around here have moved on. That or they've died. I did find a couple of people who remembered me, but they don't know anything about a big American who's come through this way. What about you?'

'I could find my way around the city now.'

'Well, I suppose that's something,' Matty said critically. 'If we was ever planning on moving here.'

'Don't underestimate the usefulness of geographical knowledge.'

Matty stared at him. 'So what's our next move?' he asked eventually.

Sherlock pondered for a moment. He'd been debating this question himself. 'I suppose we could go back and talk to the ticket collectors and the guards at the station here,' he said slowly, 'but they must see hundreds of passengers a day, and there's no guarantee that they would remember Mr Crowe. Besides, if he continued to be as careful as he was back in Farnham, then he would have got off at an earlier station and maybe hired a cart to bring him and Virginia to Edinburgh.'

'If he's here at all,' Matty pointed out. 'After all, you've only got a dead rabbit's head pointing you here. It's not much to go on. I still reckon we might have gone off in completely the wrong direction.'

'Despite Rufus vanishing?' Sherlock asked.

Matty shrugged. 'You've got a point. The clue was probably a good one, but now that it's got us here, what do we do? Wait for another one to come along?'

'Matty,' Sherlock said slowly, 'I've said it before and I'll say it again – you may not be a genius, but you can bring out the genius in those around you.'

'What do you mean?'

'Amyus Crowe left a clue that would bring us to Edinburgh, if we understood it properly. Why did he do that? We've not asked ourselves that question yet.'

'Because he wanted us to follow him,' Matty replied.

'Exactly. He *wanted* us to follow him. He wasn't just saying "Goodbye – I'm off to Edinburgh!" He wanted us to know exactly where he was heading, and the only reason for that was because he wanted us to come after him. He wants our help. Now we're here, he's not going to leave us dangling. He'll leave another clue around, one that will lead us right to where he is.'

'Why couldn't he do that from the start?' Matty asked.

'Because all he knew was that he and Virginia were heading to Edinburgh. Once he was here he would find somewhere to settle down in peace – somewhere he wouldn't be detected. Not a hotel then. More likely a cottage somewhere outside the town that he could rent. Once he knew his address, he would find a way of letting us know.'

'But he doesn't know where we are,' Matty pointed out.

'So he would leave a message somewhere that we could see it no matter where in the town we ended up.' He thought back to the newspaper that he had read on the train. In particular he remembered the page of classified advertisements that had so fascinated him: messages from one person to another, or one person to a group of people, either in plain language or in code. 'He'll place a classified advertisement in the local newspaper,' he said with certainty. 'He knows that's one of the places I'll look.'

'But what if we missed it? What if he put the message in yesterday?'

Sherlock shook his head. 'He wouldn't know what

day we were going to be here. If I know Amyus Crowe, he would pay for the advert to be in all week.'

Matty nodded. Either what Sherlock had said made perfect sense to him or he was willing to take it on trust. 'Then let's get a local newspaper. Let's get all of them.'

'How many are there?' Sherlock asked, wondering if they were going to have to plough their way through ten or twelve newspapers, or whether Amyus Crowe would have put the advertisement in all of them.

'Three,' Matty said. He turned to go, then turned back. 'You'll have to read 'em,' he pointed out, 'cos I can't read. And I ain't got any money on me, so you'll have to buy 'em as well.'

They found a newspaper vendor just outside the park and bought copies of all three Edinburgh newspapers for that day, then went back into the park and sat on a bench where Sherlock could read them. He couldn't help but notice that the Edinburgh murder story – the one he'd seen in the copy of *The Times* on the train – was the front-page story on all three papers. The first one – the *Edinburgh Herald* – was representative of them all:

Edinburgh police this morning arrested a suspect in the murder by poison of the eccentric businessman Sir Benedict Ventham. Sources close to the police have told us that the suspect in question is a Miss Aggie Macfarlane, cook to the late Sir Benedict and – this newspaper has discovered – sister to the notorious criminal and leader of the Black Reavers Gang, Gahan Macfarlane. It is believed that she slipped poison into his food, for reasons that only she knows at the moment.

The Black Reavers? The name of the gang struck a chord in Sherlock's mind. It made them sound dangerous, even sinister. He was about to move on to the classified section of the newspaper when he spotted the name again, this time in a report directly beneath the paragraphs on Sir Benedict Ventham's poisoning:

FIRE DEVASTATES LOCAL GREENGROCERS

The premises of Messrs MacPherson and Cargill, greengrocers, of Princes Street were burned down last night in a fearsome conflagration of apocalyptic proportions. Bystanders fought the blaze for nearly three hours with buckets of water taken from the nearby river, with little success. No casualties are reported, as the blaze occurred during the hours of darkness. MacPherson and Cargill's had been a local fixture for over fifty years. Our reporter was informed, by several members of the local populace, who wished to remain anonymous, that the greengrocers had recently become a target of the notorious Black Reavers – a local criminal gang of grim repute who demand money with menaces from local businesses . . .

He moved on to the classified section. It wasn't as large as the one in *The Times* – barely half a page. Most of the advertisements seemed to be from households requiring a maid, a cook or a butler ('references essential'), with a handful advertising lost property ('Found in King's Street, a lady's brooch – emeralds set in gold. Prospective owners must apply in writing with full description of item before collection can be arranged'). Nothing struck him as being the kind of thing that Amyus Crowe would have written.

Just in case, he checked the letters pages as well. These mostly seemed to be complaints about factual inaccuracies in previous editions of the paper, or comments on the lack of manners of the lower classes, but one letter in particular caught his eye, and he read it out to Matty:

SIR,

I write with reference to the spate of sightings recently of men and women within the city limits who can only be described as 'deceased and yet still moving'. Such events are an affront to God and speak to the perilous moral state of the population of this city. I draw to the attention of your readers the following biblical quotations:

Isaiah 26:19: 'Thy dead men shall live, together with my dead body shall they arise. Awake and sing, ye that dwell in dust: for thy dew is as the dew of herbs, and the earth shall cast out the dead.'

Revelation 20:13: 'And the sea gave up the dead that were in it; and death and Hades gave up the dead that were in them: and they were judged every man according to their works.'

I ask them to consider: does this not indicate that Armageddon is near, and that God will soon judge us all? Repent your sins, before it is too late!

Yours faithfully, Geo. Thribb *Esq.*

The letter made Sherlock think about the two skeletal figures that he'd seen – the one in the tavern the night before and the one in the street only half an hour ago. Was this what the letter was referring to? Was there a spate of people who looked like dead bodies walking the streets and, if so, what did it mean?

He pushed the thought aside. Interesting though these speculations were, they didn't help with the immediate task – finding Amyus Crowe and Virginia, or Rufus Stone.

In the *Edinburgh Star* the classified adverts were skewed more towards notifications of upcoming dances (or 'cèilidhean', as they seemed to be known), lost pets and horses for sale. One in particular caught his attention:

'Parakeet missing, can recite entirety of *Hamlet* and selected poems of Tennyson. Reward paid for return.' A parrot that could recite the whole of *Hamlet*? Sherlock couldn't believe it.

It was in the *Edinburgh Tribune* that he found what he was looking for. Nestled among the usual set of advertisements was one that immediately stood out.

THE SIGERSON HOTEL

Find the ideal place to rest and relax. Tell us your dreams and we will make them come true. Two days in our care will work wonders. Mr and Mrs Cramond, the proprietors, are committed to satisfying your every whim.

Locate us near Kirkaldy Town, in Fife.

'That's it,' Sherlock said, pointing to the advertisement.

'I can't read,' Matty explained patiently.

Sherlock read the advert out to Matty, who frowned. 'Bit long-winded,' he said, 'and a bit creepy as well. Don't strike me as the kind of place ordinary people stay.'

'It's not a real hotel,' Sherlock said.

'How do you know?'

Sherlock indicated the first three words. 'The *Sigerson* Hotel. My father's name is Siger – Siger Holmes. That makes me Siger's son. The advert is aimed at me.'

Matty looked dubious. 'Could be a coincidence. Maybe there *is* a Sigerson Hotel.'

'Possible,' Sherlock conceded, 'but these adverts are

paid for by the word. There are a lot of words here – more than you need to tell people how good your hotel is, but enough to contain a hidden message.'

'So Mr Crowe and Virginia are in Kirkaldy Town.' Matty scowled. 'That's miles away. I thought they were supposed to be in Edinburgh.'

'The mention of Kirkaldy is a red herring. That's not where they are.'

'Then where are they?'

Sherlock shrugged. 'I don't know. I have to decode the message.'

He looked at it again. If it had been a set of random letters or numbers then he would have tried a substitution cipher, the way that Amyus Crowe had taught him. Substitution ciphers were based around the principle of substituting one thing for another – replacing every letter *a* with a number 1, for instance, every letter *b* with a 2, and so on. Decoding them, if you didn't know what the substitution strategy was, depended on knowing the relative frequency with which particular letters occurred in normal writing. *E* was the most common letter, followed by *t*, *a*, *i*, *o* and *n*. So all you had to do was look for the most commonly occurring letter or number, and replace that with *e*, then work your way down the list – although you did need quite a large sample of code to break in order to have a good chance of getting it right. Scanning the message, though, Sherlock realized that it wasn't a substitution cipher. For one, it made a strange kind of sense. It read as an advertisement. Replacing the letters of a sentence or a paragraph with other letters would result in a completely scrambled set of meaningless words. So the code had to be something else. He took a pen out of his pocket and quickly scribbled down the initial letters of the words in the margin of the newspaper, but he only got a little way – *f t i p t r a r* . . . – before he realized that he was on the wrong track.

Perhaps it was the last letters, he thought. He scribbled another set of letters – *d e l e o t d x* . . . No, that didn't look right either.

Perhaps he should start from the end, rather than the beginning. He tried both options again – first letters and last letters – but all he got for his trouble was *f i t k n u l* . . . and *e n n y r s e* . . . Unless Amyus Crowe was deliberately confusing the issue by writing in a foreign language, Sherlock was on the wrong track.

Maybe he should be looking at words rather than letters. He tried every first word of a sentence – *find tell two mr locate* – then every second word – *the us days and us.* With the proviso that the second one sounded a bit like bad poetry, it was no good.

He sighed and bit the inside of his lip, aware that Matty was intently watching what he was doing. He was running out of ideas. Maybe this thing was too complicated for him to decipher.

Something was nagging at the back of his brain. He tried to force himself to relax, to stop thinking so that the thought could work its way to the surface. He had tried first words of sentences, and second words. What if . . . what if he tried the first word of the first sentence, the second word of the second sentence, and so on?

He knew the advertisement so well by now that he could write down the words from memory.

Find us in Cramond Town.

'Got it!' he whispered.

'What?'

'They're in a place called Cramond,' he said.

Matty looked dubious. 'I thought you said Cramond was the name of the people who owned the hotel.'

'There *is* no hotel,' Sherlock explained again. 'It's a code. Mr Crowe had to get the name of the place in there, but he made it look like something else – a person's name – and he then distracted attention from it by referring to a real place – Kirkaldy.'

'All right – where *is* this Cramond?'

Sherlock pulled out the map he had bought from the bookshop. On the reverse side of the Edinburgh map was a map of the surrounding area. In the top right-hand corner was an index relating to a grid of letters and numbers around the edge. He scanned down the index until he found Cramond – not without a little flash of pride – and then checked the grid reference on the map. 'It's on the coast,' he said. 'Just a few miles away. We can probably get someone to take us there in a cart.' He folded up the map and the newspaper, putting them into his pockets. He felt a sense of relief and weariness wash over him. He'd done it! He'd located Amyus and Virginia Crowe!

Now came the hard part – finding out why they had left, and persuading them to return . . .

A movement over Matty's shoulder made him glance past his friend. Two men were approaching. One held something in his hands: it looked like an empty sack. It took a moment for Sherlock to identify him as the smallpox-scarred American he had seen in Farnham, and then again at Newcastle Station. A chill ran down his spine, and he felt his heart suddenly speed up. His eyes flickered sideways, to Matty's face. He was just about to tell Matty to run when he noticed that the boy was staring over Sherlock's shoulder. His eyes were wide and scared.

More men must have been coming up behind Sherlock – probably including the man with the missing ear and the ponytail. Sherlock was about to push Matty left and dive right himself when the man behind Matty realized that they'd been spotted, rushed forward and threw the sack over the boy's head. Sherlock reached out to tear the sack away, but the world went dark as something heavy dropped over his head and covered his face. Hands grabbed him and pushed him off his feet.

CHAPTER TEN

The sack smelled strongly of pipe tobacco, and Sherlock found himself choking on a combination of the heat, the lack of air and the pungent odour. A small amount of light filtered through the gaps in the material, but not enough for him to see out. The hessian weave rubbed roughly against his forehead, his ears and the back of his neck. He could feel the skin being rubbed away, leaving sore patches behind. He was going to have some serious scrapes when he got out.

If he got out.

His wrists and ankles had been quickly and expertly bound with rope, tight enough to cut off the blood supply. Arms were wrapped around his chest and around his legs. He was being hoicked around like a sack of barley, carried rapidly across the park before anybody spotted what was going on. The same thing must have been happening to Matty. He tried experimentally kicking out with his left foot, but the grip around his legs tightened before he could move more than an inch. It was like having leather belts strapped around him. Perhaps this was what it was like to be crushed to death by one of those big snakes they had in South America – anacondas, or pythons, or whatever they were.

He opened his mouth to yell for help, but a fist impacted beneath his ear. A red spike of agonizing pain flashed through his head like lightning, leaving a sick ache in its wake. He felt as if he was going to throw up, but he knew that if he did so with his head in the sack then he was going to have to live with the consequences, so he swallowed several times, forcing his stomach to calm down.

Tiny flecks of tobacco had got into his mouth while it was open. He could feel the strands between his lips and his teeth, and sticking to his tongue. The bitter taste made him gag again, and he desperately swallowed more saliva. He knew that people not only smoked tobacco but chewed it as well. How could they stand it?

His fingers prickled with pins and needles as the blood fought to get past the ropes that bound his wrists. The fingers themselves felt as large and as tight as sausages frying in a pan.

The men carrying him changed their grip. For a moment Sherlock wondered what they were doing, but then the grip around his chest and legs loosened and they swung him back, swung him forward again, fast, and let go. He flew helplessly through the air, not even sure which way was up and which was down, waiting what seemed like an eternity to hit – what? Grass? Pavement? The surface of a river or a canal?

Half expecting to suddenly find himself sinking in cold water, he bounced on a soft surface and rolled until he hit a wooden board at right angles. The inside of a cart lined with straw? It seemed likely. He heard something hit the straw beside him, and a second later a heavy object thudded into him with enough force to drive the air from his body in a sudden *whoosh*!

Matty.

'You all right?' he called through the hessian sack, but before Matty could answer something struck Sherlock in the ribs. Waves of sickening pain radiating outwards across his chest. He gasped. Matty, sensibly, didn't reply. Maybe he couldn't. Maybe he was unconscious.

Not a word had been spoken by the men who had taken them, but the message was clear: stay still; don't struggle; be quiet. Any deviation from those rules would be punished.

Still, at least they were both still together. That counted for something. While he was alive and in possession of his senses and his mind, Sherlock was confident that he could find a way out of most situations.

His deduction that they had been thrown into a cart was borne out as they moved off. The way Sherlock was lying, his head was facing in the direction of travel. He quickly worked back over his memories of the past minute or so. He'd been facing Matty, in the park, with the gate towards Princes Street off to his left. When the sack was put over his head he had been snatched off his feet and carried with his head facing forward and to the right, *away* from the gate and Princes Street. He had been thrown into the cart head first, so that meant the cart was almost certainly heading away from Princes Street, away from the centre of Edinburgh.

As they travelled, Sherlock tried to keep a running tote of the various turns they made – which direction they turned, and roughly how long it had been since the last turn. The mental effort of counting and remembering gave him something to do other than panic, and if he ever had to retrace the journey then the information might be vital.

Eventually the cart stopped. Hands grabbed Sherlock and pulled him roughly upright. He was tossed over someone's shoulder and carried away. He could hear the footsteps, so they weren't on grass. Stone, or hard earth? The man who was carrying him stumbled a couple of times, so perhaps he was walking across cobbles and some were loose. That was more information that might come in useful.

Sherlock's fingers felt as if they were burning with lack of blood now. His mind was filled with images of the flesh blackening and falling off. Desperately he tried to force his mind to think about something else. The footsteps! They had changed – the man who was carrying him was walking on wood now, and the light filtering in through the gaps in the sacking was darker, cooler. He was inside some kind of building.

The sound of the footsteps on the floorboards changed, becoming more hollow. At the same time, Sherlock felt that he was being tipped up, head higher than his feet. He was being carried up a set of stairs.

At the top of the stairs things levelled out again, and the footsteps crossed more floorboards. The sound was different from downstairs, however. The floorboards creaked more, as if they were unsafe.

The man carrying him suddenly let him drop. Sherlock had less than a second to prepare himself for the impact. His left shoulder hit the floor first, and he cried out. The pain made him bite his tongue. He tasted blood.

Another impact, beside him – Matty, getting the same treatment. He didn't cry out, but Sherlock could hear him moaning.

Something sharp and metallic slid between his palms. Before he could react, it sliced upward and the ropes around his wrists fell away. A moment later the ties around his ankles went the same way.

He reached up and pulled the sack off his head.

Steely grey light dazzled his eyes, and he blinked several times. He was in a room about the size of his aunt and uncle's dining room, but that was where the similarity ended. This room was bare floorboards and cracked plaster walls rather than carpets and curtains. The green stain of mould bloomed across the peeling remnants of wallpaper. Holes in the walls exposed the wooden lathes beneath. Some of the floorboards were missing, and rat droppings were spread across the remainder like tiny black stones. The ceiling was largely bare of plaster, and the rafters showed through like ribs. Rain had trickled in through the holes and left puddles on the floorboards, adding to the general feeling of neglect and decay.

As Sherlock struggled to his knees the newspaper slid from his pocket and dropped to the rotting floorboards. He could see the word *Cramond* written in the margin. Horrified, he looked up. Three men were in front of a broken window, two of them standing and the one in the centre sitting with his hands on a walking stick that was set in front of him, but the way the light flooded around them left them looking like charcoal stick figures sketched on paper. Sherlock screwed up his eyes, trying to make out their faces, but it was no good. The light was too strong.

Matty was curled up a few feet away. A sack, similar to the one that had been covering Sherlock, was still tied around his head and shoulders. For a moment Sherlock couldn't see any movement, and his heart lurched sickeningly as he wondered if his friend was dead, but then he saw that Matty was breathing shallowly. He was alive, but probably unconscious.

Given what Sherlock suspected was going to happen in the room over the next few minutes, unconsciousness seemed like a good option.

He looked past Matty. A chair had been placed to one side of the three men. Rufus Stone was tied to the chair. He looked at Sherlock and smiled. The smile might have been more reassuring if there weren't swollen lumps on his forehead and cheeks and if his fingers hadn't been covered with blood. They looked like someone had been working on them with pliers.

'Let me explain how this will work,' a quiet, almost gentle voice said. Sherlock thought it was the man in the middle. His accent was similar to that of Amyus Crowe – he was obviously American. 'I have no compunction about hurting children. I have done it before, and I will do it again. I do not enjoy it, but if it is necessary then I will cause you immense pain in order to get what I want.'

'And what is that?' Sherlock asked. 'I don't have any money, you know.'

The man didn't laugh, but Sherlock could hear a trace of humour in his voice as he answered: 'I have no use for your money, boy. I have more money than I know what to do with. No, I want information about your friend Amyus Crowe and his daughter, and that is something you *do* have.'

'I don't know anything,' Sherlock said, trying to inject as much conviction into his voice as he could. He squinted, trying to make out some features on the man's face or his clothes against the bright light behind him. All he could tell was that the cane the man was resting his hands on had a strangely large head on it.

'Then you will die in agony. It is that simple. You are about to experience a great deal of pain, but the more true answers you give me, the longer you will live and the less pain you will be in. Now, I have a series of questions to ask you. They are very simple questions. You will answer them just as simply, with no attempt at lying or obscuring the truth.'

Sherlock's gaze fell on the newspaper. He had to stop the man seeing it. 'What happens if I don't know the answers?' he asked, brain racing as he tried to work out what to do. He jerked his eyes away from it. Just looking down might draw attention to it.

'A good question,' the man conceded, 'and one that has exercised my mind on many occasions in the past. I have, as you can probably guess, conducted many, many interrogations like this. Fortunately I have a solution. You see, we have been watching you for some time. Several of the questions I am going to ask you, I know that you know the answers to. Several of the questions I am going to ask you, *I* already know the answers to. You, however, don't know what I know. You can't risk lying – that is, unless you enjoy pain. Your best option is to tell me the absolute truth. The chances of your fooling me are slight, because on some of the questions I will know, for absolute certain, if you are lying to me – even if you say, "I don't know." Now, are we clear about the rules?'

Sherlock thought for a moment. The way the quiet man had laid out the problem was elegant and simple. If Sherlock decided to lie, or to claim ignorance, then there was a statistical chance that he might be caught out. The things Sherlock didn't know were how many questions the man was going to ask, and how many of those he already knew the answer to. If the answers were ten and one then Sherlock might still have a chance to keep Amyus Crowe's hideaway secret. If the answers were ten and five, then his chances were much slimmer.

His logical mind clambered all around the problem, trying to find a way through it, but it was seamless. The man asking the questions had the upper hand. He'd thought it all through.

'Do you understand the rules?' the man said. His voice was just as gentle as before. 'I will not ask again.'

'Yes, I do,' Sherlock said, edging his foot to one side as if shifting position to make himself more comfortable. He nudged the newspaper into one of the puddles of rainwater that had come through the holes in the ceiling.

The man turned his head slightly, so that he was looking at Rufus Stone, and something about the way the light illuminated his face puzzled Sherlock. 'It goes without saying,' he added, 'that I will tolerate no interruptions from the sidelines. Are we clear?'

Stone nodded his bruised and bloody head, but Sherlock was too concerned with what was happening with the newspaper to pay attention to his friend. The water was beginning to soak into the pages, but a quick hand could pull it out of the puddle.

He risked a glance down. The ink had began to run, erasing the letters that he'd written in the margins of the page. Within a few minutes even the printed text would be indecipherable. He breathed a sigh of relief and turned his attention back to the quiet man's face, trying to gauge whether the man had seen anything. Sherlock was suddenly struck by the fact that there was something *wrong* with his skin. There seemed to be marks on it, but he couldn't see what they were.

'Then let us begin.'

The man raised a hand from his walking stick. Sherlock saw with shock that the head of the cane was a golden skull, gleaming in the light from the window, but he only glimpsed it for a second before the men on either side moved forward. Stepping over Matty's inert form they grabbed Sherlock by his arms and hauled him to his feet. The floorboards creaked and bent with the strain.

The men were both holding ropes with loops at the end, made with slip knots. One of the men – the earless one with the ponytail – threw his loop over Sherlock's head and pulled it tight around his neck. He threw the other end of the rope over one of the bare rafters and pulled it tight. Rufus struggled against his bonds in protest, but the man nearest him casually cuffed him with the back of his hand. Rufus fell back, groaning.

Sherlock felt the rope tighten beneath his chin, choking him. Instinctively he rose up on tiptoe to try to lessen the strain, but the other man – the one with the smallpox scars – was slipping the loop on his own rope beneath Sherlock's feet and tightening it around his ankles.

'I suggest,' the quiet man said in a calm, reasonable voice – the kind of voice that a vicar might use when asking for a cup of tea – 'that you take a tight hold on the rope that is above your head. In a few seconds your life will depend on how tight a grip you can keep. Plus, of course, on how truthfully you answer my questions.'

Abruptly the man holding the rope that was around Sherlock's neck pulled on it. The noose tightened, yanking Sherlock off his feet. He grabbed for the rope above his head and hung on for dear life. The strands were rough beneath his fingers, but he could feel his palms becoming sweaty, and he knew that if his hands slipped then he would be left dangling by his neck, and he would suffocate.

His toes dangled in the air inches from the floorboards. The man pulled harder, and Sherlock rose into the air, still hanging on to the rope above his head with both hands. His vision was turning red, but he could just about make out the shape of the man who was holding the rope crossing the room and tying it to an exposed lathe.

'Now,' the quiet man said, 'let us begin.' He cleared his throat. 'What is the nature of the relationship between you and Amyus Crowe?'

'I . . . don't . . . know . . . anyone . . . with . . . that . . .

name . . . !' Sherlock gasped between precious breaths of air.

'Now I know that to be a patent falsehood,' the quiet man said. He raised his hand an inch above his walking stick. As Sherlock looked down he could see the man who had slipped the rope around his feet crouch down, reach into the shadows behind him and pull out a stone the size of Sherlock's head. String had been tied and knotted around the stone, and one end of the string was attached to a fishing hook. The man hoisted the stone in one hand and stuck the fishing hook in the rope that hung loose from Sherlock's ankles. Then he let go of the stone.

The weight of the stone suddenly transferred itself to the rope and thus to Sherlock's feet, dragging him down, stretching his muscles and tendons and pulling the noose tighter around his neck. He clamped his hands even more tightly around the rope, trying desperately to keep himself from choking.

'On the assumption that you may be congenitally stupid and you may not have understood the rules,' the quiet man said, 'I will repeat the question. The penalty for lying should be obvious by now. As you will already have worked out, I *do* know the answer to this question: what is the nature of the relationship between you and Amyus Crowe?'

'Teacher!' Sherlock gasped.

'Good. Thank you.' A pause. 'Now, the second question – where is Amyus Crowe now?'

Sherlock's vision was narrowing down into a fuzzy tunnel. His blood was thundering in his ears, but the question still reverberated around his mind. He couldn't answer it – surely he couldn't answer it! But if he didn't . . .

He had no choice. He couldn't give Amyus and Virginia away.

'Don't . . . know . . .' he choked.

The quiet man sighed. 'Another falsehood. You would not have come all this way if you did not know where your teacher is. Are you stubborn, or just foolish?' He raised his hand again, just an inch off his knee.

Despairingly Sherlock tried to kick out with his feet to hit the crouching man in the head, but the weight of the stone that was pulling his ankles downward was too great. The man reached into the shadows again and pulled out another rock as large as the last. It was similarly tied up with string, with a fish hook dangling off the string.

The rope was already pulling Sherlock's chin up. His fingers were beginning to cramp. He wasn't sure how much longer he could hold his body up and stop the rope from cutting off his air supply.

The man by Sherlock's feet hooked the fish hook into the rope and let go. The heavy stone *clunk*ed against the one that was already hanging there. Sherlock felt as if he weighed twice as much as he had when the rope around his neck was first pulled tight. The muscles of his shoulders and arms were shaking with the strain of taking his weight. His heart was hammering within his chest, and his vision had narrowed to a coin-sized circle in the centre of a red-tinged darkness. The rope around his ankles was digging deep into the flesh, and the weight felt as though it were dislocating his legs. The man crouching by Sherlock's feet shifted position, and Sherlock distinctly heard the floorboards creak beneath his feet. Similarly, the man who had pulled Sherlock off his feet took a step to his right, and once again Sherlock could hear the floorboards creak beneath the man's weight. Even to his ears, blocked as they were by the desperate rushing of blood, that creak spoke of a possible sudden splintering in the near future. Those boards were old and rotten. That gave him an idea.

But he had to time it perfectly, otherwise it would not work.

'You seem to singularly misunderstand your situation here,' the quiet man said. His voice seemed to be coming from a long way away. 'The pain must already be immense, and I cannot see you surviving more than one or two more questions. I admire your fortitude, I really do, but are your friends really worth the torment? At the end of the day, would they die for you?'

Sherlock had to force the words through his constricted throat one by one. 'Doesn't . . . matter . . . what . . . they . . . would . . . do.' He gasped for breath. 'Matters . . . what . . . I . . . do!'

'Ah, a man of principle. How rare – and how pointless.' The quiet man sighed. 'I will ask again, and this time I really do suggest that you give me an answer that I can use. Where is Amyus Crowe now?'

'I . . . don't . . . *know!*' Sherlock ground out.

The quiet man raised his hand again. Sherlock's head was canted at such an angle by the weight of the stones pulling on his feet and the noose pulling on his throat that he couldn't see downward, but he could hear the scrape of stone on wood as the man crouching at his feet pulled another rock out of the shadows. How many did he have there?

A pause, as the man attached the rock to the rope, and then he released it. The sudden jolting pain was so immense that it was as if Amyus Crowe himself was holding on to Sherlock's legs and pulling. Sherlock's arms were on the verge of being wrenched from their sockets as he held on to the rope above his head in a desperate attempt to stop his entire weight from coming down on the noose. Even so the rope around his neck was biting in so deeply that he could hardly breathe. The problem was that he had to make things worse if he wanted to escape.

With the last vestiges of his energy he clenched his right hand on the taut rope above his head and tensed the muscles of his arm as tight as he could. Then he let go with his left hand.

The entire weight of his body and the three rocks

was suddenly taken by his right hand, and his neck. Before his fingers could slip from the rope, leaving his neck to bear the entire weight, he whipped his left hand down and delved into his trouser pocket. His fingers closed around the handle of Matty's knife – the one his friend had used to carve a hole in the vats, back in Josh Harkness's tannery, and that Sherlock himself had used to connect up the pinholes in Amyus Crowe's cottage wall to form the shape of an arrow. Pulling the knife out, he flicked it to open the blade. Sensing, rather than seeing, the men to either side of him move closer to stop whatever he was doing, he lunged upward, carving an arcing path with the knife.

The blade sliced through the taut rope above his head. Suddenly the noose was less tight and he was dropping free, air rushing into his lungs as pure and as cool as spring water. The rocks hit the floorboards. A fraction of a second later, Sherlock's feet hit the rocks. The combined weight of the rocks and his plummeting body, along with the weight of the two men who were already standing there, was too much for the rotten wood. It splintered and broke, creating a hole that the three of them fell through, directly into the room below.

Sherlock twisted his body as he dropped, bringing his knees up so that he fell on top of the two men. Floorboards scraped his skin as he fell. The men hit the floor with a sound like an explosion. The floorboards collapsed under the sudden impact, dropping them into the dank earth beneath. Surprised by the sudden absence of darkness, rats and cockroaches fled in all directions.

Scrambling clear, Sherlock desperately tugged at the noose around his neck. It loosened to the point where he could pull it over his head and throw it to one side.

He kept shifting his glance between the men and the hole which he had created above, but the men weren't doing anything apart from moaning and writhing in pain and nobody appeared looking down through the hole.

He pulled the rope from around his ankles. The flesh was swollen where it had bitten in, and he suspected that his neck looked the same way, but he didn't care. He was free!

He stood up, and immediately collapsed. His legs wouldn't take his weight. He knew he couldn't stay there, on the floor, so he tried again. And again. It was just a question of willpower, he told himself. His body would do what he told it to do, not the other way round.

On the fourth attempt his legs stayed more or less straight, apart from a tremor in the muscles. He took a deep breath and staggered across the room towards the stairs. It never even occurred to him to run out of the house. Matty and Rufus Stone were up there, and they were helpless, defenceless. He had to rescue them, no matter what the risk to his own life.

Climbing the stairs was possibly the hardest thing he had ever done in his life. His muscles screamed at the effort, and twice he nearly fainted. When he got to the top he entered the room where he had been tortured with the knife held out in front of him, ready for a fight, but the quiet man had gone. Vanished. It wasn't clear to Sherlock how he had got out – the window was closed and the only way out was the stairs that Sherlock had just climbed – but he had left. Only Rufus Stone and Matty remained.

Matty was still curled up with the sack over his head. Sherlock looked over at Rufus – bloodied, but smiling – and Rufus nodded towards Matty. 'See to him first, lad,' he said. His voice sounded like he was talking through a mouthful of walnuts – a result, Sherlock supposed, of the beating he had received. 'I feel like I've gone several rounds with a bare-knuckle pugilist – and believe me, I am more than familiar with that experience – but I'll keep. The boy's not moved since he was thrown down there. He might need your help.' He shook his head admiringly. 'That was an amazing piece of improvisation, by the way. If I live to be a hundred years old – which, by the way, I have every intention of doing – I doubt that I'll ever see anything like that again.'

Sherlock went over and knelt beside Matty. Worried about what he might find, he reached out to pull the sack gently from the boy's head. Matty's blue-grey eyes stared up at him in amazement.

'You're all right,' Sherlock breathed.

'I'm always all right,' Matty replied.

'I thought . . . you weren't moving, so . . .'

Matty smiled. 'I've learned that in situations like this, best thing to do is be like a hedgehog – curl up into a ball and wait for everything to settle down. Failing that, be like a badger – attack everything wildly, biting and scratching as much as you can.'

Sherlock pulled Matty to his feet, and together they set about freeing Rufus Stone from his bonds. Sherlock was worried about the amount of blood on Rufus's hands, face and shirt, but the violinist shrugged it off. 'I've had worse scrapes falling off roofs,' he said, 'although I won't be playing any *pizzicato* notes on the violin for a while. What happened to those two thugs? Are they likely to come back?'

Sherlock went gingerly over to the hole in the floor, aware that the rest of it might collapse at any moment, and gazed down into the room below. The men were still crumpled on the floor, in the hole that their bodies had made. They were groaning, but they didn't look like they would be moving at any stage in the near future. 'I can see them,' he replied, 'but I don't think we need to worry about them. Not just yet, anyway.'

'Fair enough. Ah, Sherlock, my admiration for you knows no bounds.'

'What happened?' Sherlock asked. 'We lost you at Newcastle.'

Rufus grimaced. 'They were on to us from Farnham,' he said. 'From what I overheard, they found Amyus Crowe's cottage empty and set someone to watch it in case he came back. It was that fellow with the ponytail and the chewed-off ear.'

Sherlock frowned. 'I didn't see him. We searched the house.'

'He was hiding outside somewhere. He'd made a hole in the side of the house and run a speaking tube from it, along the ground to his hidey-hole. He could hear everything you said.'

'A speaking tube?' Matty asked, puzzled.

'The kind of thing the captain of a ship uses to talk to the engine room – a ribbed and waxed canvas tube. If you speak into one end, then someone with their ear against the other end can hear you clearly over hundreds of yards.'

'Who'd've thought?' Matty muttered, but Sherlock was kicking himself. He'd seen a tube just like that leading away from Amyus Crowe's cottage, but he had thought nothing of it at the time. He vowed then and there never again to ignore something that was out of place or unusual.

'He overheard you two in the house,' Rufus continued, 'then he crept out after you and heard you talking about Edinburgh in the paddock.' He shook his head. 'Once he notified his compatriots, all they had to do was keep track of us on the journey up to King's Cross and then on to the train. They decided to take one of us at Newcastle so they could find out where exactly in Edinburgh Amyus Crowe was hiding – if indeed you'd got it right and he was in Edinburgh.' Ruefully he looked at his bloodied hands. 'They found out that I didn't know anything more than the fact that he was somewhere in the city, so they kept me quiet and took me along for the ride just in case they could use me against you somehow. We were on the same train as you, but the man in charge – the one who asked you the questions – had booked a whole compartment so they weren't disturbed, and they waited until the platform was empty before they got off. Once we all got to Edinburgh they set about finding a base to operate out of and give you two time to make contact with Mr Crowe – or him with you. Come this morning they decided to take you and find out if you knew anything more than me. Which apparently you didn't.'

'Actually,' Sherlock said, 'we do.' He glanced at the newspaper on the floor – now a sodden mass. It didn't matter – he had memorized the message. 'What we still don't know is why they are after Mr Crowe.' He shifted his gaze to Rufus's hands. 'Are you . . . are you going to be able to play the violin again?'

'Worried about your lessons? No refunds, lad.' Rufus held his hands up in front of his face and flexed his fingers experimentally. He grimaced at the pain, but kept doing it. 'The muscles and tendons are intact. The cuts and bruises will heal, in time. I won't be attempting any Paganini in a hurry, but the rest of the repertoire is mine to command.'

Sherlock looked around. 'What happened to the man who was asking the questions? The one with the walking stick with the gold skull on top?'

Rufus frowned. 'Didn't he go past you? I thought he went for the stairs.'

'I didn't see him.' Remembering the man's hand, caught in the light from the window, Sherlock added, 'What was wrong with his skin?'

'Ah, you noticed that?' At Sherlock's nod, Rufus went on: 'He had tattoos all over: face, neck, hands, arms – everywhere.'

'What kind of tattoos?' Sherlock asked.

'Names,' Stone said. 'People's names. Some were done in black ink, but a few were in red. One in particular, across his forehead, was in red ink and larger than the rest.' He looked up, meeting Sherlock's gaze. 'It was Virginia Crowe's name,' he said.

CHAPTER ELEVEN

Sherlock's heart went cold, but before he could ask Rufus why Virginia's name should have been tattooed on the quiet man's forehead the musician raised an eyebrow, as if he'd just caught up with something that had been said a few moments before. 'You know where Amyus Crowe is?'

'He left a message for us in the newspaper,' Matty replied. 'It was coded, but we worked it out.'

Sherlock gazed at Matty and raised an eyebrow at the 'we', but Matty just smiled back innocently.

'Well done.' Rufus looked around. 'We should get out of here before our friend comes back.'

They went down the stairs together and across the ground-floor room, detouring around the two thugs. They were still writhing in pain and groaning. Rufus stopped and stared at them for a moment. There was a glint in his eye that suggested he was thinking about paying back some of the pain they had caused him, but he turned away and kept moving. 'We could question them,' he said thoughtfully, as if he was still tempted by the thought, 'but they look like hard nuts to crack.'

'I dunno,' Matty said, following his gaze. 'They look like they're pretty cracked already.'

Rufus led the way out into daylight. The sky was covered by a metallic sheen of cloud, casting a grim light on their surroundings. Sherlock looked around curiously. He had assumed that they'd been inside a house, but looking back at the building the three of them had emerged from, and the other buildings around, he could see that he'd been wrong. The buildings, which were grouped together, were six floors high and as long as half a street. The blocks were separated by narrow alleyways that were like straight paths between vertical cliff faces. The ground floors were lined with doors, one after another after another, and the upper floors with windows, more than half of which were missing their glass. The buildings looked soulless and empty, more like ants' nests than places where people lived.

'What are these places?' Sherlock asked.

Unexpectedly it was Matty who replied. 'Tenements,' he said. 'I remember 'em from the last time I was here. Find 'em all over the place, you do. They're cheap places for poor people to live, but you end up with only two rooms to call your own, stacked up with other people's rooms like birdhouses. Everyone's rooms look the same – same front doors, same plaster, same window frames. The people who live there try an' make 'em individual-like, with curtains an' flower pots an' stuff, but it's like decoratin' one beer crate in a pile of crates wiv a bit of ribbon. Just draws attention to how borin' it is.' He sniffed. 'An' they all end up smellin' of rottin' rubbish and boiled cabbage.'

'The place looks deserted,' Rufus observed. 'A perfect temporary base of operations for our transatlantic captors. I wonder how they heard about it.'

'I 'eard a rumour,' Matty continued, 'last time I was 'ere, that the local authorities was tryin' to move people out of the tenements. 'Parently they wanted to sell the land off to build factories on, or posh mansions or somethin'. People I talked to told me that the authorities would start a rumour that some illness, like consumption or the plague, had broken out in a tenement. They'd move everybody out to the workhouse, then they'd knock the tenement down an' build on the land. Make a lot of money that way, they could.' His voice dropped to a whisper. 'I 'eard that sometimes, if there weren't any places left in the workhouse, they'd brick up the alleyways in an' out of the tenements an' leave the people inside to starve, but I don't believe that.'

'The trouble is,' Rufus said thoughtfully, 'that we don't have any idea where we are, we have no way of getting out and there's nobody to ask for help.'

Sherlock looked around. He had the map still in his pocket, but it was no use. 'I think we were carried from the cart to the block from over there,' he said, pointing to an alleyway between two of the blocks. 'We didn't turn any corners, and that's the only straight route.'

'Cart'll be gone by now,' Matty observed darkly. 'That bloke who was askin' the questions will've taken it.'

Rufus shook his head. 'He had his own carriage. That's how he brought me here. Just him and a driver. The driver stayed in the carriage.'

'With the two men who kidnapped us from the park still in the tenement block,' Sherlock finished, 'the cart should still be here.'

The three of them looked at each other for a moment, then rapidly headed for the alleyway that Sherlock had pointed out. The alleyway opened out on to a dirt road that led away into the distance. On the other side of the road was a stretch of unkempt ground where a handful of bony, hollow-eyed horses were grazing on thistles and weeds. Sherlock couldn't help but compare the scene with Amyus Crowe's cottage back in Farnham: a beautiful, rustic location beside a field where Virginia's well looked-after horse grazed contentedly. Here, everything seemed to be a dark inverse of that familiar place: rows of identical prison-like blocks next to a patch of wasteground where horses that might be Sandia's forgotten siblings had been left to die.

Glancing into one of the tenement doorways, Sherlock caught sight of a movement. He squinted, trying to see what it was. A curtain fluttering in the wind? A pigeon or a seagull roosting?

Something white moved against the darkness inside the doorway. More quickly this time, Sherlock realized that it was a skull. The deep sockets of the eyes, the hairless surface of the head, the sharp edges of the cheekbones and the sinister grin of the teeth – another dead man was staring at him!

The figure moved back into the shadows before Sherlock could point it out to Matty or Rufus Stone. He scanned the row of doorways frantically. *Was* he going mad? Most of them were empty, but – yes, there! Another thin white figure stood half in shadow, watching him. It moved back into darkness as soon as it realized it had been seen.

Were these creatures connected with the Americans who had kidnapped the three of them, or was this some kind of hallucination born out of a breaking mind?

He gazed over at Matty, and saw that the boy was staring at the tenement doorways as well. Matty turned his head to look at Sherlock.

'Did you see them?' Sherlock asked desperately.

Matty nodded. 'They're dead men walking, aren't they? They're following us. They *want* us.'

'I don't believe that dead men can walk.'

'Why not?'

'You've seen dead rabbits on butchers' slabs, and dead fish in costermonger's?'

'Yeah. So?'

'They never move. Not ever. When you're dead, the vital spark has gone from you. Vanished. The only thing left is flesh, and that decays. Dead animals don't come back to life, so dead people don't come back to life.'

Matty looked unconvinced. 'I ain't got time to argue wiv you,' he said.'

'Come on!' Rufus called. 'We need to get out of here before they come back!'

On the side of the road a cart had been left, its horse tied to a stunted tree. The animal looked in considerably better condition than the ones in the ground across the road.

'That,' Rufus said, 'is our ride home – if we knew which way home was.'

'I memorized the route out,' Sherlock said. 'I can just reverse the times and the turns, and we can work out the way back to our hotel.'

'But we'll have to put a sack over your head,' Matty murmured. He looked up at Sherlock and smiled. 'So the conditions are the same as on the journey out. Otherwise you might get it wrong.'

Sherlock and Matty climbed into the back of the cart while Rufus clambered in the front. He flicked the reins experimentally and the horse started off as if someone had fired a gun. It didn't seem to like being near the tenements.

Sherlock stood up behind Rufus's shoulder, clutching on to a wooden bar, and tried to reverse the route that had brought them there. He assumed the cart was travelling at about the same speed, so all he had to do was remember the turns and the rough times in his head and then start the list at the bottom and work upward. Of course he had to change the turns around. A right-hand turn heading from the city centre to the tenements would be a left-hand turn heading back.

His neck was throbbing, and his ankles had been scraped raw by the rope. Whenever he took a breath he could feel a catch in his throat, as if the cartilage had been pushed in. Worse than the physical damage, however, was the feeling of helplessness that had flooded over him when he was hanging there, in the tenement room. He'd been close to death before, but he'd always felt that there was something he could do, some way he could fight. Before he had remembered the knife in his pocket – *Matty's* knife – he had been completely at the quiet man's mercy. He had been moments from a painful and protracted death.

If he hadn't kept Matty's knife, if his friend hadn't told him to hang on to it, then he wouldn't have had any way out. He would be dead by now.

On such trivial things survival can rest. The thought made him feel uneasy. He looked at Rufus, who was also injured, and wondered if he felt the same.

It took half an hour, and two wrong turns, before they were back at the park near Princes Street.

'Right,' Rufus said. 'Where now?'

Sherlock looked at Matty. 'Do you want to tell him?' he challenged. 'After all, *we* worked it out.'

'Nah.' Matty smiled. 'You go ahead.'

'They're hiding in a place called Cramond. I've looked on the map, and I know the way. It'll probably take us an hour or so to get there.'

'We'll grab some food first,' Stone said, 'and clean ourselves up. I don't know about you lads, but I'm starved.'

After they had done both, Matty purloined a scarf from somewhere, and Sherlock used it to cover the marks on his neck. Then, with Sherlock directing, Rufus steered the cart out of the city. It took a while to get past the houses and out into the countryside, and for the first half-hour or so Sherlock was aware of the dark shape of Edinburgh Castle looming over them, perched on its massive crag of rock. The low grey skies matched Sherlock's mood. What had started as an adventure to find his friends now seemed like something much darker and more unpleasant. There were people out there who wanted to hurt Amyus Crowe, that much was sure. The question was, why? But whatever the reason, it looked as if Sherlock had unwittingly led them right to him. All he could do now was to get to Amyus Crowe before his enemies could work out where he was.

Sherlock looked back along the road as they moved. He was looking for carts or carriages or horses keeping their distance but not dropping too far back. He couldn't see anything, but he felt that he had to do more to identify possible followers. Twice he got Rufus to pull off the road and hide the cart behind a barn for twenty minutes while he carefully watched every vehicle and rider that went past. He didn't recognize anyone, and nobody looked confused at the fact that the people they were following had suddenly vanished.

At one point, while they were waiting, Sherlock leaned across to Rufus. 'I thought you might have been taken by the Paradol Chamber, back on the train,' he said.

'Why would you think that? We haven't seen hide nor hair of them since Moscow – apart from that attempt they made to have you diagnosed insane and locked away.'

Sherlock grimaced, remembering. 'I thought I saw Mr Kyte at Newcastle Station. He was standing behind a pile of luggage, and he was staring straight at me.' He paused, aware of a tightness in his chest. 'I thought maybe the Paradol Chamber had decided to take some kind of revenge against us for messing up their plans. I think they still want to get even with me, and with you.'

'Be that as it may,' Rufus said, shrugging, 'I didn't see Mr Kyte on the station. If I had, I would have taken that great red beard of his and shoved as much of it as I could as far down his throat as I could reach. Take my advice, Sherlock – never trust a red-headed man, or a red-headed woman. They're born for trouble.'

'Virginia has red hair,' Sherlock pointed out.

Rufus turned to fix Sherlock with a warning expression. 'In that case, my friend, you have a problem.'

Uncomfortable at the way the conversation had turned back to him, Sherlock said quickly, 'What do you think these people want with Mr Crowe?'

'The same thing you seem to think the Paradol Chamber want with us – revenge.'

'But what's Mr Crowe done to them?'

'Amyus Crowe is a complicated beast,' Rufus replied. 'On the one hand he's civilized and fair-minded and very genteel. On the other . . .' He paused. 'Let's put it this way – I think if we knew more about Mr Crowe's past we might not like everything we found.'

'He told us that he used to be a spy for the Union against the Confederacy during the War Against the States,' Sherlock protested. 'And after that he was responsible for tracking down Confederate criminals who had looted and pillaged civilian towns during the War.'

'Yes,' Rufus admitted, 'he did tell us that. But he didn't tell us the lengths he went to in order to recover those criminals, and he didn't tell us how many of them he managed to bring back to face trial and how many happened to die in shootouts before he could take them captive. Remember, Sherlock, the man is a bounty hunter. He hunts men for money.' He sighed. 'Except that in this case it would appear that men are hunting him, and not for money. They want payback.'

'You don't like him, do you?'

Rufus smiled. 'Ah, you picked up on that, did you?

No, he's not the kind of man I would choose to sit with over a tavern table, with beer in our glasses and tobacco in our pipes. I don't think we would have much to talk about, but I think we would have a lot to argue about. I have a strong respect for the sanctity of human life, whereas I think Mr Crowe would have no problems in taking another man's life for little provocation. What's worse, he doesn't like music.'

Sherlock was quiet for a while, digesting what Rufus Stone had said. He couldn't find fault in his logic or his description of Amyus Crowe, but neither could he square the harsh words with the genial smile that he had seen on Mr Crowe's face or the way he had taken Sherlock under his wing and looked after him. Were all people like this – complicated, not easily understood? If that was the case, what about Rufus Stone himself? Or Mycroft?

Or himself.

He thrust the thought aside. He would rather believe that what people displayed on the surface was what they really were.

'How many of these Americans do you think are over here in England, hunting Mr Crowe?' he said eventually.

'Impossible to say,' Rufus mused. 'There were three in the tenement room. Add that to the driver of the leader's carriage – assuming he was part of the gang, and not just someone hired for the day – and we get two left that we know of. Trouble is, there might be others we *don't* know of.'

'There were two carrying me,' Sherlock said.

'And two carrying me,' Matty added.

'So that's at least four people still at large. Problem is, if the man in charge came over here with money, then he could just hire whatever support he needed of any nationality. There's people in every major town and city in the British Isles that would murder their own grandmothers for an evening's drinking and gambling.' He sighed. 'There's no end of bad men out there, and a precious shortage of good men to fight them.'

'That's all right,' Sherlock said. 'One good man is worth ten bad ones.'

Matty snorted, and Rufus eyed him sceptically. 'If only the world worked that way, things would be a lot better.'

'When I grow up,' Sherlock murmured, 'I'm going to *make* them better.'

'You know,' Rufus said, smiling at him strangely, 'I think you just might. You and your brother between you, but in radically different ways.'

'But I'm not going to work for the Government like Mycroft does.'

'Why not?' Matty asked.

'I don't like taking orders,' Sherlock said darkly. 'Not from anyone. I know that sometimes I have to, but I don't like it.'

When they got back on the road there was nobody in sight. It looked as if they had got away from the city without being spotted.

The landscape was a mixture of rough patches of scrubland and outcroppings of rock. The terrain undulated such that they were never on a level road for more than a few minutes, and their path detoured to get around some of the bigger rocky areas.

Cramond was on the coast: a collection of granite cottages with thatched roofs. Virulently green moss erupted from between the stone blocks of the cottages, looking like some kind of seaweed that had been deposited on shore by a storm and was not only clinging on to life but thriving. The air smelled of salt, and seagulls cried out like abandoned babies.

As the cart rounded the side of a hill Sherlock suddenly saw the sea laid out beneath them. The sun caught the tops of the waves and made them glitter in a hypnotic pattern, points of light dancing on a grey-green background. Closer to the shore, waves broke in parallel lines of white foam that appeared from nowhere, ran for a while and then vanished again.

'Well, this is Cramond,' Rufus said as they began the descent into the village. 'Any idea where we go now?'

'We could always ask if anyone's seen a big American bloke with a white suit and a white hat,' Matty piped up.

'I think he would have dumped the distinctive clothes,' Sherlock observed. 'And we've both been with him when he's gone into taverns and other places to ask questions, and done it in an English accent so good that he might have been brought up a few miles from London. No, he's got the hunter's skill of being able to blend with the background so well that you just don't notice him until he wants you to. By now he'll have picked up a Scottish accent so perfect that you would think he was born in Edinburgh.'

'So I repeat the question,' Rufus said. 'Any idea where we go now?'

Sherlock thought for a moment. 'We know that he wants to be found by *us*, because he left a coded message for us. So he'll have left a trail that only we can follow, or he'll assume that I can work it out. He won't be staying in the centre of the village, because he would be too visible. Despite anything he does with his accent and his clothes, he can't disguise his height. Virginia is with him as well. So he'll find a place out by itself, and he'll probably keep Virginia hidden away.' He let his mind run loose on the various parameters of the problem. 'He won't rent a cottage on the main roads in and out of the village,' he mused, 'because there would be too much chance of passing people seeing him. He would choose somewhere high up, so that he would be able to see anyone coming well in advance, and so that he would have the advantage of height. Anyone who found him would have to approach slowly, uphill, while he could throw rocks and stuff downhill at them.' He frowned. 'He might choose a place on top of a hill, so that he and Virginia could escape in any direction if they were attacked, but that would mean attackers would be able to come at him from any direction while he could only watch in one direction at any time – or two if Virginia was helping him. No, it's more likely that he would choose somewhere towards the top of a hill but in a cleft or a dip or something, so that anyone coming at him would be forced into approaching from the front.'

'That narrows it down,' Rufus said. 'We can ask around for cottages that meet that description.'

'There's a better way,' Matty said.

'What's that?'

'Kids my age.' Matty thumped his chest in emphasis. 'In every town an' every village there's kids like me. They go everywhere an' see everything. You can't stop 'em. Just find one an' slip 'im a tanner. He'll know where Mr Crowe is hiding.'

'Better than that,' Sherlock added, 'he's probably paying them. Mr Crowe knows that urchins –' he glanced at Matty apologetically – 'go everywhere and know everything. He'll be slipping them a tanner each himself to watch out for strangers. They'll be watching out for us, as well.'

Enthused by this strategy, they headed towards the centre of the village. Whenever they passed either an individual kid with unkempt hair and dirty clothes or a group of them together, Matty slipped off the cart and went to talk to them. Each time he came back he shook his head and said that they weren't talking, but Sherlock couldn't help notice that whenever their cart was pulling away, the lone kid or one of the group would slip off. They all headed in more or less the same direction.

'Should we follow one of them?' Rufus asked after a while. The cart was parked on a stretch of dirt road near the centre of the village.

'No,' Sherlock and Matty said together.

'They're probably reporting back to another kid, an older one who acts as a central point for messages,' Sherlock explained.

'He'll send a runner to Mr Crowe,' Matty added. 'If we get near that older kid, he'll just up sticks and run for it, and then we'll be back at square one.'

'Given the scale of Mr Crowe's intelligence network,' Sherlock said, 'we're better off waiting here. Once the messages get to him, he'll send someone to check us out.'

Sure enough, some time later a dirty, untidy child approached them. His feet were bare and almost black with dirt.

'Afternoon!' Rufus said, touching his forehead.

'Got some questions for you,' the boy said in a thick Scottish accent.

'Go ahead.'

'What's the name of the lassie's horse?'

'The lassie?' Sherlock asked.

'The girl,' Matty explained. 'Virginia.'

'Oh.' Sherlock raised his voice. 'It's called Sandia.'

'Aye. An' what's the name of *your* horse?'

Sherlock smiled. It had become a joke between him and Virginia. 'He didn't have a name for a long time, but eventually I called him Philadelphia.'

'Aye,' the lad confirmed. 'An' what's *your* middle name?'

'Scott,' Sherlock said. 'I'm Sherlock Scott Holmes.'

'Come on then. I'll take you where you want to go.' As Rufus flicked the reins to get the horse's attention, the kid added, 'Best leave the cart. We're headed uphill.'

He led the way off the road and upward, scrambling from rock to rock or clump of grass to clump of grass. Sherlock, Matty and Rufus followed as best they could. The way was steep, and Sherlock's abused body found it hard to cope. After a few minutes his breath came in gasps and he could feel a rasp deep in his chest. His ankles started aching, where the rope had pulled on them, and after ten minutes spikes of pain were lancing up his calf muscles. But he kept on going. He had no choice. He could tell that Rufus was struggling too.

Their path led them past several cottages that were perched on the hillside, looking down on the town and on the sea. Every now and then Sherlock looked over his shoulder at the scenery. The sea was a slowly billowing sheet – grey now, seen from above, rather than the green that it had been when looked at on the way into the village – and he could see darker areas where, he guessed, the sand beneath the surface dropped suddenly away. The line where land met water was a stone quayside, and fishing boats were tied up along it, their masts dipping and bobbing as the waves rolled in. All in all it was an extraordinarily peaceful sight. Despite the pain in his legs and in his chest, Sherlock felt something inside him loosen its tight grip on his heart. Matty seemed to feel the same.

They passed a stone chapel and a graveyard – the highest point of the village proper. After that they were ascending through tall grass and thistles. The sound of seagulls crying accompanied them. Glancing backwards, to the sea, Sherlock realized that they had climbed so high that he was looking down on the seagulls.

After twenty minutes of hard hiking they came to an area where the hill rose up on either side of them and they were walking into a narrowing gorge where the ground sloped up slightly ahead but rocky cliff faces loomed on their left and right. Over his shoulder the boy said, 'Difficult climb up ahead. Get ready.'

He was right. After a few hundred feet of gradually rising ground, with the cliff faces closing in on both sides, they came to a section where the ground ahead of them rose sharply for a stretch of perhaps ten feet. It wasn't as steep as the cliff faces to either side, but it was still pretty steep. There was no choice but to scramble up using hands and feet. Once they got to the top, Sherlock looked back. He was surprised how high they were. Far in the distance he could see the dark line where grey sky met grey ocean.

The way ahead narrowed even more, and jinked around to the right so that the point of the gorge – if it even came to a point – was hidden. They kept trudging on, exhausted by the climb.

Sherlock looked back again after a few minutes. He could see the edge of the place where they had scrambled up, but nothing beyond that apart from the sky. The ground dropped away too steeply.

Finally, once they had moved beyond the jink in the gorge, a lone cottage came into sight. Built of the usual grey granite, weather-beaten by years of storms, it nestled into the hillside as if it had grown there. The cottage was set back into a V-shaped notch where the canyon came to an abrupt end, and the ground in front of it was littered with rocks of different sizes that had fallen from the cliffs over the years. On either side, steep faces of rock rose up to the point where the hillside began again. If this was where Amyus Crowe was hiding, Sherlock approved of his choice. The only approach to the cottage was uphill, and from the front. To either side and at the back there was a sheer face of rock. Anyone trying to climb down it would be risking their life.

The boy leading the way stopped within sight of the cottage windows. He stood there, with Sherlock,

Rufus and Matty clustered behind him, until one of the windows opened and closed again. A signal that it was safe to approach. Sherlock suddenly had a picture flash into his mind of Amyus Crowe sitting in the cottage with a large gun in his hand, pointed out of the window. If someone had approached the cottage without stopping to be identified or being signalled to continue, Sherlock had no doubt that he would open fire.

The boy turned round and said, 'The big man says it's all right to go in.'

'Thank you,' Sherlock said. On an impulse he delved in his pocket and took out a half-shilling. 'We appreciate the help,' he added, holding the coin out.

The boy looked at it wistfully. 'The big man pays us well enough,' he said, keeping his hands by his sides. 'He says that anyone who takes coins from two masters can't be trusted by either one of them.'

Sherlock nodded and pulled his hand back. 'Good advice,' he said.

The boy walked off downhill, whistling.

'What now?' Matty asked.

'Now we find out what all this is about,' Sherlock said as he set off towards the cottage.

CHAPTER TWELVE

Those last few yards were perhaps the hardest that Sherlock had ever walked. He didn't know what kind of reception he was going to get – whether Amyus Crowe was going to be pleased to see him or not, he didn't know if Virginia was going to be there or whether she had been hidden somewhere else, and most of all he didn't know whether Mr Crowe and Virginia were ever going to return to Farnham or whether this was just a temporary pause before they left the country. He didn't have enough evidence on which to base a deduction, and that made him uncomfortable.

He reached the door, heart pounding. It was closed. He knocked.

'Come on in,' a familiar voice called.

Sherlock pushed the door open and led the way in. It took a few seconds for his eyes to adapt to the darkness inside – a deliberate ploy on Crowe's part, he assumed. When he could see properly, he realized that Amyus Crowe was standing on the far side of the room. He was wearing a dark suit and holding a gun.

'Well done,' Crowe said. 'You solved the riddles. Ah thought you would.'

'It wasn't hard,' Sherlock said, shrugging.

'Not for you, perhaps.' Crowe switched his gaze to Sherlock's companions. 'Young Master Arnatt, welcome to mah temporary accommodation. And Mr Stone as well – make yourselves at home, all of you. Ah'll stay within sight of the window if you don't mind. Ah'm not expecting any more guests, but a man can never tell when visitors might arrive. Can I offer you a drink – some water, perhaps?'

'After that walk,' Rufus Stone said, 'a drink would be most welcome. I don't suppose you have any beer? Or cider, perhaps? A flagon of cider would go down very well just at the moment.'

Crowe smiled. 'Ah might be able to find somethin' of that kind around.' He raised his voice. 'Virginia, you can come out now. We have guests.'

A door behind Crowe opened and Virginia slipped into the room. Her hair seemed to glow like fire in the relative darkness. Her eyes were fixed on the floor, uncharacteristically shy, but she raised them after a few seconds and looked at Sherlock.

And then she was racing across the floor towards him, and her arms were around his neck, and she was kissing him. He'd dreamed about what kissing her would be like, but the reality was so much more than he had ever imagined. The weight of her body in his arms, the warmth of her lips locked against his, the smell of her hair . . . he felt overwhelmed. His mind was unsure what to do, but he suddenly realized that his body was already kissing her back without instructions.

She broke contact suddenly, not pushing him away but stepping back. He might have taken it as a rejection except for the fact that her hands were resting on his arms. She gazed at him from those bottomless violet eyes, and he saw that she was on the verge of tears.

'You came looking for us,' she whispered.

'I had to,' he said simply. The words came out of nowhere, unplanned. 'I can't live without you.'

'Much as ah hate to break up this reunion,' Amyus Crowe rumbled, 'there's a whole heap of talking that needs to be done, an' I do believe that Mr Stone might expire here on the mat if he don't get a drink inside him. Ginnie, be a darlin' and get refreshments for our guests.'

Virginia's hands squeezed Sherlock's arms for a second, and then she let go. She backed away, still maintaining eye contact. He felt as if he could drown in those eyes. It was as if she was sending him a message, but he didn't know what it was. Perhaps she didn't either. Perhaps the important thing was that there *was* a message, not the content.

Virginia dropped her gaze, and Sherlock felt like a puppet whose strings had suddenly been released. He turned to look at the rest of the room, at the others, and the world seemed to have changed. Everything looked the same, but it was different. He couldn't explain it.

Amyus Crowe was staring at him with a strange

expression on his face. He raised a shaggy eyebrow. 'A handshake will suffice for me, if that's all right with you.'

Sherlock smiled. 'I'm glad you're all right,' he said. 'I'm glad you're *both* all right. When we found your cottage was deserted, we were worried.'

Crowe nodded. 'Couldn't be helped. Ah got wind that someone was in the vicinity askin' 'bout me and mah girl. Normally ah'd go in search of the people askin' questions an' ask them some of mah own, but when ah heard the descriptions of the fellows doin' the askin' ah decided that discretion was the better part of valour, an' made a run for it.'

'They're as dangerous as that?' Stone asked. 'I have to say that young Sherlock here dealt very well with two of them – a black-haired fellow who appears to be deficient in the hearing department and a friend of his with a face like a potato.'

'That'll be Ned Fillon an' Tom Payne.' Crowe suddenly seemed to realize that he was still holding the gun and placed it on a table by his side. 'They ain't anything more than small fry. It's the man they work for that scares the bejazus out of me.'

'I think we met him,' Sherlock said. 'I couldn't see his face, but I heard him speak. He talked really quietly.'

'I saw him,' Stone said, 'and I really wish I hadn't. He had tattoos all over. People's names.' He looked briefly at Virginia, but Crowe shook his head slightly, warning Rufus off. Only Rufus and Sherlock noticed.

'Bryce Scobell,' Crowe said heavily. 'So he's here.' He sighed. 'Ah was hopin' that he might have just sent his men over to find me, but ah guess ah was too optimistic in that regard. He wants me so badly that he's made the journey from America himself. You saw him in Farnham, ah suppose?'

'I'm afraid he followed us here,' Sherlock admitted. 'To Edinburgh.'

Even in the dim light Sherlock could see that Crowe's face seemed suddenly to grow paler and even more immobile than usual. To Sherlock the signs were clear. Crowe was in the grip of some strong emotion. His hand reached out to rest on the pistol on the table, and his gaze flickered towards the window, through which the approach to the cottage was visible. 'Ah would have expected,' the big American said, choosing the words carefully, like a man stepping on stones to cross a dangerous river, 'that you'd cover your own tracks well enough that he couldn't come after you. Does he know about this cottage?'

'No.'

'It's only a matter of time.' Crowe shook his head angrily. 'Sherlock, how on earth could you be so careless as to let him follow you?'

'He heard Matty and me talking about Edinburgh before we even set off,' Sherlock said nervously. 'He had some kind of listening tube in the cottage.'

'Ah.' Crowe nodded. 'Clever.'

'He kidnapped Rufus on the train,' Matty added, 'and then he kidnapped me and Sherlock, but we escaped.'

'Escaped?' Crowe's face twisted into a grimace. 'Ah doubt it. He let you go.'

Matty was affronted. 'Sherlock broke the legs of those two men – Fillon and Payne.'

Crowe shrugged. 'If that enabled him to follow you here, Scobell would consider that a small price to pay.'

'He was torturing me for information,' Sherlock pointed out. 'It would have been easier just to keep on torturing me until I talked rather than trade two of his men for the information.'

Crowe didn't look any less angry, but his hand moved away from the pistol. 'Perhaps,' he conceded. 'Are you sure you weren't followed here?'

'Very sure,' Sherlock said firmly.

'What's so bad about this Scobell bloke?' Matty asked. 'Apart from the fact that he likes hurting people. There's blokes in *this* country who like hurting people. Can't imagine this Scobell is much worse.'

Sherlock nodded in agreement. Matty's words put him in mind of Josh Harkness, the blackmailer whom Mrs Eglantine had been working for. Harkness had been a nasty piece of work; could Bryce Scobell be that much worse?

'There's a load of different examples ah could give you,'

Crowe replied, 'but ah'll let one suffice.' His eyes seemed not to be looking at Sherlock, or any of the others, but to be fixed on something that only he could see. 'Scobell was a Lieutenant Colonel in the Confederate Army. He weren't right in the head, even then. Ah don't think there's a word for what he was, what he *is*. Not *evil*, exactly, but he don't have emotions like guilt, or regret, or shame like the rest of us. He don't even feel things like anger or happiness. He just seems to sail through life with a complete indifference to anythin' except his own survival. He's convinced that he's the most important thing in the world, and that everythin' else exists to make his life easier an' better.' He sighed heavily. 'Ah first heard about him when he was sent to deal with an uprisin' among the native tribes. They'd taken advantage of the confusion surroundin' the War Between the States an' they were attackin' families, settlers, anyone they could isolate an' kill. Scobell was under the command of Colonel John Chivington at the time, and they were sent with a troop of militia to stop the Arapaho an' the Cheyenne from mountin' these attacks.'

Virginia came into the room with a tray containing five glasses and a plate of oatcakes. None of them had even seen her leave, so caught up were they in her father's story. She gave the beer to Crowe and Rufus Stone, then passed glasses of water to Sherlock and Matty. Everyone helped themselves to the oatcakes.

'This was about five, six years back,' Crowe went on.

'Chivington used to be a pastor in the Church, but his forbearance for his fellow man didn't extend as far as the Indians. He hated them with a passion most men reserve for scorpions an' rabid dogs. Scobell, his second-in-command, didn't hate them, but he regarded them as a lower form of life that didn't belong in his world. Between the two men there wasn't a single friendly thought. Under Chivington and Scobell, the militia attacked not just the Cheyenne and the Arapaho but the Sioux, the Comanche and the Kiowa as well.

Crowe sipped at his beer. Nobody broke the heavy silence in the room.

'The Indians were gettin' the sharp end of the stick,' he continued, 'an' they decided they wanted peace, so a meetin' was arranged with the authorities. The Indians left the meetin' thinkin' they had a peace treaty, but nothin' had actually been signed. Few days later, a chief named Black Kettle camped his people near Fort Lyon. They weren't doin' anybody any harm – they was just followin' the buffalo along the Arkansas River. They lived off the buffalo, you see – used them for meat, for clothes, for oil, for everythin'.'

Crowe halted for a moment and looked out through the window. His hand moved towards the gun, but whatever he had seen must have been innocent – a bird, maybe, or an animal crossing the open ground – because he pulled his hand back and started speaking again.

'They reported to Fort Lyon, just like they was

supposed to, and then camped on Sand Creek about forty miles north. Their camp was in a dip in the ground, surrounded by low hills. Not long after they arrived, Chivington and Scobell rode into Fort Lyon and told the garrison commander that they was goin' to attack Black Kettle's tribe. The garrison commander told them Black Kettle had already surrendered, but Scobell persuaded him that this was an ideal opportunity to rid the world of more Indians. He seemed to be able to influence people like that. Next day Chivington led his troops, most of them drunk, I've heard, and surrounded the camp. On Scobell's advice, Chivington took four artillery pieces with him.'

Virginia slipped into a seat next to Sherlock. Somehow her hand ended up in his. He squeezed it reassuringly, and she squeezed back.

'Seeing the militia gatherin' around him, Black Kettle flew a white flag of peace over his tent. Without givin' any warnin', an' without consultin' with Chivington, Scobell gave the order to attack.'

Crowe paused, and the momentary silence in the room was like something heavy and alive.

'It was a fire storm of death an' destruction descendin' on them from the skies,' he whispered. 'Men, women, children – all of them massacred by the artillery fire an' by rifle fire. They had no chance to defend themselves. An' when the artillery had run out of shells an' the rifles had run out of bullets, Scobell led his men into the camp an' they killed every last one, by beatin' them with the butts of their rifles, an' with their knives. Every last one.'

'Someone must have taken action,' Sherlock said, shocked. 'I mean, Chivington and Scobell broke the peace treaty.'

Crowe laughed harshly. 'What peace treaty? There weren't any signed bits of paper to refer to.' When Sherlock opened his mouth to say something else, Crowe raised a hand to stop him. 'Chivington was hauled up in front of a military tribunal a year or two later and forced to resign from the Army. Scobell went absent without leave, an' has been on the run ever since.'

'But . . . *children?*' Virginia whispered. 'Why? It doesn't make any sense.'

'When he was asked at the military tribunal why children had been killed, Chivington replied, "Because nits lead to lice." Funny thing is, ah reckon ah can hear Bryce Scobell's voice there, speakin' through Chivington. Ah reckon Scobell had much more influence over his superior officer than people thought at the time.'

'And I'm guessing,' Rufus Stone said, 'that you were sent to bring Scobell back to face justice.'

'That, or mete out some justice of mah own choosin',' Crowe said evenly. 'Ah was given that authority by President Andrew Johnson himself.' He shook his head. 'Ah nearly caught Scobell three times, in different places 'cross the States. Ah lost several good men in firefights along the way.'

'What happened?' Matty asked, breathless.

Crowe stared over at him. 'Ah'll give you an example of what Scobell is like,' he said. 'Cincinnati, three years ago: ah'd tracked Scobell down to a room in a boarding house. We surrounded it and burst in. He'd already left, but the woman who owned the place was sitting there, on the bed. She was holdin' a stick of dynamite an' a match. When she saw us, she struck the match and lit the dynamite.' He paused, shaking his head. 'We only just cleared out of the room in time. The explosion killed her, of course. Found out later that Scobell had kidnapped her daughter – said he'd kill her if she didn't act as a livin' booby trap for us. An' she believed him.'

'What happened to the daughter?' Matty asked.

'Oh, he let her go. He had no further use for her. Course, she was left without a mother, but Scobell didn't care nothin' about that.'

Sherlock stared at Amyus Crowe. There was something the big American wasn't saying.

'Why did he change tactics?' Sherlock asked. 'It started out with you chasing him, but it ended up with him chasing you. What happened?'

Crowe stared levelly at Sherlock. 'There ain't much gets past you, is there, son? You're right. Something did happen. Ah said ah lost some men in firefights an' traps an' the like. Scobell lost somethin' too. He lost . . .' He paused, and looked up at Virginia. 'Ah've never told you this, Ginnie. Ah reckon you'll think the less of me for what ah'm about to say, but that can't be helped. It's the truth, so help me God.'

He took a breath, obviously having to force himself to continue. Sherlock found that he was holding his breath, waiting for what came next.

'Bryce Scobell had a wife an' child. Ah don't believe he ever loved either of them. Ah don't believe he's capable of love. But ah think he came closer to real emotion with them than with anyone else. Maybe it was more like possessiveness – ah don't know for sure. But the thing that happened was, we cornered Scobell an' his bodyguards at a farmhouse in Phoenix. They started firin' when they saw us, an' we fired back. In the crossfire, two of mah people were killed, and so were Scobell's wife an' son. We'd had no idea they were there. Scobell escaped, like he always did, but he took an oath that day that he would make me pay for what ah'd done.' He grimaced. 'A month later a message arrived for me. It was from Scobell. He told me that he'd kill mah wife an' mah child an' he'd make me watch. He told me exactly what he'd do. It weren't . . . the kind of thing that would occur to any normal, God-fearin' person, but ah knew Scobell – ah knew that once he set his mind to a thing, then that thing would happen. With the permission of President Johnson ah took a leave of absence from mah duties an' came here.'

'And now he's followed you,' Sherlock said in the silence that followed Crowe's admission.

'As ah said, once he sets his mind to somethin', that thing happens.'

'You could have asked for help,' Rufus Stone pointed out. 'Mycroft Holmes would have provided guards for your cottage, I'm sure. If not, we could have recruited some people locally to help.'

'For how long?' Crowe asked. 'Even if Mr Holmes provided us with round-the-clock bodyguards, he couldn't keep them there forever. At some stage they would have been taken away an' placed on more important duties.' He shook his head. 'Bryce Scobell is a patient man. Patient, and very, very clever. He would have waited until everyone had gotten bored an' tired, an' then he would have struck.'

'But you've faced dangerous men before,' Sherlock pointed out. He was confused. He didn't understand why Amyus Crowe hadn't stayed to fight. Crowe had always seemed to Sherlock to be a man who confronted difficulty rather than running away from it. Secretly he felt a bit disappointed. 'I was there in the tunnels beneath Waterloo Station when you took on that man who wanted to kill me. You nearly broke his neck, and you didn't seem the slightest bit frightened. What's so different about Scobell?'

'Ah *have* faced dangerous men before,' Crowe agreed. 'Ah've gone up against some of the toughest, hardest men in the world in mah time, but Bryce Scobell is a different bucket of catfish entirely.' He sighed. 'It's difficult to describe, but there's something . . . not human about him. Most people are wary of bein' hurt, of bein' damaged, an' that gives you an advantage in a fight, but he ain't. He just don't care. Ah'm not sayin' he don't *feel* pain, cos he does, but he just shrugs it off. It don't interest him. An' he don't *remember* the pain neither. If you punch a normal man in the face enough times he'll stay back, not wantin' to get hit again, but Scobell – hit him the first time an' he'll remember the fact that he was hit, but he don't seem to learn from the pain. He don't seek to avoid it next time. Knock him down an' he just gets up again, an' again, an' again. He keeps comin' back at you, like some kind of mechanical creation.' He shook his head. 'Ah'm not makin' much sense, ah know, but facin' Bryce Scobell is like facin' some dark force of nature. He's unstoppable. That would be bad enough if he was stupid, but he's one of the cleverest men ah know. He thinks several moves ahead, like he's playin' chess, an' he gathers people around him who are like him.'

'I don't understand about the names tattooed on his skin,' Virginia said suddenly. She had been quiet up until that point. 'Why would he *do* that? What does it *mean*?'

'It's a fixation with him,' her father replied darkly. 'Ah was told that when he joined the Confederate Army he only had three names, tattooed on his arm. Someone asked him what they were. He said they were the names of men he'd killed.' He paused and shook his head sadly. 'He was only eighteen. He'd had them indelibly inscribed on his skin, along with the dates. Said he wanted to make sure he never forgot them.' He shrugged. 'Course, in war you rarely know the names of the men you kill, so he'd leave a gap an' do his best to find out who they were, where they were from, based on their regiment. After the end of the War Between the States he spent a considerable sum of money tryin' to get the names of all the Union soldiers who died in particular places, at particular times. He even tried to find out the names of the Indians he killed. Had Black Kettle's name tattooed right across the nape of his neck. He's obsessed with the idea.'

'What about the ones in red?' Rufus Stone asked. 'As if I didn't know.'

Crowe eyed him darkly. Sherlock assumed he was tacitly warning Rufus not to mention Virginia's name. 'Those are the people he's going to kill but hasn't got around to yet,' he said slowly. 'Planning for the future, ah guess. He's makin' a statement that there are people out there whose days are numbered. When they're gone, he has the name tattooed over in black.' He peered out of the window again. 'Ah'm told he's got mah name in red on his forearm, right where he can see it every day.'

Rufus Stone was frowning. 'For a supposedly

intelligent man,' he mused, 'this Bryce Scobell seems to have missed a trick. I mean, he's on the run from you, he's on the run from the whole US Government, and he deliberately makes himself more and more recognizable. If I was him I'd dye my hair blond and keep out of sight, not tattoo more and more names on myself.'

'It's a compulsion,' Crowe explained. 'The man can't help himself. An' it's amazing' what a pair of gloves an' some stage make-up on the face an' neck can accomplish.'

'So what's the plan?' Matty asked. 'What do we do?'

'We don't do anythin',' Crowe replied. 'Ginnie an' I, we leave the country. Head somewhere else. Change our names. Change our descriptions, as much as we can. You three go back to Farnham an' try to forget about us.'

The words hit Sherlock like blows. His gaze slipped across to Virginia. 'I don't think we can do that,' he said quietly.

Rufus Stone frowned. 'I don't understand. Why did you leave the clues to bring us to Edinburgh if you don't want our help?'

Crowe closed his eyes momentarily. 'Because ah wanted to say goodbye properly,' he said. 'An' because ah wanted to explain, face to face, why ah was runnin' away. Ah wanted you to understand the scale of what ah'm up against. Scobell will keep comin', an' keep comin', and keep comin' until he succeeds. An' even if ah try to turn the tables an' hunt him down, he's too clever. He'll cover his tracks an' hide until I stop lookin'; or worse: he'll lure me into a trap.'

A silence followed as each of them tried to come to terms with what Crowe was saying.

'There's two problems with all that,' Sherlock said eventually.

Crowe raised an eyebrow. 'An' what're they then?'

'The first,' Sherlock continued, not put off by Crowe's attitude, 'is that this man, Bryce Scobell, will keep on coming after you. If he's as clever and as dedicated as that, then he will find you wherever you go, no matter how long it takes him.'

'You're right,' Rufus Stone said, nodding.

'What's the other problem?' Matty asked.

'It's that you're treating this like you would treat any hunt.' Sherlock paused for a moment, trying to collect his thoughts into some kind of order. 'I know, from what you've taught me, that you treat men as if they were animals. If you're hunting them you try to predict their movements based on their habits, and you look for the signs of their presence – the signs they can't help leaving, the way that animals leave tracks.'

'Ah've always believed that mankind is just a different kind of animal,' Crowe conceded, 'an' many's a time ah've used that fact to mah advantage. What's your point?'

'My point is that Bryce Scobell isn't an animal. He's turned the tables. He's treating *you* as the animal, and he's tracking *you*, and that's spooked you. Your usual way of dealing with a situation won't work. The game has been reversed.'

'You're saying he's cleverer than me?' Crowe challenged, his eyes flashing beneath his bushy grey brows.

'Yes,' Sherlock said simply. 'So if the game has been reversed, let's change the game. If Scobell is a better hunter than you, let's not make this a hunt. If he's a better game player than you, let's not make it a game. Don't let him choose the fight. Change the rules.'

'Easier said than done, young man,' Crowe rumbled, but the expression on his face suggested that Sherlock had surprised him.

'If he's looking for you,' Sherlock said, 'then don't hide. Don't do what he expects. Stay in the open. He'll wonder what you're doing. He'll assume it's a trap and he'll back away.'

'And then what?' Crowe challenged.

'And then he'll make a mistake, and you can turn the tables on him.'

Crowe nodded slowly. 'When the game is a hunt and you're losing, change the rules.'

'When the man you're up against is cleverer and more ruthless than you,' Sherlock amplified, 'make sure that the game doesn't depend on the winner being the cleverest or the most ruthless.'

Crowe smiled and opened his mouth to say something, but there was a sudden *thump* from the roof of the cottage. Crowe's gaze snapped upward, his hand already on the pistol, then he looked through the window again. Sherlock followed his gaze. The narrow enclosed hillside that sloped away in front of the cottage was empty, deserted, but something in the air had changed. A smell. Something . . . burning.

'Smoke!' he said. 'I smell smoke.'

Amyus Crowe moved swiftly across to the window. 'Nothin' out here.'

Sherlock looked towards the door out to the rest of the cottage. Was it his imagination, or was there a faint haze in the atmosphere out there?

'It's Scobell,' he said. 'He's set fire to the cottage!'

'But how?' Rufus snapped. 'Nobody's come near! And how on earth did he find us?'

'They didn't have to come near,' Sherlock replied. 'He's dropped something burning on to the thatched roof from the cliffs above the cottage! That's dry straw – it'll go up in seconds!'

CHAPTER THIRTEEN

'Come on!' Matty yelled. 'We need to get out!'

Sherlock moved to take Virginia's hand, wanting to make sure she got to the door safely, but Crowe grabbed at his shoulder. 'Scobell will be out there, son!' he shouted. 'He'll have rifles. He'll pick us off like rabbits!'

Sherlock had a mental flash of the decapitated rabbit back at Amyus Crowe's Farnham cottage. He didn't want to end up like that.

'We don't have a choice,' Rufus Stone said. 'If we stay here we'll be burned alive.'

They could hear the fire catching hold in the straw thatch now – a crackling sound, like sticks being broken by some giant hand. Smoke was drifting in through the open door. Already it was hard to breathe, hard even to see.

'I don't think he wants to kill us in the fire,' Sherlock suddenly said.

Crowe stared at him questioningly.

'He wants to take his revenge on you. A fire isn't good enough for him – especially if he can't be sure from the remains if you were even here.'

'So what's he trying to do?' Rufus Stone asked, struggling not to cough.

'Flush us out into the open. He'll have men waiting further down the hill. They'll have guns, and they'll take us prisoner when we run out.'

'But that's the only option we've got!' Matty cried.

Crowe shook his head. 'Not quite. There's a path that leads up the rock face, away from the house, if we can get down the slope that far. It's hard to spot, but I know where it is.'

Stone covered his mouth and coughed. 'The trouble will be in getting there,' he said. 'Scobell's men won't let us get too far from the house before they take us.'

'I think I've got an idea.'

Sherlock ran for the door to the outside. Crowe and Rufus were moments behind him, with Matty and Virginia just behind them. Sherlock threw the door open. The sudden blast of fresh air sucked the smoke out in a billowing plume that would immediately alert whoever was watching from the rocky crags above – as Sherlock was sure they would be doing.

All over the ground in front of the cottage were the rocks of various shapes and sizes they had passed on the way in. Twenty feet ahead of that was the point where the ground dropped sharply away for ten feet or so – the point where they had had to scramble up using hands and feet. Somewhere past there, hidden by the sudden drop in the ground, were Scobell's men.

'Help me!' he shouted, and set to work dislodging one of the bigger stones.

Realizing what he was doing, Rufus and Crowe threw themselves against two more rocks – even larger ones. Matty and Virginia joined Sherlock, trying to get his one moving.

Sherlock set his shoulder against the boulder and heaved. His throat and his ankles throbbed where the rope had bruised the flesh, but he ignored the pain and kept pushing. The boulder shifted before his weight, rising up slightly and pivoting on a point on its front edge.

'We've got it!' he yelled.

Something whistled past his ear and buried itself in the ground by his side. He let go of the boulder in surprise, and it fell back into its crater with a *thud* that he could feel through the soles of his feet. He looked at the new object in surprise. For a moment he thought it was a stick, but there were feathers stuck to the back. He pulled it out of the ground. The front end was sharp, like an arrowhead.

He stared upward. Silhouetted on top of the V-shaped cliff into the bottom of which the cottage was set he could see men holding cross-shaped objects in their hands. They were aiming at Sherlock the way they might aim a rifle.

They were crossbows. Sherlock hadn't seen one before, but he'd seen pictures. It was like a small bow, but on its side, and made of metal rather than wood. It could fire bolts – like small arrows – very fast, and with enough power to punch through metal armour.

'Get out of the way!' Matty yelled, pulling him back towards the cottage.

'He's not trying to shoot us – he's trying to spook us into running!' Sherlock shouted, pulling away from Matty and rugby-tackling the stone with all his weight. 'They don't want us dead, remember!' The stone shifted again, pivoting forward, teetering on the point of rolling down the hill.

Which was exactly what Sherlock wanted.

More crossbow bolts hit the ground around him, but he ignored them. He gave the boulder one last push, using all his weight and all his strength. It rolled over on to the grass – and kept on rolling down the slope, gathering speed as it did so, bouncing slightly as it hit bumps in the ground. Amyus Crowe got his rock moving as well – a bigger one that rolled heavily rather than bounced, creating a furrow of grass and earth as it moved. But it did move – faster and faster.

Rufus Stone's boulder started to move, but instead of following the other two down the widening slope it veered sideways, towards the rocky walls of the V-shaped canyon. For a moment Sherlock thought it was going to stop dead, but it hit the wall and rebounded, catching two smaller stones on the way and dislodging them from where they sat.

The boulders, rocks and stones vanished over the edge of the slope. Seconds passed with no response – and then he heard a flurry of shouts and screams from below. Sherlock imagined the boulders smashing into a line of Bryce Scobell's men like a bowling ball hitting skittles, breaking legs and smashing people aside. He smiled grimly.

'More!' he shouted, and immediately got both hands beneath another rock and levered it out of the ground. It came out easily. He hoisted it up to his shoulder and threw it like a shot-putter. It hit the ground and bounced away downhill until it was out of sight. Matty and Virginia sent smaller stones the same way, while Amyus Crowe and Rufus managed to dislodge two more huge boulders.

Two more bolts struck the ground around them, splattering earth everywhere, but the shooters had realized that their distractions weren't working. For a moment Sherlock worried that they might start shooting *at* the four of them, rather than around them, but that didn't seem to be part of their orders. The shooting continued sporadically, but no longer felt dangerous.

The shouting and screaming from below was reaching banshee proportions now. Sherlock didn't know how many men Scobell had down there, but it sounded like they were all either incapacitated or otherwise distracted. They would have been expecting a handful of desperate runners whom they could easily subdue, but instead they'd got an avalanche of rocks.

'Come on!' he yelled.

With Crowe, Virginia, Matty and Rufus behind him,

he piled down the slope after the rocks. The gradient seemed steeper than it had on the way up, and he could feel himself accelerating out of control. He nearly slipped in the wet grass. He tried to slow himself down, but Amyus Crowe careered into his back, pushing him onward.

As they scrambled down the ridge, he saw the remnants of Bryce Scobell's ambush. There were five men located in a dip in the ground. Four of them were cut and bleeding. It was impossible to tell how badly hurt they were, but two of those four were trapped beneath the boulders that Crowe and Stone had sent hurtling down the slope. The fifth was trying to help his companions, but he didn't seem to know which way to turn. Crossbows lay scattered around them.

Sherlock ran right through the ambush before they were even aware that he was there. He looked back over his shoulder to see Crowe and Rufus slow down, shepherding Matty and Virginia past them, before they speeded up again, taking up the rear. One of Scobell's men blindly groped for a crossbow, but Crowe kicked it out of his reach as he passed.

They raced on, leaving the ambush behind them.

The occasional bolt still pocked the ground or pinged off the rocks, fired from the cliffs above, but the range was too great and the angle was wrong and Sherlock knew, just *knew*, that they weren't a threat.

He felt exhilarated as he ran. *He* had rescued Amyus Crowe!

'Ginnie! Sherlock! *Here!*'

Without stopping, he looked over his shoulder. Amyus Crowe was standing at the bottom of a barely discernible set of steps in the cliff face fifty yards behind him. Sherlock had completely missed it as he had run past, and so had Virginia, but Rufus Stone and Matty were already scrambling up it. This must be the hidden path that Crowe had mentioned! Sherlock skidded to a halt at the same time as Virginia, ready to turn and go back to where Crowe was standing, but just as he was about to move three of Scobell's men came running down the rocky slope behind Crowe. There was blood on their clothes and their faces – they were the remnants of the ambush team – and they looked ready to kill, despite what orders they might have been given by Scobell. They wanted revenge for the rock attack.

Crowe saw the way Sherlock was looking past him and turned round. Sherlock saw the immediate tension in his shoulders. His head snapped back towards Sherlock and Virginia, and his eyes were wide with a mixture of fury and terror. He had obviously done the same mental calculation as Sherlock. The men were running downhill. If Sherlock and Virginia ran back to where Crowe was standing, they would be running uphill. There was no way they could get to Crowe before Scobell's men did. Despite Sherlock's admiration for and trust in his friend and mentor, he didn't think that Crowe could take three furious men by himself. Especially if they were armed.

'Go!' he shouted. 'Look after Rufus and Matty! I'll take care of Virginia!'

'I *can't*!' Crowe yelled. His face was white with shock.

'You *have* to!' Sherlock yelled back. He turned to Virginia, who was looking back and forth between Sherlock and her father. 'Trust me – we have to keep going down.'

She looked at Amyus Crowe. His face was despairing. Eventually, after a time that felt like hours but must have been less than a second, he nodded.

Virginia turned and ran towards Sherlock. Crowe scrambled up the hidden path, surprisingly fast for a man of his bulk.

Virginia grabbed Sherlock's hand and ran with him, flying down the slope, pulling away from their pursuers.

Sherlock looked back, once, over his shoulder as they ran. Amyus Crowe, along with Rufus and Matty, was out of sight, hidden by the rocks. The pursuers had seen Crowe climbing. Two of them followed, while the other kept on going.

The slope began to level out ahead of them. To his left, Sherlock caught sight of the chapel that he'd seen on the way up. They would soon be back in the town. Could they evade their pursuers there, or were Scobell's men already waiting?

Still clutching Sherlock's hand, Virginia pulled him

towards the chapel. 'Maybe we could hide there,' she panted.

They scurried behind a moss-covered gravestone that was leaning at a perilous angle. There was barely room for them both. Sherlock had to move close to Virginia so they could fit without being seen. He could feel her breath on his neck: warm and fast.

Boots clattered on the rocks, then disappeared.

'What now?' Sherlock asked after they had heard nothing for a few minutes.

'I think we need to meet up with my father and Rufus and Matty. Somehow.'

Sherlock nodded. 'All right.'

He turned his head. Her eyes were only an inch away from his.

He wanted to kiss her, but instead he just said, 'Let's go.'

The gorse and the heather were rough underfoot. The stems kept catching on Sherlock's shoes as they trudged across the moorland. Virginia's shoes were a lot more practical than his and he had to struggle to keep up.

They both looked around as they walked, checking the buildings behind them and the low wall they were slowly approaching in case anyone had seen them, but they were alone. The whole landscape seemed strangely deserted. Sherlock worried that a figure would spring up from somewhere, point at them and shout, but nothing happened.

The setting sun cast their shadows across the heather, purple on purple. The air was cold, and it smelled of flowers. Despite the lateness of the year a handful of bees buzzed slowly around, moving from bloom to bloom in search of pollen.

'What are you thinking?'

He turned his head. Virginia was looking at him questioningly. She had noticed his preoccupation.

'I was just thinking about bees,' he explained.

'Bees?' She shook her head disbelievingly. 'We're separated from our friends, we're on the run from a gang of murderers and you're thinking about bees? I don't get it.'

He shrugged, suddenly defensive. 'I understand bees,' he said. 'They aren't complicated. They do whatever they do for obvious reasons. They're like little clockwork machines. They make sense.'

'And you don't understand people?'

He kept walking, not answering for a moment. 'Why is any of this happening?' he asked suddenly. 'Because Bryce Scobell decided that he didn't like the American Indians and decided to wipe them out instead of just moving somewhere there weren't any Indians? Because your father was sent to catch him and became obsessed with finding him no matter how many people he lost along the way? Because Scobell became obsessed in turn with taking revenge on your father and followed him to England instead of hiding peacefully somewhere else in the world? I don't understand any of it! If people just acted logically, then none of this would be happening now!'

'Scobell is mad, according to my father,' Virginia said quietly. 'He doesn't have any morals, any scruples. He does whatever he needs to in order to get what he wants.'

'The madness aside,' Sherlock said quietly, thinking about his own father, 'that's the only thing about this whole business I do understand. It's a very logical attitude.'

'It's only logical if you're the only person who acts that way,' she pointed out quietly. 'If everyone in the world acts that logically, then everyone fights everyone else, civilization falls apart, chaos ensues and only the strong survive.'

They walked on in silence for a while. Sherlock could feel Virginia staring at him, but he didn't have anything to say.

A sudden movement and a burst of noise startled them both, but it was just a bird launching itself from cover and flying away.

By now they were nearly at the stone wall that they had seen earlier. Sherlock looked over his shoulder once more, expecting to see the same empty landscape he had seen every other time, but there were people moving down by the chapel. At that distance he couldn't tell whether they were locals or Scobell's men, but he wasn't willing to take a chance. Before he could do anything, Virginia grabbed him by the arm and pulled him towards the wall. It was only waist high, and she jumped over it lithely and vanished from sight. He vaulted the wall and dropped down beside her.

Sherlock got to his knees and peered over the top of the wall, looking down the slope. There were still people around the chapel.

'Come on,' Virginia urged. 'We need to keep moving. We need to get to my pa.'

'All right,' he said, 'but carefully. Stay out of sight.'

Together they scurried along in the wall's shadow, keeping low so that the stones shielded them from anyone looking in their direction.

Sherlock peered ahead. In the distance, across an undulating stretch of ground, was a wooded area.

'Come on,' he said. 'We need to get to cover before nightfall.'

Despite being rife with tension the walk towards the trees was quiet and even boring. Sherlock was exhausted after all that he'd suffered that day, and he found that just putting one foot in front of the other, over and over again, was one of the most tedious things he'd ever had to do. Every now and then he would stumble over a stone, or put his foot in a pothole, and he would nearly fall over – much to Virginia's amusement.

He kept alert for movement that might mean they had been spotted, but apart from the birds that circled in the sky and the occasional rabbit the only thing that Sherlock saw was a majestic stag standing on a rise in the ground. Its antlers spread like small trees stripped of their leaves. It stared impassively at them, head turned to one side. When it was certain they were not a threat it lowered its head to the ground and began to eat the heather.

The sky dimmed from blue to indigo and from indigo to black as they walked. Stars began to twinkle: first one or two, and then, within a few minutes, too many to count.

Remembering the stag, and how it had casually dismissed them from its mind to chomp at the vegetation, Sherlock realized that he was hungry. No, he was *starving*. Apart from the oatcakes at Amyus Crowe's cottage, he hadn't eaten since breakfast.

Virginia was biting her lip. She looked hungry too.

What were his options? Try to chase a rabbit down the next time one broke from cover? Unlikely that he would succeed. Throw Matty's knife – which was still in his pocket – and hope to hit a rabbit? He didn't know much about throwing knives, although he'd seen it done at fairgrounds, but he suspected that the knives had to be carefully balanced so that they spun smoothly, end over end. Matty's knife had a handle that was much bulkier than the blade. He wouldn't be able to aim it properly.

He remembered the first ever lesson that Amyus

Crowe had given him, back in Hampshire in the woods that surrounded Holmes Manor. Crowe had taught Sherlock which fungi were safe to eat and which were poisonous. If he could find some mushrooms, then they could eat. He glanced around. There wasn't much chance of finding them in open moorland, but perhaps when they got into the trees he could find some growing on rotten logs in piles of leaf mould.

He looked up to see how far they were from the wood. The treeline was probably half a mile away.

'Look,' Virginia said. 'We can sleep there for the night.'

Sherlock followed the direction in which she was pointing. At first he saw nothing, but then he spotted a small stone building in the shadow of the trees. For a second he thought it was someone's house, but after a moment he noticed how small it was, the absence of glass, and the door-less entrance. It was a hut, built to shelter shepherds from storms.

'Well spotted,' he said.

'Any chance of some food?' Virginia asked. 'I'm starved after all that walking.'

Sherlock thought for a moment. He supposed he could safely leave Virginia for a bit while he scouted for mushrooms.

He told her so. She looked sceptically at him. 'Mushrooms? You tryin' to poison me?'

'Trust me – your dad is a good teacher.'

She raised an eyebrow. 'He may be a good teacher, but are you sure he knows what he's talkin' about?'

'Only one way to find out.'

'Look, why don't I collect some wood and get a fire going while you get the mushrooms? It'll save time.'

'Are you sure you'll be all right? There are people after us.'

She stared at him, an eyebrow raised. 'I can look after myself.'

They checked inside the stone shelter. Just one room, and leaves had drifted into the corners, but it seemed secure enough. There was even a small wood-burning brazier, along with a couple of battered saucepans and some metal plates.

'Are you goin' to be long?' she asked.

He shrugged. 'As long as it takes. You want dinner, don't you?'

She smiled. 'I've never had a man actually go an' *gather* dinner for me before, 'part from my dad. I kinda like it.'

He couldn't help himself. 'What about *buy* you dinner? Has anyone ever done that? Apart from Mr Crowe, I mean?'

She shook her head. 'Nope.'

'Or *cook* you dinner?'

'Nope.'

He smiled. 'I'll be back as soon as I can.'

The trees closed in around him within moments:

trunks as thick as his body that erupted from tangles of roots and reached up towards the sky, forming a lacy ceiling with their branches. The thin light of the moon filtered down from above as he walked. Twigs seemed to grope for his face. Trailing strands of moss – or perhaps fine spider webs – brushed his cheeks and forehead, and he kept having to push them away. An owl hooted, and he could dimly make out the occasional sound of something larger – badgers, ferrets, maybe the odd deer – pushing its way through the undergrowth.

Somewhere off in the distance, a twig snapped as if it had been stepped on. Leaves rustled. Was it the wind, or a person?

He tensed, fearing that Scobell's men had tracked them down, but a moment's thought convinced him otherwise. He could still hear the owls and the passing animals. If Scobell's men were around, the wildlife would have been more cautious.

Remembering the Edinburgh tenement, and the faces of dead men that had been staring out at him from the darkened doorways, he began to feel a flutter of panic in his chest. Were there dead men stalking him through the forest? Were they even now clustering around the door of the shepherds' shelter, ready to burst in and attack Virginia? His heart started to race. He began to turn around, ready to race back to save her, but he stopped and took a deep breath. This was stupid. He put a firm mental hand on the panic in his chest and pushed downward. Dead men did not walk. There were no such things as ghosts. They weren't *logical*. They were just *superstition*. Amyus Crowe had taught Sherlock a lot over the past year, but whatever Sherlock had learned had been built on top of a basic scepticism that was part of his character. There had to be a reason for things happening. There had to be a cause. Things that were dead were *dead* – they didn't keep moving. Death was the absence of life. Whatever he had seen back in the tenement, whatever he and Matty had seen in Edinburgh, it wasn't dead men.

Feeling better, he kept on walking. If he was hearing anything in the woods apart from the breeze then it was scurrying animals. The rest was just his imagination drawing the wrong conclusions from small amounts of evidence. Speculation in the absence of correct information was, he decided, a fruitless occupation. If he was going to come to conclusions in future, he was going to make sure they were based on evidence.

He entered a small clearing. In the light of the moon that flooded down from above he could see a cluster of mushrooms pushing through the loam and the leaf mulch of the forest floor. He approached and knelt beside them. They were bright orange in colour, and their edges were wavy, like lettuce leaves. He recognized them as chanterelles. Pulling as many as he could from the ground, he stuffed his jacket pockets.

A few feet away he found some morels, their

honeycomb-like interior structure and brown colour unmistakable. Across the other side of the clearing, a few feet into the trees, he found a fallen trunk on which was growing a mass of the distinctive white strands of Lion's Mane mushroom.

Arms and pockets full, he set off back for the shelter. He had enough to keep the two of them going until the morning. If he could find some water then he could boil them in the saucepans. That started him thinking – were there any herbs growing nearby that he could use to flavour the water?

His mind occupied with thoughts of how he was going to impress Virginia with his culinary skills, he walked up to the hut.

'I'm back!' he called softly, in case she was sleeping. 'And I've got dinner!'

He stepped into the shelter, where Virginia had got a fire going in the stove. By its light, he saw that she was asleep, curled up on the ground. She had found some rushes or reeds from outside, and had piled them up underneath her head as a pillow. She had also piled more of them up for Sherlock, just a few feet away from her own head.

He wasn't sure what to do. He supposed he could prepare food and then wake her up, but it had been a long hike uphill, and they had more walking ahead of them in the morning. Best that she slept now.

He dumped the mushrooms on the ground and

sat beside Virginia. Something about the fresh air and the long walk through the woods had quelled his own appetite as well. They weren't going to die of malnutrition if they missed one meal. He could cook the mushrooms when the sun came up.

He stared at her face. She seemed so relaxed, asleep. Her lips were curved in a slight smile, and her expression was calmer that he had ever seen it. Usually there was a watchful look on her face, especially when she was looking at him, but now it was as if he was looking at her with everything wiped away apart from the real Virginia. The girl that he so desperately wanted to know better.

He reached out a hand and brushed a strand of hair away from her eyes. She stirred slightly and made a noise, but she didn't wake up.

He watched her for a while, mesmerized by her incredible beauty. It was difficult looking at her when they were together in daylight, because she would spot him staring at her and stare straight back, or ask him what he was looking at, but now he could admire her for as long as he liked.

Eventually he stretched out beside her, his head on the rushes that she had left for him. He felt himself drifting off to sleep. Despite the danger, despite the situation that they were in, he felt happy. He felt as if he had found the place where he belonged.

He fell asleep so gradually that he didn't even realize when it happened, but he woke up suddenly. Sunlight was streaming through the doorway. He must have turned over during the night, because he was facing in the opposite direction, away from Virginia.

He turned back, and felt his heart freeze.

There was no sign of Virginia. Three white skeletal figures were standing in the centre of the room. They stared at him with wide, lidless eyes set deeply in shadowed sockets. In their hands they held curved blades, like the sickles that farmers use to slice through wheat when harvesting it.

He scrabbled desperately for the door, but thin arms grabbed him from behind. The fingers looked like twigs against the sleeves of his jacket, but they were as hard as bone, and they hurt as they dug into his flesh.

CHAPTER FOURTEEN

Sherlock struggled wildly, trying to break free, but the fingers of his attackers were immovable. One of them held a knife to his throat. It had a tarnished blade, as if it had been buried in the ground for years. The message was clear, and he stopped struggling.

The figures turned Sherlock over unceremoniously. He noticed with a shiver of fear that their clothes were ragged and mouldy, as though they too had been underground for a while. Buried.

They bent and grabbed his feet, hauling him unceremoniously into the air. They were strong, despite their appearance. He was carried from the shelter like a sack of corn. None of them said anything, but he suddenly realized that he could hear them breathing. One of them wheezed like an asthmatic, while the others sounded just like ordinary men would if they were carrying something heavy. Dead men didn't need to breathe, Sherlock told himself. They didn't *smell* as if they were dead. Sherlock knew the cloying, awful smell of rotting flesh: he'd found enough dead animals in the woods in his time. Looking at these things, they should have reeked to high heaven, but all he could smell was sweat. So they weren't dead men. Just men who *looked* like they were dead. But *why*? And what had they done with Virginia?

He looked down at where their thin hands were clutching at his shoulders. White marks were rubbing off on the material of his jacket. Make-up? On their *hands*? He breathed a sigh of relief. He hadn't really thought they were dead, but it was a relief to have his deductions confirmed. He supposed it made sense: if you wanted people to think that you were dead, then you needed to look the part. White hands and white faces indicated a lack of blood circulating. If people saw them only at a distance, as Sherlock had till now, it was convincing.

They were carrying him downhill, away from Cramond. He caught sight of the occasional upside-down face as he was jolted along. This close he could see beard stubble poking through the white make-up on their cheeks and necks. He could also see how bits of thin paper had been stuck to their skin to resemble dry, peeling flesh, how the clever use of shading made it look as if their bones were poking through their skin, and how one of them had markings painted on his cheeks that, at a distance, would look like the grinning teeth of a skull. It was all theatrics and pretend. Dressing-up games.

'Tell me where we're going!' he demanded.

The 'corpse' holding his right arm looked down at him and grinned. His teeth were stained green, like moss, but even that was make-up. 'You come with us,' he grunted in a voice that sounded like it was bubbling up through mud. 'You see Clan Chief of the Dead.'

'You're not dead,' Sherlock said. 'You're just pretending.'

The 'corpse' kept on grinning. 'You sure about that?' he asked. 'You bet your life on it?'

Sherlock had no answer to that.

They carried him over rough ground for what seemed like an hour. He kept looking around to see if he could see Virginia, but if she was being carried as well then she was ahead of him and out of sight. He hoped that she'd managed to escape.

Eventually he was thrown on the back of a horse. His arms and legs were tied together with a rope running beneath the horse's stomach, and his belt was fastened to the saddle so that he didn't slip underneath the animal while they were riding. One of the 'corpses' mounted the horse, and they started to gallop away.

The repetitive thumping impact of the horse's rump in his stomach and the heavy odour of the horse itself made Sherlock feel sick. He was constantly on the verge of sliding beneath the horse, where its massive legs would pound into him over and over again until his bones were smashed to fragments. He clenched his arms and legs as tight as he could, trying to stay where he was.

His head was jolted up and down so much that he couldn't see what was flashing past. He was dimly aware, though, that there were other horses ahead of him and behind. Was Virginia on one of them? As his discomfort got worse and worse, he hoped that she wasn't.

The noise made by the horse's hoofs changed. They weren't riding on earth any more; they were riding on stone. He heard echoes, as if they were surrounded by hundreds of horses. They were inside some kind of stone courtyard. The horse slowed to a halt. Sherlock was thrown forward, and the rear of the saddle hit him in his side, knocking the breath from him.

Hands grabbed him. A knife cut through the ropes holding him on to the horse. He was carried again, face down this time, too weak and nauseous even to lift his head. All he saw were cobbles, and the occasional edge of a stone wall.

And flickering shadows. The whole place appeared to be lit by torches.

Where *was* he? He remembered the granite shape of Edinburgh Castle, looming above the town. Surely they hadn't ridden far enough to be back in Edinburgh? Were there other castles around?

Sherlock was carried down a corridor and into a room. He heard barking and growling. On the far side of the room was a fenced-off area. Men were looking into it with avid interest, some of them exchanging money. Through gaps in the fence Sherlock could see two dogs – big ones – fighting. They leaped at each other, tearing at ears with their teeth and scratching at eyes and skin with their claws. In the flickering torchlight he could see blood spattered across the floor. Some of it was fresh, but some of it was dried. Dogs – and maybe other things – had been fighting there for a while.

He was carried out of that room and into another one. There was no fenced-off area here – instead, men and women were gathered around a rough circle that had been chalked on the flagstones. In the centre of the circle, two men warily stalked each other. They were stripped to the waist, and their chests gleamed as if they had been oiled. One of them had fingernail marks ripped down his torso. The second man suddenly stepped forward. He crouched, grabbing the first around the waist, lifted him in the air and threw him to the ground. The crowd went wild, yelling and cheering.

Moments later Sherlock was being carried out of that room as well. The next had a walkway round the edge and a rectangular pit in the middle, like a swimming pool. Except that there was no water, and a waist-high fence made of wide wooden panels ran all the way round the edge of the pit. Sherlock could smell a rank, feral odour.

Something made a snarling sound. Sherlock realized that there was an animal corralled in there. It had obviously heard the men carrying Sherlock, because it threw itself against the fence. The wooden panels shook. What was *in* there?

The men scurried for the far door, obviously terrified of whatever the beast was.

Sherlock was taken into a large room and dumped on the ground.

He lay there for a while, staring upward. His arms and legs felt three inches longer than they had been. He could feel bruises all over his body. All in all, he thought, he wasn't really in a position to do any damage to anyone.

The ceiling was white plaster separated into squares by wooden beams. It looked old, and it looked impressive, but there were massive strands of cobwebs in each corner, hanging like grey rags.

Sherlock closed his eyes and listened. He could hear the crackling of a fire – logs splitting in the heat – and a background murmur that sounded like a whole group of people waiting for something – whispers, giggles, the shuffling of feet. The sound of an audience waiting for a show to start. He could smell sweat, and food, and underneath it all the rank odour of the animal in the pit in the previous room.

Eventually Sherlock pushed himself to a sitting position and looked around.

He was in a stone hall. Flaming torches hung from the walls, illuminating everything with a flickering red-tinged light. Tapestries hung between the torches, looking like old moth-eaten bits of carpet. Interspersed between the tapestries and the torches were the stuffed heads of animals, mounted on shield-like plaques. Most of them were stags with spread antlers, but there were also some wolves with their jaws open, exposing their teeth, and something that Sherlock could have sworn was a bear. He supposed he should be glad there weren't any men's heads on the wall.

Ahead of him was a dais, and on the dais was a chair. It looked like it had been hewn by hand from a massive tree trunk. Sitting on the chair, *lounging* on it, as if he was a king in the centre of his court, was a man who was as big as Amyus Crowe, but where Amyus Crowe was usually a symphony in white – white hair, white clothes, white hat – this man was a concerto in black. His mane of hair, wild eyebrows and unkempt beard were the colour of night. The checked jacket and the kilt he wore were mostly black as well, with occasional lines of red or white. Like Crowe he must have been in his late fifties or early sixties, but like Crowe he looked as if he could beat several younger men at a time in a fight.

Several men stood behind him. They looked like boxers, or wrestlers – heavily muscled, with flattened noses and thickened, misshapen ears. They too were wearing jackets and kilts of the same black-checked cloth. Clan tartan – wasn't that what Matty had said it was called? Did that indicate they were all part of the same clan?

The man in the chair gazed down at Sherlock with a raised eyebrow.

'So,' he said in a Scottish brogue so thick that Sherlock could have cut it with a cake knife, 'this is the other bairn the Yankees are looking for.' He raised a hand and gestured to one of the men behind him. 'Bring the youngster's friends here. Let's have a little family reunion before the inevitable and tragic separation.'

The man nodded and walked off through an arched doorway. While they waited, Sherlock took the opportunity to look around. Gathered on either side of the dais was a mixed group of people who were staring either at Sherlock or at the man in the chair. There were men, women and some children, but they all had the look of people who survived by their wits – hard, watchful eyes, and skin that had seen a lot of sun and rain. They weren't dressed in tartan. Instead their clothes were a mixture of the patched and the threadbare. Where Sherlock saw a jacket and a pair of trousers that actually matched he guessed it was either by accident or because they'd been stolen together. Among the rabble that clustered around the dais, Sherlock noticed several of the white-faced, skeletal figures. The rest of the crowd didn't seem to mind their presence – unlike the people in the tavern. They were fully integrated, not avoided, chatting with their companions. They weren't acting in the distant, corpse-like manner Sherlock had noticed before. He didn't know why they were dressed the way they were, but there had to be a reason for it.

A ripple of interest ran through the crowd, and they turned towards the archway. Seconds later, Crowe, Virginia, Rufus Stone and Matty were pushed through.

They glanced around, orienting themselves. Seeing Sherlock in the centre of the room, Crowe headed over towards him.

'Son,' Crowe nodded as Sherlock climbed to his feet. 'Ah worked out when ah saw they'd taken Ginnie that they'd gotten you as well.'

'I'm sorry I couldn't protect her,' Sherlock apologized.

Crowe shook his massive head. 'Ain't nothin' you could've done,' he said. 'These folk are organized. They took us at the top of the cliff an' brought us here.'

Sherlock frowned. 'I'm guessing they're not Bryce Scobell's men,' he said. 'They look more like locals, like Scotsmen.'

Crowe nodded. 'Ah suspect they're a local criminal gang based around Edinburgh. We seem to have fallen into their hands, though ah ain't quite sure why or what they want.'

The man who had been sent out to get them stepped towards Crowe. 'Nae talkin',' he growled, and reached out as if to cuff Crowe around the ear. Crowe calmly caught his hand and bent it backwards until the man screamed and dropped to his knees.

'Ah don't much like bein' manhandled,' he said quietly, 'an' there's been a whole load of that already. Grateful if you could stop.'

The man on the ground struggled to get to his feet, and two thugs from behind the bearded man on the chair started forward towards Crowe, but their leader raised a hand.

'Leave him be, for the moment. He's got spirit. I admire that in a man.' He nodded at Crowe. 'Stand down, Mr Crowe. I could throw all my lads at you at once, I suppose, and that would certainly be fun to watch. As you can see, we do like to watch a good fight here – watch and place bets. Problem is that you'd return a few of them damaged and I need them for other things.'

Crowe faced up to the big black-bearded man. 'You have the advantage of me, sir. You know my name, but ah don't believe we are acquainted.'

The man stood up. He was even taller than Sherlock had thought, and his chest was as wide as a beer barrel. 'My name is Gahan Macfarlane of the Clan Macfarlane, and I have a wee business proposition to put to you.'

Something about the name 'Macfarlane' struck a chord in Sherlock's mind. He'd heard that name recently. But where?

Crowe smiled, but there was little humour in his expression. 'You don't strike me as a businessman,' he replied. 'More like a bully an' a criminal.'

Macfarlane smiled back. 'Strong words from a man who's outnumbered. There are many kinds of business, my friend, and many kinds of businessman. They don't all wear frock coats and top hats.'

'So which particular kind of business are you in?'

'Oh, I have a bonny portfolio of interests.' Macfarlane

stared around at his court, and they duly laughed. 'Let's just say I work in insurance and have done with it.'

'This,' Crowe said darkly, 'would, ah guess, be the kind of insurance where local shopkeepers pay you a certain amount every week to ensure they don't have . . . accidents.'

'That's correct,' Macfarlane acknowledged. 'And you would be surprised how often those shopkeepers have accidents very shortly after they decide they can't afford my particular kind of insurance any more. It's a dangerous world out there. Shops catch fire all the time, and shopkeepers get beaten up by roving gangs of roughs for no reason at all. As I see it, I'm providing a public service by protecting them from these perils.'

Crowe turned to Sherlock. 'Extortion,' he said simply. 'Innocent struggling shopkeepers paying money to stop this man from sending his thugs in to destroy their stock, beat them up and set fire to their premises. It's an ugly way to make a living.'

Macfarlane shrugged. 'It's nature, red in tooth and claw,' he said. 'Every animal has something that it's scared of, something that can kill and eat it. It's no different here in Edinburgh. The locals avoid paying their taxes to the Government whenever they get a chance. The shopkeepers sell beer and bread to the locals, but they water down the beer and adulterate their bread with sawdust to save some flour. I come along and take my own cut from the shopkeepers. It's the chain of life, my friend.' He smiled. 'They call us the Black Reavers,' he said proudly. 'And we're known and feared from here to Glasgow!'

The name was familiar to Sherlock from the Edinburgh newspaper reports. The Black Reavers were the criminal gang that was feared so much. 'So who are *you* scared of?' he asked boldly. 'Who takes their cut from you?'

Macfarlane moved his shaggy bearded head to look at Sherlock. 'I'm at the top of the food chain in these parts, laddie,' he said grimly. 'There isn't anyone I'm scared of.' He glanced back at Crowe. 'And give me my due – I don't get involved in prostitution, or blackmail, or kidnapping, or anything like that. Nothing that affects bairns, by the by. I leave that to the lower classes of criminal. I have my standards.' He shrugged. 'Maybe a little pickpocketing or breaking and entering every now and then. Or some of the men who work down at the docks get a little careless with the occasional crate, it smashes on the dock and some stuff gets scooped up and taken away. I don't organize the crimes, or carry them out, but I do take a cut from the pickpockets and thieves for the privilege of being able to operate on my territory.'

'A criminal with morals,' Crowe mocked. 'How touchin'.'

'A criminal with a practical attitude,' Macfarlane rejoined. 'The police get more exercised over kidnapping, blackmail and murder than they do over theft and extortion. I try not to attract their attention.'

'So there *is* someone higher up the food chain than you,' Sherlock pointed out.

Macfarlane scowled. 'Even the bear avoids disturbing the wasp's nest,' he snapped.

Interesting, Sherlock thought. The man was touchy on that point.

He looked around at Macfarlane's court of bullies, thugs, pickpockets and thieves. And of course the skull-faced 'corpses' scattered among them. 'But what's the point of pretending you have dead people under your command?' he continued. 'I mean, it's very well done, very convincing, but I don't understand what it's for.'

'I rule through fear, laddie,' Macfarlane replied simply. 'People pay me extortion money because they fear what will happen to them if they don't. I've found that they fear me more if they think I have powers they don't understand. Sometimes they try to stand up to my men – try to get them to back down, or try to pay them off – but how can they threaten or bribe a corpse? If they think I can control the dead they will live in mortal fear of me, and they'll keep paying.' He laughed. 'There's some that don't call us the Black Reavers any more – they call us the Black *Revivers*, on account of the fact that we revive the dead!'

'But they're just people dressed and made up to

look like corpses,' Sherlock pointed out. 'Don't people *realize?*'

'People believe what they want to believe. Edinburgh is a dark place. People here *want* to believe that the dead can walk. What with Burke and Hare, the buried parts of the city and all the ghost stories associated with the castle, my work was half done for me already.'

'Fascinatin' though this is,' Crowe said, 'ah don't quite see what we have to do with your fine little business set-up. We're not thieves, we're not pickpockets an' we're not shopkeepers. What exactly are we doin' here?'

'Ah,' Macfarlane said. 'That's an interesting question. Word reached my ears that someone new to the area was looking for a party of people. They were looking for a big man with white hair and a funny way of speaking who was travelling with a girl with red hair who was dressed like a boy. In fact, the word that reached my ears suggested that the girl might even be disguised as a boy, but that she could be recognized by the unusual colour of her eyes.' He gestured towards Crowe and Virginia. 'And here you are – a big man with white hair and a funny way of speaking and a girl with eyes the colour of gorse in flower. Once I was told you'd been seen in the area of Cramond I decided to take a look at you myself. I wanted to see what was so valuable about you.'

'Valuable?' Crowe said. His face was grim. He seemed to know where the elliptical conversation was heading, and Sherlock had a good idea as well.

'Oh, didn't I mention? There was talk of a reward offered for the man and the girl I described. Alive, of course. Five hundred pounds was spoken. That's a significant sum in these parts. There was no reward for them dead. In fact, there was a specific threat made of retribution if they were killed by accident.' He smiled at Crowe. 'I don't know who you are or who you annoyed, but someone is very keen to get their hands on you. Not that it matters, but do you want to tell me why they want you so badly?'

Crowe locked gazes with Macfarlane. 'Everythin' is scared of somethin',' he rumbled.

Macfarlane nodded. 'Bold words,' he said. 'But you're here, and you don't seem too frightening to me. I've sent a message to the man who was offering a reward for your capture. He'll be here soon. Then we'll see what we see.'

'What about the boys?' Crowe asked, jerking his head towards Sherlock and Matty. 'You said you never hurt bairns. They got caught up in this by accident. Ah'd be obliged if you could see your way clear to lettin' 'em go. There's no reward for them, an' you have mah word as a gentleman that ah'll be less trouble to you if you let them go.'

Macfarlane considered for a moment. 'It's true that I'm not a man who countenances violence to bairns,' he said thoughtfully.

'I won't go!' Sherlock blurted out.

Crowe rounded on him. 'You will if ah say so, son,' he hissed. 'You don't know what Bryce Scobell is capable of.'

'But—'

Crowe raised his hand. 'No more discussion. Better two of us stay to confront Scobell than all four of us. Ah'd feel easier in mah heart if ah knew that you and young Matthew were safe.' He turned to Macfarlane. 'Well? Do we have a deal?'

Macfarlane stared at Crowe for a while. 'On the one hand, you're right – there's no specific reward offered for the two laddies. On the other hand, they're resourceful, and I think that, despite what you say, you might be more inclined to cooperate if I keep them here. So, no, there is no deal. I hold all the cards at the moment, and there's no reason for me to give any of them up in a hurry.'

Something was still tugging in the depths of Sherlock's mind about the name 'Macfarlane'. He tried to give it space to come through, to make itself more obvious. Something he'd heard recently? No, something he'd *seen*.

'That murder case!' he said suddenly as the memory broke through to the surface of his thoughts. 'The one where Sir Benedict Ventham was killed.' He tried to bring the images of the newspapers into focus in his mind – the one he'd read on the train from Farnham to London, and the one he'd read in the park at the head of Prince's Street. 'The woman who was arrested – *her* name was Macfarlane, and the newspaper said she was connected to the Black Reavers.'

A hush seemed to settle over the room. Macfarlane's face turned thunderous. 'Mah wee sister,' he growled. 'To have that happen to her! She's not even guilty! She wouldn't hurt a fly!'

'She's related to a criminal gang leader,' Crowe growled. 'Ah presume the police just took one look at her family tree an' threw her into jail.'

Macfarlane stood and walked forward, stepping off the dais and coming right up to Crowe. The two men stood face to face, nose to nose. They were both the same height, and had the same impressive build and the same mane of hair. The only differences between them were that Gahan Macfarlane's hair was black instead of white.

'She isn't guilty of any crime,' he said quietly, his words dropping into the expectant quiet of the room like stones into a still pool of water. 'She always hated the line of business that I'd gone into. She's a God-fearing lass, and nothing could ever change that.'

'Things can happen,' Crowe said, equally quietly. 'Perhaps this Sir Benedict Ventham attacked her, and she had to protect herself.'

'She wrote to me.' Macfarlane wasn't blinking. He was staring straight at Crowe, daring the big American to continue finding reasons why his sister might be guilty. 'She swore to me on the Bible that she didn't do *anything* that might have resulted in his death, and that she mourned his death like she mourned the death of our own dear father. I believe her.'

'In that case,' Sherlock said loudly, '*I* have a business proposition for *you*.'

CHAPTER FIFTEEN

Macfarlane stared at Crowe for a long moment, as if he hadn't heard Sherlock speak, then swivelled his head until he was looking directly at him. 'Go on, laddie. Astound me.'

'If we can clear your sister's name, show that she's innocent – you let us go. You don't give us to Bryce Scobell.'

Sherlock could hear a murmur of disbelief run around the room.

Crowe had also turned to look at Sherlock. In contrast to Macfarlane's calm, almost serene expression, he was frowning as if he was wondering what Sherlock was up to. Sherlock had to admit that he wasn't sure himself.

'Let me get this right,' Macfarlane said slowly. 'You want to . . . what? *Investigate* the murder? Look for things the police might have missed? And you seriously think you can collect enough evidence to convince the police that young Aggie is blameless in this crime?'

Sherlock shrugged. 'What have you got to lose? If we fail to prove her innocent, then you give us to Bryce Scobell and collect your blood money. If we succeed, and she's released, then you get your sister back. Either way, you win.'

Macfarlane smiled, as if amused at Sherlock's confidence. 'You're a little young to be a copper, lad.'

Sherlock's mind flashed back to the time, some months before, when his brother Mycroft had been accused of murder. The police hadn't been interested in investigating the crime: they had a suspect right in front of them, and enough evidence to convict. It was Sherlock who'd had to find the real killer.

'The police see what they want to see,' he said bitterly. 'They see what's *easiest* for them. I don't get distracted by the obvious. I can see things they can't.'

Macfarlane stared at him without speaking. His expression was a strange mixture of dismissive scorn and faint hope. There was something in Sherlock's voice that was working on him.

'I believe you can, at that,' he said eventually, 'but I'm going to need more than that before I let you loose to investigate. This might just be a way of getting you somewhere you can make a run for it.'

'Not when you've still got my friends captive,' Sherlock pointed out. He glanced around, desperately looking for something – anything! – which he could use to persuade Macfarlane that he could do what he said.

'You said some of your men work at the docks?' he asked.

Macfarlane nodded.

'What if I could tell you which of your men work on the docks and which don't. Would that convince you?'

'Just by looking at them? Not asking them any questions?' Macfarlane shook his head. 'I can't see how you'd be able to tell.'

'Line up twenty of your men,' Sherlock said. 'Don't even tell me how many of them work at the docks. I'll work it out.'

'Let's make it more difficult,' Macfarlane said. 'You can't look at their hands either, just in case you were hoping for rope burns or the like.'

Sherlock shrugged. 'If that makes you happier.'

Macfarlane moved away from Amyus Crowe as if he had forgotten that the big American was even there. He pointed at various people in the crowd. 'You, you and you – over there, against the wall. Dougie, you too. And you, Fergus . . . Hands behind your backs, all of you.'

While Macfarlane was selecting his twenty men, Rufus Stone gestured to Sherlock. 'Are you sure about this, Sherlock? Can you do it?'

'I think so,' Sherlock replied. 'I'm not sure there's an alternative. We need to find some leverage to get him to release us. If you've got a better idea . . . ?'

Rufus shrugged. 'Not off the top of my head.'

'All right,' Macfarlane announced. 'Let's see your party trick.'

Twenty men were arranged along the wall, all with their hands behind their backs. They ranged from one of Sherlock's age to a handful in their sixties. They all had dirt ingrained in their necks and in the backs of their ears, and crude blue tattoos on their forearms. Some had long hair down to their shoulders, some had ponytails and some just had stubble covering their scalps.

Sherlock went up to one end of the line. Instead of walking along and looking at their faces and their clothes, which he suspected Macfarlane was expecting him to do, he crouched down and examined the first man's shoes as closely as he could. He could hears titters of laughter from the crowd of thugs and thieves, but he ignored them. On hands and knees he scuttled along the line, checking shoes and boots and the turn-ups of trousers.

When he got to the end of the line, he straightened up. The men in the line were all craning their necks, looking at him with fascination and, in some cases, suspicion, while the rest of the crowd were talking among themselves and pointing at Sherlock.

'Right,' he said. He walked back along the line, pointing to five of the twenty men. 'You, you, you, you and . . . yes, you. Step forward.' He glanced across at Macfarlane, who was watching him with fascination. 'These five all work on the docks on a regular basis. The other fifteen don't.'

'You're right. You're absolutely right.' He gestured to the men to return to the crowd. 'How did you know?'

'They work near salt water,' Sherlock said, 'and that's what gives them away. They must get splashed with the water from the docks on a regular basis. I've noticed it before. Seawater does two things. When it soaks into shoe leather and dries out it leaves white marks behind, where the salt has been deposited in the leather itself. Also, when drops of water collect in the turn-ups of trousers and then evaporate, they leave crystals of salt behind. These five men either have white marks in their shoe leather or salt crystals in their turn-ups, or both.'

'I'm suitably impressed,' Macfarlane admitted. 'You seem to have your wits about you, which is more than I can say for the coppers investigating the murder of which my sister is accused. All right then – I'll take you up on your offer. Have to tell you, though, that you haven't got long. It's –' he checked his watch – 'nine o'clock now, give or take. A meeting's been arranged with the men who want your American friends here for two o'clock this afternoon. You've got five hours, no more and no less.'

Sherlock glanced at Amyus Crowe, then at Virginia's white face, then at Matty. Matty gave him a smile and a thumbs-up.

'If that's all I've got, then that's how long it will take,' he said grimly, hoping he could live up to the boast.

Macfarlane gestured to one of his men. 'Dunlow, you know the lie of the land. Get a carriage out front right away. You and Brough go with the kid. Take him to the big house first. If he tries to make a run for it, go and find him. Whatever happens, get him back here for two o'clock. Understand?'

The men nodded.

'The butler at Sir Benedict Ventham's house is a . . . client of mine,' Macfarlane told Sherlock. 'Tell him you're working for me and he'll let you in to look around, although I can't think what you'll find now.'

'Neither can I,' Sherlock murmured. He went to leave with Macfarlane's man, Brough, but turned back to smile at Virginia. 'I'll come back for you,' he said.

'I know you will,' she replied.

Brough was a thin man in his thirties with a scattering of freckles across a bald head. His lips were twisted in a sneer, as if he could smell something unpleasant. He accompanied Sherlock back through the rooms he'd been carried through before. Whatever was in the pit was snuffling around behind the fence on the far side as they passed, but in the next room the two men were still fighting, trading blows slowly while standing close together, not moving anything apart from their arms. They looked exhausted, and their faces were swollen and covered with blood. The dog fight had ended, and the crowd who had been gathered around it were dispersing. Money was still changing hands.

They headed towards the door to the outside, emerging into a weak, watery sunlight that was filtering through rain-heavy clouds. Sherlock turned around to look at the building they had left. Based on the flagstones, the tapestries, the animal heads and the flaming torches, he was expecting an old manor house at the very least, perhaps even a castle, but he was amazed to see that it was just a large and anonymous wooden warehouse set among other warehouses. The area looked deserted. It was probably located somewhere near the docks where those men worked. From the outside the building looked like somewhere that sacks of grain would be stored, not the central base for a criminal gang. More disguise, he supposed. Anything could be made to look like anything else, if you took enough trouble over it.

Dunlow was already waiting outside. He was older than Brough, shorter and wider, but he gave the impression that his bulk was largely muscle rather than fat. The two men led Sherlock to a black carriage.

Half an hour later they drew up outside a building made of grey stone and with a long roof of black slate tiles. The windows were barred. A carving in the stone above the door read *Edinburgh and Lothian Police*.

'This is where the boss's sister is being kept,' Dunlow said. His voice sounded like stones grinding together. He looked uncomfortable at being so close to a police station. 'Let me go in and see if they'll let you talk to her.'

'Is that likely?' Sherlock asked. 'I mean, I'm not a relative or anything, and even if you claim I *am*, they'll know as soon as I open my mouth that I'm not Scottish.'

'There's a fine trade goes on in these parts in letting citizens with spare change observe criminals in their cells,' Dunham replied darkly. 'The middle classes like to see the poor in police custody – it lets them sleep more securely in their beds. I'll slip the sergeant a shilling and tell him that you're the son of a visiting English lord. He'll be happy to let you have ten minutes alone with her, no questions asked.' He saw Sherlock's shocked expression and snorted. 'What, you think the police are any better than the criminals? The only difference is that they have uniforms and we don't.'

He walked off into the police station and came out five minutes later.

'There's a constable on the desk who'll take you to the cells,' he said. 'Be out in quarter of an hour, otherwise they'll want another shilling.'

Dubiously, Sherlock entered the police station. It smelled musty, unpleasant. A uniformed constable was indeed waiting just inside the door. He had mutton chop whiskers and a bushy moustache. 'This way,' he said gruffly, without making eye contact. 'Fifteen minutes to look at her and talk to her. No funny business, you hear?'

'No funny business,' Sherlock agreed, without knowing quite what he was agreeing to.

The cells were down a set of stone steps that had been worn into curves by generations of feet. They reminded Sherlock uncomfortably of the time he had visited Mycroft in a police station in London. He hoped that this visit would have as successful an outcome as that one.

The constable stopped in front of a door and unlocked it with a large key from a hoop on his belt. He pushed the door open and gestured Sherlock in. 'Fifteen minutes,' he warned. 'She spends most of her time crying, so I don't think she'll do anything stupid, like attack you, but you can't tell with this sort. If she makes a move towards you, bang on the door. I'll be just out here, waiting.'

Sherlock entered. The door closed behind him, and he heard the key turn in the lock. He was alone with a potential murderer.

The potential murderer was lying on a metal bed that seemed to be attached to the wall by hinges and chains. She looked up at him. She was about thirty-five years old, with hair like straw and blue eyes. There was something about the shape of her face that reminded Sherlock of her brother, although she was smaller and more delicate. Her face was dirty, and streaked with tears, and her clothes were crumpled, as if she had slept in them – which she probably had.

'I don't need a priest,' she said. Her voice was weak, but firm. 'I am not yet ready to make my peace with God.'

'I'm not a priest,' Sherlock said. 'Your brother sent me.'

'Gahan?' She pushed herself upright. There was panic in her eyes. 'He mustn't get involved. He *mustn't.*' She glanced towards the door, as if the constable might be listening outside. 'If the police think he has anything to do with this, they will chase him to the ends of the Earth and never rest until they catch him!'

'Don't worry,' he reassured her. 'He's not involved. I asked him if I could come to see you. I want to find out what happened.'

'What happened?' She looked away, eyes filling up with tears. 'Sir Benedict is dead, and the police think I did it, sir. That's what happened.'

'And did you?'

She looked back at him, shocked. 'I couldn't kill Sir Benedict! I'd worked for him for twenty years. Sir, he was like a father to me!'

Sherlock nodded. 'All right – then why do the police think that you killed him?'

She put her head in her hands. 'Because I am his cook. Or at least, I *was* his cook. I prepared all of his food. And he was poisoned, or at least that's what they say. So if he was poisoned, then I must have done it. It stands to reason, doesn't it?'

'But other people must have touched his food, or carried it, or been able to access it, surely?'

She shook her head. 'Sir Benedict was very . . . untrusting. He believed that his business rivals were out to destroy him. He was convinced that they would attack him, or poison his food if they could. There were guards all around the house to prevent anyone getting in or setting fire to the place, and he took one with him whenever he left the house. All the doors and windows were locked and barred, and the only person he trusted to cook and serve his food was me.' She made a slight sighing sound. 'It was like a prison sometimes, and yet I was happy there. I'd been working for him for a long time, and he knew that I would never do anything to hurt him. Besides, he put it in his will that if he died of natural causes then I was to inherit five *hundred* pounds. The same was true for the butler, the maids, the gardener and all the guards he employed as well.' She sniffed. 'He knew that nobody could pay any of us to hurt him, or to let them into the house.' She sniffed. 'Not that the money was the reason why I wouldn't have done anything.'

'So you prepared his food – by yourself – and you took it to him? Alone?'

'That's right,' she confirmed. 'And I collected all the raw ingredients myself. Bought all the herbs and vegetables and milk from the market, and picked the meat from the butchers' slabs. And I baked all his bread myself too.'

'So if the meat or the vegetables were poisoned, then anyone in the area buying them would have died as well – and nobody did.'

'That's exactly the case, sir, and that's why I'm in here now, facing the gallows.'

Sherlock checked his watch. Time was ticking away. Bryce Scobell was only a few hours from meeting Gahan Macfarlane. 'And are the marketplace and the butchers' shops the only places you got the raw ingredients?'

'Yes.' She caught herself, hesitating. 'Except for the occasional rabbit. The gardener catches them in traps. He'd bring them to me, still warm, and I'd gut and skin them. Sir Benedict loved a bit of rabbit in cream-and-mustard sauce – ordered it a couple of times a week, he did.' She sniffed, on the verge of tears again. 'That was what they reckoned killed him. They fed a dog with the remains of his dinner, and the dog died as well.'

'Interesting. His last meal was rabbit in cream-and-mustard sauce?'

She nodded.

'And you prepared it all yourself?'

'That's right. I bought the cream in the market, along with the mustard seeds. The gardener provided the rabbit himself. It was still warm, so I knew it had only just been killed.'

Sherlock racked his brains for something else to ask. Nothing sprang to mind. He looked at the woman as she sat there on the hard metal bench, her face tearful, grief-stricken, and yet hopeful. She was depending on him to prove her innocent, just as Amyus and Virginia Crowe, Matty Arnatt and Rufus Stone were depending on him. He couldn't let them down, but he couldn't see how Aggie Macfarlane could be anything else but guilty. If what she had told him was true, then Sherlock couldn't see any way that the meal could have been poisoned. Yet if Aggie Macfarlane was guilty, wouldn't she have given him a story that provided some chance that the food might have been poisoned by someone else? She was likely to be convicted and hanged because of her own honesty.

'I need to see the house,' he said lamely, 'to look at the scene of . . . of the crime. If I find anything out, I'll let you know.'

He left her there, in the cell, staring after him with newly kindled hope in her eyes.

He told Dunlow and Brough that he wanted to visit Sir Benedict Ventham's manor house next. They raised their eyebrows, but they set off without a word.

The journey took another twenty minutes. Sherlock checked his watch at least five times, counting the minutes and the seconds.

They turned off the road and into a driveway that curved up to a large, forbidding house. Instead of stopping at the front, the carriage kept going, past the house and down a side road to the back.

'Servants' entrance,' Dunlow explained.

They got out of the carriage, and with Dunlow in the lead and Brough bringing up the rear they walked towards a door at the back of the house. It opened as they got to it. A tall, thin man with a pencil moustache stood there, looking at them. He was dressed in striped trousers and a black jacket. His left cheek appeared to be slightly swollen, and Sherlock wondered if he had been in the middle of eating something when they turned up.

'What in heaven's name are you two doing here?' he hissed. 'I've paid your employer his blood money this week. Get out of here!'

'Macfarlane wants this kid here to see the place where Sir Benedict died.'

'This is not a tourist attraction,' the man said. 'We do not conduct sightseeing tours.'

'Are the police here?'

The butler shook his head. 'They said they already have everything they need.'

'Then there's no reason you can't show us the room where your boss died, and the kitchen where the meal was prepared. Or do you want to explain to *my* boss that you don't want to?'

The butler hesitated. He looked at Sherlock. 'Just the boy, then, and only for a few minutes. No more than that.'

Dunlow looked at Sherlock.

'That should be enough,' Sherlock said.

The butler led the way into the house, moving from the servants' area, where the walls needed painting and the carpet was threadbare, to the main part of the house, where the paint was immaculate and the carpets were so thick and so comfortable it was like walking on clouds. He led Sherlock into the main hall. A grandfather clock was set against one wall. It ticked loudly, counting down the seconds. The butler turned to one side, into a dining room. Sherlock noticed that he was chewing something.

'This was where Sir Benedict died,' the butler said. He nodded to a chair at the head of the table. 'Sitting there, he was.'

The smell of tobacco drifted across to Sherlock as the butler spoke. That explained the swollen cheek – he was chewing tobacco.

'Who brought the food in?' Sherlock asked. He already had the cook's answer, but he wanted to check that she had told him the truth.

'Aggie Macfarlane.' The butler's lips wrinkled. 'Very close to Sir Benedict, she was. Too close, if you ask me. She came in carrying the plate like everything was normal, but she knew that there was poison in it.'

'You're sure she poisoned the food?' Sherlock asked.

The butler scowled. 'Who else could have done it?' he asked.

That was a fair question, and Sherlock was asking himself the same thing. 'What about the plate?' he asked. 'Could the plate have been coated with poison?'

The butler paused before answering, and Sherlock noticed that he was shifting the chewing tobacco from one side of his mouth to the other. 'The cook had strict instructions always to wash the plate just before she dished up the meal,' he said eventually. 'Everybody was aware of that. There would be no point in poisoning the plate.' He paused, thinking. 'And I was told that the police fed a dog with some of the food – not from the plate, but from the oven dish she'd cooked it in. The dog died. That surely must mean that it was the food that was poisoned, not the plate.'

'Yes,' Sherlock said slowly, 'but that means the food was poisoned before it was cooked. Why poison the food and *then* cook it? The poison might be destroyed by the heat of the oven. It makes more sense to put the poison on the food after you've served it up.' He felt a little flutter of excitement in his chest. This was the first real evidence he had that Aggie Macfarlane might actually be innocent. It wasn't enough to clear her name with the police, but it suggested to Sherlock that he was on the right track.

The clock in the hall made a sudden noise as the cogs and gears inside shifted. Sherlock glanced at its face. He *needed* to be on the right track.

'I need to go to the kitchen,' he said.

'Follow me.'

As they walked back through to the servants' area he checked his watch. Ten thirty in the morning. Two and a half hours left – and half an hour of that would be wasted in getting back to Macfarlane's warehouse. He was running out of time.

The kitchen was almost identical to the one at Holmes Manor – a large table in the centre stained with years of use, a big range with plenty of oven doors, a dresser stacked with plates and dishes, a rack hanging from the ceiling where the bodies of pheasants and rabbits dangled, a large, square sink . . . all the usual paraphernalia of the culinary arts. There were no dirty plates or food-encrusted saucepans – either Aggie had tidied up as she went along or she hadn't been arrested straight away.

He wasn't going to learn anything here.

'The rabbit that was poisoned,' he said. 'I need to see where it was caught.'

'That,' the butler sniffed, 'is not my area of expertise. My domain is *in*doors, not out. I will fetch the gardener.' He walked across to a door that led outside, to the garden, and opened it. He spat the tobacco out of his mouth in a brown stream that hit the ground to one side of the door and called, 'Hendricks! Come here!'

The butler turned back to Sherlock. 'Hendricks will answer any more questions you might have. Now, if you will excuse me, I have a new position to seek.'

He walked off, leaving Sherlock alone. Sherlock stood there, in the kitchen doorway, gazing out on the well-tended garden, aware of the dark odour of the tobacco rising up from where the butler had spat it out. He felt slightly sick at the smell. He couldn't see the point in tobacco – either smoking it or chewing it. They were disgusting habits. He had no intention of doing either when he grew up.

A figure appeared at the end of the path, through a gap in the hedge. He was in his forties, with short salt-and-pepper hair and beard, dressed in a dark green jacket and moleskin trousers. 'Did someone call?' His voice was a rich Scottish brogue, completely unlike the butler's strangled accent.

'Are you Mr Hendricks?'

'Just Hendricks will do.' He glanced at Sherlock's clothes. 'Sir,' he added. 'What can I do for you?'

Sherlock debated whether to try to explain who he was and what he was doing, but after a moment's thought he decided just to tell the man what he wanted and leave it at that. 'The rabbit that you caught – the last one Aggie Macfarlane cooked for Sir Benedict – I need to see where you caught it.'

Hendricks stared at Sherlock for a moment. 'Fair enough,' he said eventually. 'Best come with me then.'

Sherlock checked his watch. This was all taking too long! Time was running short, and the lives of his friends were on the line!

CHAPTER SIXTEEN

Hendricks led the way along the path and through a gap in the hedge. On the other side was the edge of a stretch of woodland, still within the estate's boundaries. He set off, trudging with easy steps, not looking to see if Sherlock was following.

Sherlock checked his watch again. Coming up to eleven o'clock, and all he was doing was walking in the countryside. He wasn't going to make it!

The gardener came to a stop by a grassy bank. On the other side of the bank the ground dropped away to a natural depression, roughly circular in shape, that was bereft of trees. Around the edges of the bank Sherlock could see dark holes – rabbit burrows, he presumed.

He had a sudden flash of memory – the rabbit's head in the burrow, back in Farnham. The thing that had started his journey off. It seemed so long ago now, but it had only been a few days.

'This is where I laid the traps,' Hendricks said. He wouldn't look at Sherlock, but instead gazed into the distance. 'Used a looped snare attached to a bent sapling. The rabbit puts its head through the snare and triggers it, and the sapling pulls the snare tight and lifts the little critter off the ground. I check the snares every couple of hours.'

Sherlock gazed at where the snare had been, but he wasn't sure what it could tell him. On a whim, he moved across to the bank where the rabbit burrows were. He bent down to check the nearest one. There was no sign of a rabbit, but he did notice some plant stalks that were lying just inside the mouth of the burrow. For a moment he assumed that they were the remnants of a meal that the rabbits had brought back to the burrow, but then he realized that couldn't be the explanation. He'd never seen rabbits move food from one place to another – they always ate wherever they could find grass growing. He bent and picked up one of the stalks. There were flowers at one end, like purple bells, and the other end had been cut. These plants had been deliberately put there, in the mouth of the burrow. But who would do that?

'Do you recognize this?' he asked, holding the stalk up where Hendricks would see it.

'Foxglove,' the gardener said, glancing at the stalk and frowning. 'Be careful of that, sir. "Dead Man's Bells" they call that. Just a nibble of one of them leaves can kill you. There's some as say that just breathing in near the plant can kill you, but I don't put much stock in that. Been walking these woods for years, I have, and never had a problem.' He frowned 'Not seen much foxglove neither. Quite rare round here.'

'Why would rabbits be eating poisonous plants?' Sherlock asked. 'Surely animals avoid poisonous plants.' He turned the stem in his hand. 'More to the point, why would someone put a poisonous plant where a rabbit can't help but find it?'

'They do say,' Hendricks said, 'that rabbits are immune to foxglove.' His face was contorted, as if he was thinking something through. 'Don't know if that's true or not, but if it is . . .'

'If it *is* true,' Sherlock said, his thoughts racing ahead of his voice, 'then the poison in the foxglove might build up in the rabbit's meat. That might poison anyone who ate the rabbit!'

He glanced up to meet Hendricks's gaze. The gardener was staring at him, the frown still darkening his face. The thought occurred to Sherlock that if it was Hendricks who had left the foxglove plants by the burrow, hoping that the rabbits would eat them and the poison would build up in their meat, and if he had then given the rabbit to Aggie Macfarlane, knowing she would prepare it for Sir Benedict to eat, then the gardener had committed a particularly devious murder. He might want to stop Sherlock telling anyone about it. He tensed his muscles, preparing to spring up and run if Hendricks made any move towards him.

But no – if Hendricks was a murderer, then why tell Sherlock what he needed to know to solve the crime?

'Someone deliberately left the foxglove here, for the

rabbits to eat?' the man asked. 'So the chances were that if I caught a rabbit, its flesh would already be poisoned?'

Sherlock nodded. 'How long would it take for the poison to build up?'

'A week,' Hendricks said. 'Perhaps two. But . . . who would *do* something like this? Something this *barbarous*?'

Instead of answering, Sherlock glanced at the ground. The earth was hard – too hard to retain any impression of shoes or boots. He might know *how* the crime had been committed, but that information was useless without knowing *who*.

He wanted to check the time, but he stopped himself. Knowing how little time he had left wasn't going to make him think any faster.

His gaze was skittering around the area of the burrows, looking for something, *anything* that might be important, when he suddenly realized that there was something unusual on the ground. It was brown and dry, and looked a bit like a long, straight worm. He stared at it for a few moments, wondering why a dead worm would be laid out as straight as that, before he realized.

It wasn't a worm. It was the mark left where someone had spat a mouthful of tobacco and saliva.

He glanced at Hendricks. The gardener had followed Sherlock's gaze and was staring at the tobacco stain.

'Do you chew tobacco?' Sherlock murmured.

'Can't say I ever picked the habit up,' he replied. 'I

don't chew tobacco and I don't smoke it. But I know who does.'

Sherlock remembered the butler, back at the house, and his mouthful of tobacco, and also the way he had claimed that the garden and the woods weren't his area of expertise. If that was true, why had he been out here, all this way from the house?

'You need to go to the police,' Sherlock said. 'Tell them what you found.'

'What *you* found,' the gardener said grudgingly. 'I should have seen all this, but I didn't.'

Sherlock shook his head. 'The police won't listen to me – I'm a kid, and I'm not local. There's more chance of them believing you. If you want Aggie Macfarlane to be released, you need to tell them everything.'

'Aye. I will.' A corner of his mouth turned up. 'I've always had a soft spot for Aggie. I'll do whatever I can to get her out. But what about you?'

Now Sherlock did look at his watch.

Ten past one. He had less than an hour to make it back and convince Macfarlane that he could clear Aggie's name.

'I have to run,' he said. 'I need to be somewhere else in a hurry.'

And he did run. He ran all the way back to the house, to where Dunlow and Brough were waiting for him. Before he even got to the carriage he was shouting, 'Quick! We need to get back!'

As he climbed into the carriage, which was already pulling away, Sherlock glanced back at the manor house. He thought he saw the butler staring at him from a downstairs window, but the carriage was jolting too much to be sure. As they drove away Sherlock couldn't help thinking about Mrs Eglantine. Were all staff who ran households potential murderers?

He kept his watch in his hand as the carriage rattled through the streets, lanes and alleys of Edinburgh. His heart was pumping, and he could feel a pressure in his ears and temples. He wanted to jump out of the carriage and *run*, but that wasn't logical. It wouldn't have done any good. The carriage was already going faster than he could.

He hated waiting. He hated relying on other people. He wanted to be *doing* something.

He glanced out of the window for the thousandth time. Walls, windows, street signs and street lamps flashed past, blurring into an amorphous mass. He was sure Edinburgh was a wonderful place, but at the moment he hated it.

He realized that they were getting close when he started to see warehouses rather than ordinary houses go past. As they slowed to a halt he jumped out and sprinted towards the particular warehouse he recognized from earlier. Macfarlane's base.

'Kid,' Dunlow shouted, 'wait for us!' Sherlock pelted full speed through the front door. Men standing guard tried to stop him, but he managed to evade their reaching hands. He left a wake of shouts and yells behind him as he ran onward through the dog-fighting room and through the room where the two men had been boxing.

'I've done it!' he cried as he sprinted into the room where Macfarlane held his court. He spotted Amyus Crowe, standing protectively next to Virginia, and Rufus Stone, and Matty. Their gazes intersected on him, amazed, as he skidded to a halt in front of Macfarlane's dais. 'I've *done* it!' he repeated. 'I know who killed Sir Benedict Ventham, and it wasn't your sister! It was the butler. I don't know why, but I know it was him.'

'That's good news,' Macfarlane said. There was something grim about his voice, and his previous good humour had evaporated. 'I owe you, laddie, as we agreed. The problem is, I'm not in a position to pay and you're not in a position to collect.'

Sherlock was about to ask what he meant, to point out that they had a deal, but he suddenly realized that most of the eyes in the room weren't looking at him or at Macfarlane, but were looking past him, towards the door. Already knowing what he was going to see, he turned round.

Ten men were standing along the wall, invisible to anyone looking into the room. Nine of them were pointing crossbows at Macfarlane and his men, and at Sherlock. The tenth man stood calmly a pace in front of the others. He was below average height, and had short hair brushed neatly across his forehead. His clothes were tailored to a perfect fit. He rested his hands on a black wooden cane, the point of which rested on the floor between his feet. The head of the cane was a golden skull. All of this Sherlock noticed in a flash, but it was the man's face and hands that fixed his attention. There wasn't a square inch of skin that didn't have a name tattooed on it. From where he stood Sherlock could see 'Alfred Whiting', 'Cpl Bill Cottingham', 'Winnie Thomas' and 'Paul Fallows'. They were all written in black, but prominently tattooed in red across his forehead was 'Virginia Crowe'.

'Bryce Scobell,' Sherlock said calmly.

'We meet again,' Scobell said in his curiously precise, curiously gentle voice. 'Apologies. I know that my appointment was later on this afternoon, but I just could not wait any longer. Mr Crowe and his beautiful daughter have been on my mind, and on my skin, for quite some time now.' He gazed at Sherlock. His eyes were so black that Sherlock couldn't tell the pupil from the iris. 'You caused me significant trouble yesterday. Two of my men were crippled by your actions.'

Sherlock looked along the line of Scobell's men, but couldn't see any casts or bandages.

'Oh, you won't see them now,' Scobell continued. He had a small smile on his face. 'Like horses, I have them put down when they are injured.'

'Then why do the rest stay working for you?' Sherlock

asked. 'If I were them, I wouldn't take the risk.' As he was speaking he let his gaze run up and down Scobell's body, looking for something – anything – that might give him an edge if it came to a fight, or anything he could use to influence the man verbally, but there was nothing. There were no clues to anything on Scobell's person. He might just as well have been a walking, talking mannikin.

'They fear what will happen to them if they leave, of course,' Scobell replied, 'and I reward them well enough to compensate them for the risk. If there is one thing I have discovered about people it is this: nobody ever believes that *they* will die. Others around them, yes, but each person privately believes that they personally are invincible.'

Sherlock's attention was caught by the golden skull on the top of the cane. The dark hollows of the eye sockets seemed to be staring at him. He thought he could see something on the top of the skull, a slot of some kind, but before he could work out what it was Scobell had lifted the cane up so that the end was pointing directly at Sherlock's face. His finger moved slightly, pressing into the skull's left eye socket, and a slim blade sprang out of the end of the cane. The point hung in space, half an inch from Sherlock's right eye.

He felt sweat bead on his forehead.

'There is,' Scobell said, still in that horribly gentle voice, 'no time for pleasantries and polite badinage, I fear. I am on a tight timetable, and there is something

I have been promising myself for a few years now. Revenge, they say, is a dish best served cold, but I have been waiting so long that my revenge has congealed on the plate.' He gazed at Crowe. 'You owe me. You owe me for the death of my wife and child.'

'Let the boys go, Scobell!' Amyus Crowe shouted from the dais. 'They've done nothing to offend you. It's me you want.'

'On the contrary,' Scobell replied, 'they cost me several of my best men. I will have my revenge on them later, but first I will see to your beautiful daughter – not so beautiful when I have finished with her, I promise you – and then I will deal with you.'

Gahan Macfarlane stepped forward. 'This is my place,' he growled, 'and you are a guest in it. I give the orders here.'

Scobell slowly let the end of the cane sink down to the floor. He pushed down on the golden skull, and the blade slid back into the cane.

Sherlock heard a *click* as it was caught by some kind of spring mechanism so that it was ready to jump out again when needed. His attention was still caught by the slot on the top of the skull. What *was* it for?

Scobell gazed calmly at Macfarlane. 'I hold all the cards,' he pointed out. 'You have done nothing to offend me – yet – but whether you live to see another day depends on your making sure that you continue that way.'

'You do *not*,' Macfarlane roared, 'give orders in my—'

Before he could finish the sentence, Scobell raised his free hand. One of the men behind him moved his crossbow slightly, and pulled the trigger. With a metallic *twang* the bow released, sending a bolt flying through the air. It hit Dunham in the centre of his chest. He stared at it for a moment in horror, then fell forward to his knees. He looked up at Macfarlane and tried to say something, but instead he slumped sideways to the flagstones.

'I give orders wherever and whenever I please,' Scobell said, his voice as calm as if he was buying a newspaper.

Sherlock glanced around, taking in everything that he could see, calculating whether or not he could use it to change the dynamic of the situation. Scobell's men had the advantage, and Sherlock couldn't see any way out. Another few minutes and he would lose both Virginia and Amyus Crowe. A few minutes more and he would be dead too, along with Matty and Rufus Stone. He *had* to do *something*.

His gaze moved over Gahan Macfarlane. The big Scotsman was staring at Sherlock. He glanced at the doorway to the previous room, then back at Sherlock again. Then he nodded.

What was he trying to say?

Sherlock remembered the pit in the centre of the room next door, and the creature that was penned inside.

Was that what Macfarlane wanted him to think about? He didn't know what the creature was, but judging by the dog fight and the boxing match in the other rooms, and by the various animal heads that hung from the walls here, Macfarlane liked to see people and animals fighting. Whatever was in the pit was likely to be big and fearsome. Macfarlane probably set dogs against it, or possibly even people, wagering not on whether they would win but on how long it would take them to die.

It gave Sherlock an idea, but he had to get to it first.

'It's time,' Scobell said. 'The names on my forehead and on my forearm have been red for too long. It is time to have them covered in black ink.'

As Scobell stepped forward, Sherlock's eyes fixed again on the gold skull on his cane. The cane had a blade in the end, activated by one eye socket. But the skull had *two* eye sockets . . .

He reached out and jammed his forefinger in the skull's *right* eye socket.

A blade erupted out of the slot in the skull and through Scobell's hand. He screamed: a high-pitched, shocked noise that paralysed everyone in the room apart from Sherlock. He pushed past Scobell and towards the door to the previous room – the one with the beast trapped in the pit. Scobell's men regained their wits and tracked him with their crossbows as he ran, but he was already through the doorway when they fired. He heard the bolts whizzing behind, and screams as some of them found a mark. Scobell's men were shooting each other by accident.

There was chaos in the room he had left, cries and shouts and sounds of people running, but Sherlock was more concerned with what was ahead of him: the swimming-pool-like pit, and the waist-high wooden panels that lined the edge.

The creature in the pit roared. Sherlock heard the thudding of paws and the clicking of claws as whatever it was rushed towards his side of the pit.

He grabbed a panel and pulled it upward. It was loosely bolted to the floor and resisted for a moment, but in his desperation his strength was such that he tore it loose. He didn't have the luxury of failure. The panel was perhaps fifteen feet long and three feet wide, and so heavy that he had difficulty in manoeuvring it, but somehow he managed to turn it and throw it into the pit so that one end was left on the edge by his feet, right in the gap where the panel had been fastened.

He had made a ramp so that whatever was in there could get out.

It was the only thing he could think of that could even up the odds.

With a roar, a massive shape surged out of the pit and loomed above him, shaggy arms wide and claws spread like handfuls of knife blades. It was a bear – a brown bear – and it must have measured ten feet from its tail to the tip of its nose. Its eyes gleamed red with rage and madness. God alone knew where Macfarlane had got it. Probably he'd had it since it was a cub. The chances were that it had been penned up for years, taunted and abused and forced to fight, and now it was free.

It swiped at Sherlock with a massive paw. Sherlock dropped to the floor and rolled beneath it, just as Scobell's remaining men burst through the doorway looking for him. The bear forgot about Sherlock. It saw the men, and it saw their crossbows. It remembered all the pain it had suffered.

And it attacked.

Sherlock rolled over the edge of the pit. As he was falling he could hear screams from Scobell's men and terrifying roars from the bear.

The impact with the floor of the pit drove the breath from his body in a *whoosh*. His vision filled with stars. It took him a moment to recover. He rolled over and stood up cautiously, looking around. The sides of the pit were about fifteen feet deep, and it was littered with bones. Some were old, but some were fresh and bloody. Sherlock could have sworn that some were human.

He climbed carefully back up the ramp. The bear had gone into Macfarlane's main room, but five or six of Scobell's men were lying on the ground just inside the doorway. It was hard to tell exactly how many there were, given the state they were in.

Cautiously Sherlock moved into the doorway.

Most of Macfarlane's men had run. Macfarlane himself was still there, on the dais by his throne, with Rufus Stone, Matty, Amyus Crowe and Virginia clustered around him. They were watching what was happening in the centre of the room with horror.

The remainder of Scobell's men had been pulled apart by the bear's claws. They had obviously tried to stop it: their crossbows had been fired, and there were bolts sticking out of the bear's fur, but that hadn't helped them at all. Having dealt with them, the bear was rearing over Bryce Scobell. It was nearly twice his height. There was no trace of fear on Scobell's face. There was no trace of pain either, despite the blood that was streaming from his right hand where the blade from the cane had sliced through it.

'Get out of my way,' he said with just a tinge of annoyance in his voice. 'I have business to attend to.'

The bear swiped at Bryce Scobell with a deadly paw. The sharp claws caught in his chest, picking him up like a rag doll. He flew across the room and hit the wall. As Sherlock watched, his body slid, broken and crumpled, to the ground. His expression was as calm, as uninterested, as it had always been, and now would always remain.

The bear scented the group of people on the dais. It dropped to all fours and stalked towards them. The growl that rumbled deep in its chest reverberated through the floor.

Sherlock moved up behind it. He knew he had to

stop it, but he didn't know how. One of the crossbows dropped by Scobell's men lay by his feet. It hadn't been fired. He bent and scooped it up. Five or six bolts were already sticking out of the bear's body, but maybe Sherlock could hit a vulnerable spot. Did bears even *have* vulnerable spots?

Gahan Macfarlane took a step forward, but Amyus Crowe put a hand on his shoulder. Macfarlane looked at the American, frowning. Crowe moved past Macfarlane, stepping off the dais. He walked forward, towards the bear. Matty and Rufus Stone were frozen. The bear padded towards Crowe, growling. Sherlock could see Virginia raise a hand to her mouth. Her face was shocked, her eyes wide. She could see her father's death unfolding right in front of her.

Sherlock raised the crossbow, taking aim at the back of the bear's neck. Maybe he could sever its spinal column. He knew his chances were very slim, especially given how much his hands were shaking. But he had to do something.

The bear reared up on its back legs. It loomed above Crowe, front legs stretched wide and paws spread. It raised its snout and let out a deafening roar.

And then Amyus Crowe did the most amazing thing Sherlock had ever seen. He threw his arms wide and his head back, and he roared as well. His voice echoed through the room. With his massive chest and his heavily muscled arms and legs he seemed suddenly larger than life. He was like a bear as well, but white instead of brown – a polar bear instead of a grizzly bear.

The bear dropped its head and gazed down at Crowe. It sniffed uncertainly.

'Ah have eaten bigger bears than you for mah breakfast,' Crowe said firmly. 'Go back from whence you came, mah friend. Live for another day.'

Unbelievably, the bear sank to all fours. Even so, its head was on a level with Crowe's. It sniffed at him for a long moment, then it turned round and shambled out of the room, back towards its pit. It passed by Sherlock without even a glance, head held low.

'Now that,' Macfarlane said, breaking the silence, 'is something men would pay to see. Can I perhaps offer you a job, Mr Crowe? Fights twice weekly, payment to be agreed?'

Crowe glanced at Sherlock. He saw the crossbow, still held in Sherlock's hand, and nodded. 'Ah gave up bear-wrestlin' some years ago,' he said. 'Ah much prefer bein' a teacher. More of a challenge, ah find.'

CHAPTER SEVENTEEN

They returned home from Scotland the next day. Sherlock slept for most of the journey. He was exhausted, both mentally and physically. None of the others seemed inclined to talk. In those occasional moments when Sherlock's mind rose from the depths of sleep he found them either asleep, reading newspapers or just moodily staring out of the window. Matty dashed off the train at Newcastle and came back just as it was leaving with a paper bag full of bread rolls. That was the extent of anything momentous happening.

At Farnham they said their goodbyes as passengers disembarked around them and porters unloaded crates and boxes from the train.

'You'll be staying around?' Rufus said to Crowe, phrasing the question that Sherlock had been wanting to ask but didn't dare.

'No reason to go anywhere else now,' Crowe replied. He had his left arm protectively around Virginia's shoulders. She looked pale. 'We don't need to run any more, and we got nothin' pullin' us home.' He gazed down at Virginia and then across at Sherlock. 'In fact, we've got a shovelful of reasons to stay. As long as the cottage is still standin', an' nobody's moved into it, ah think you'll be seein' a deal more of us in the future.'

'I think I speak for all of us,' Stone said, 'when I say that I'm glad. Life would be a lot less interesting without you around, although to be fair it would also be a lot safer.'

Crowe extended his right hand towards Stone. 'You were there for us when we needed you. That's the only definition of friendship that counts, in my book. Thank you.'

Stone, taken by surprise, shook Crowe's hand. He winced at the pressure of Crowe's grip on his still tender fingers. 'I'd say it's been a distinct pleasure, Mr Crowe, but it hasn't; and I'd say don't hesitate to call on us again if you need any help, but I'm seriously hoping that you will forgo that opportunity.' He smiled, to show that he wasn't serious. 'Regardless of all that, however – you're more than welcome.'

Crowe shook Matty's hand next. 'Son, you're brave an' you're street-smart. With your instincts an' Sherlock's brainpower, you make an unbeatable combination. Thanks.'

'You're welcome, I s'pose,' Matty said, shifting uncomfortably. He wasn't used to praise, or to being the centre of attention.

Crowe turned to Sherlock. He gazed at him for a long moment, then shook his head. 'Sherlock, whenever ah think ah've gotten you figured out, you manage to surprise me. Ah'm not sure which one of us is the student and which one is the teacher any more. Ah suspect that it's more a partnership of equals now, but ah'm not uncomfortable about that. Ah'm not too old to learn.' He paused and swallowed. 'Fact is, Virginia an' I would be dead or on the run now, if it weren't for you. Ah owe you more than ah can say.'

Sherlock glanced away, out at the bustling scene of the station forecourt. 'I don't like change,' he muttered eventually. 'I like to have everything in my life familiar, and I need to know where I can find it. That counts for people as well as things.'

'Well, son, you know where *we* are. Don't be a stranger now.'

Crowe dropped his arm away from Virginia's shoulders, ready for the two of them to head off towards their cottage, but Virginia stepped closer to Sherlock.

'Thank you,' she said simply, and kissed him on the lips.

Before he could do anything apart from blush, she had turned away and was walking off with her arm through her father's.

In the station, the train's steam whistle sounded. It was ready to leave.

'I think,' Rufus Stone said, breaking the heavy silence, 'that I need a stiff tot of rum and a liniment-soaked bandage for my fingers. Or a stiff tot of liniment and a rum-soaked bandage for my fingers. Either one will do. The rum in the Farnham taverns tastes like liniment anyway.' He cocked his head as he looked at Sherlock. 'Let's delay restarting the violin lessons, eh? I suspect that your fingers will be a lot more agile than mine for a while, and I hate to be embarrassed.'

Glancing at Matty, Rufus raised a finger to his forehead and saluted. 'Until next time, Mr Arnatt.'

Stone walked off jauntily. Sherlock watched him go. He knew he should have been feeling something over all the goodbyes, but his lips were still tingling with the memory of Virginia's kiss.

'See you tomorrow?' Matty said.

'I suppose so,' Sherlock replied. 'The only thing I can think of now is sleep, and lots of it.'

Matty glanced at the crates that had been unloaded from the train. 'Looks like there's some good scoff there,' he said. 'I think I'll follow them crates for a while, just in case an accident happens and one smashes.'

Sherlock smiled. Matty was irrepressible. He would always survive, no matter what happened. In fact, Sherlock wouldn't be surprised if, in fifteen or twenty years' time, someone named Matthew Arnatt was a highly successful businessman with interests all over the country. But he would still be stealing pies off market stalls, just to keep his hand in; of that much Sherlock was certain.

'People think there's an obvious dividing line between things that are legal and illegal,' he said quietly. 'I think if

I've learned anything since moving to Farnham, it's that there *is* no line. There's a whole lot of grey in between the white at one end of the scale and the black at the other end. We just need to be careful where we stand.'

'As long as I'm closer to the white end than the black end, I'm prob'ly all right,' Matty said. He grinned suddenly, then turned and ran off.

Sherlock held on for a moment, waiting for something to happen. He wasn't sure what that thing might be, but he had a sense that the storm had paused for a moment rather than passing on. Eventually, when nobody else came up to talk to him and nothing at all noteworthy happened anywhere around him, he left, feeling somehow deflated.

He caught a ride on a farmer's passing carriage back to Holmes Manor. He jumped off at the gates and walked up the curving drive to the front door, carrying his bag of clothes and toiletries.

The door was unlocked, and he pushed it open. Sunlight streamed across the hall. The space that for so many months had seemed dark and threatening now was filled with warmth and light. It was like an entirely different house. Had he finally got used to it, or was this something to do with Mrs Eglantine's departure? Had she taken the shadows and the darkness with her?

As he stepped into the hall, a figure appeared from the dining room.

'Ah, you must be Master Sherlock,' a voice said.

Sherlock's tired gaze took in the form of a middle-aged woman with straw-coloured hair pulled back into a bun that was secured at the back of her head with a net. Her face was kind, and her eyes were brown and lively. Although she wore black there was something about her clothes that gave the impression of parties and dances rather than funerals and wakes.

'Yes,' he said. 'I've been away for a few days.'

'So the master said. He mentioned that he was expecting you back soon.' She smiled. 'My name is Mrs Mulhill, and I am the new housekeeper. I started yesterday.'

'Welcome to Holmes Manor.'

'Thank you. I am looking forward to working here very much indeed.' She glanced at his bag. 'I'm sure you have laundry that I can take. If you want to make yourself comfortable somewhere, I will bring you a tray of tea and some biscuits. The master and the mistress are out at the moment, but they will be back for dinner.'

'Tea and biscuits,' he said, 'would be wonderful.'

Leaving his bag in her care, he went across to the library. In his uncle's absence it was the place where he felt most at home. The front room was for receiving visitors, and the dining room was for eating, and he didn't feel like going up to his bedroom.

He settled down into his uncle's leather chair, soothed by the smell of the books and the manuscripts that surrounded him. On the desk he could see the pile of sermons, letters and suchlike that his uncle had asked him to sort through, before Josh Harkness, Gahan Macfarlane and Bryce Scobell had infiltrated his life. It all seemed so long ago.

The sermon in front of him was one he had already looked at – an attack by a vicar somewhere up in the Midlands on various heresies and schisms within the Church. Sherlock's gaze caught on the phrase 'Church of Jesus Christ of Latter-day Saints' halfway down the page, and it was as if a light had suddenly gone on in his brain.

Gold plates. Mrs Eglantine had been looking for gold plates, because she had overheard Sherlock's Uncle Sherrinford talking about them. She had been obsessed with the idea that somewhere in the house was hidden a stash of gold plates – a treasure of some kind – but she had never found them.

There was a treasure, but it wasn't the kind she had been anticipating.

Sherlock called to mind what he had read about the Church of Jesus Christ of Latter-day Saints – or the Mormons, as they were also known – while he was in his uncle's library. The movement had begun in America about forty years before, led by a man named Joseph Smith Jr. He had claimed that he had in his possession a sacred text called the Book of Mormon, which he told people was a supplement to the Bible. When asked where this sacred book had come from, Smith claimed that when he was seventeen years old an angel named Moroni told him that a collection of ancient writings, engraved on golden plates by ancient prophets, was buried under a hill near New York. The writings told of a tribe of Jews who had been led by God from Jerusalem to America six hundred years before Jesus was born.

Golden plates.

Sherlock felt a laugh bubbling up in his chest. Mrs Eglantine must have overheard Sherrinford Holmes talking to Aunt Anna about the golden plates of the Church of Jesus Christ of Latter-day Saints. Had he mentioned the word 'treasure' as well? Had he said to her something like, 'I shall treasure this letter, my dear, as it gives me everything I need to argue that the golden plates of the Mormons never existed,' and had Mrs Eglantine overheard the words 'treasure' and 'golden plates' and drawn a completely erroneous conclusion? Without asking her, Sherlock would never know, and he devoutly hoped that he would never meet her again, but it seemed likely. The treasure she had so diligently searched for was a chimera. A complete illusion.

Sherlock laughed again. He would tell his uncle, of course, as soon as he returned, but he didn't think Sherrinford would be too distressed by the news that there was no treasure. He wasn't a man who cared much for worldly goods.

In the midst of laughing, Sherlock smelled something sweet. It was a familiar smell, vaguely medicinal. He knew it from somewhere, but he couldn't quite place it. For a moment he thought that Mrs Mulhill had returned with the tray of biscuits she had promised, but the room was empty apart from him.

He tried to stand up, but his vision began to blur. He put a hand on the desk to steady himself, but he missed. He fell forward, head impacting on the blotter, but he didn't feel the impact. He didn't feel anything apart from a delicious lassitude. A warm mist closed in around him, and he slept.

Vague visions, like a collage of pictures, filled his mind. A black carriage. Ropes. A pad that smelled sweet and cloying placed across his mouth. The sky. A face, red-bearded and wild-eyed, that he recognized but could not put a name to . . .

When he woke up, everything was different.

He was buried in the midst of a pile of thick, tarry ropes in a small room. The walls, the floor and the ceiling were made of rough wooden planks. His head was pounding, and his stomach was lurching. The floor seemed to be moving beneath him, but it was only when he tried to push the ropes away and get to his feet that he realized that the problem was with the room, not with his sense of balance. It really *was* moving.

He pulled the door open and stepped through, still holding the frame for support.

He was looking out on the deck of a ship. Beyond the rails was a choppy grey sea flecked with white spume. There was no land in sight.

A sailor came around the corner and stopped dead at the sight of Sherlock. He sighed heavily and turned to look behind him.

'Get Mr Larchmont,' he yelled. 'We got ourselves a stowaway!' Turning back to Sherlock he shook his head. 'You chose the wrong ship to stow away on, boy.

'Why?' Sherlock asked. 'Where are we going?'

'This ain't a pleasure cruise to the Mediterranean,' the sailor said. He smiled, revealing a handful of tobacco-stained teeth. 'This is the *Gloria Scott*, and we're sailing all the way to China!'

HISTORICAL NOTES

You might think that researching a book set on the same land mass as the one where I live would be easier than researching one set in, oh, say, America or Russia. *I* certainly thought that before I started work. The strange thing is that it didn't turn out that way.

I first started thinking about setting a book in Edinburgh when I was staying there for a few days. I was doing a talk at the Edinburgh Festival, and then visiting a couple of schools and talking to the pupils about Sherlock Holmes, and me, and why I wanted to write these books. I was staying in a small hotel in the centre of Edinburgh – just off Princes Street, in fact – and every day, when I left the hotel, I looked to my right and saw the massive volcanic plug of Castle Rock, with Edinburgh Castle sitting on top of it like a solid grey cloud hanging above the city. It all looked so stunning that I couldn't help but start to picture Sherlock Holmes clambering up Castle Rock, risking his life to save someone. Probably Virginia.

What I should have done, of course, was go to the nearest bookshop and buy as many books on the history of Edinburgh as I could. But I had a lot of stuff in my suitcase, and at the time I was busy writing the previous

Young Sherlock Holmes mystery, *Black Ice*, so I didn't have time to think about the *next* book. I filed the images and scenes away in a little locked box in my mind for later. Much later.

Much later comes around faster than you expect. By the time I started to write *Fire Storm* I was back in Dorset, nearly as far from Edinburgh as it's possible to get without falling into the sea. Looking around for inspiration, I could only find Michael Fry's *Edinburgh – A History of the City* (published by Macmillan – who also publish the Young Sherlock books – in 2009, which means I probably could have got them to send me a free copy rather than buying my own). That book did, however, give me a good sense of how the city had developed and the kinds of people who lived there.

The story of the bodysnatchers Burke and Hare, which Matty tells Sherlock when they are in the tavern off Princes Street, is entirely true. Edinburgh was famed for its medical school, and there was indeed a shortage of bodies. Burke and Hare found the perfect solution to the problem – provide fresh bodies to order, by killing people. Burke was indeed hanged, and then dissected in the very place where so many of his victims had ended up, while Hare did vanish, never to be seen again.

The other story that Matty tells Sherlock – later, when they are coming out of the tenements where they have been questioned by Bryce Scobell – is not true, although it is widely believed.

> I 'eard a rumour, last time I was 'ere, that the local authorities was tryin' to move people out of the tenements. 'Parently they wanted to sell the land off to build factories on, or posh mansions, or somethin'. People I talked to told me that the authorities would start a rumour that some illness, like consumption or the plague, had broken out in a tenement. They'd move everybody out to the workhouse, then they'd knock the tenement down an' build on the land. Make a lot of money that way, they could. I 'eard that sometimes, if there weren't any places left in the workhouse, they'd brick up the alleyways in an' out of the tenements an' leave the people inside to starve, but I don't believe that.'

The tenement in question is called Mary King's Close (a 'close' being the local name for the alleyway between two tenement blocks). It's been built on, over the years, to the point where what were alleys are now underground tunnels. You can visit the place today, and hear the stories about the people who were walled up there to starve, and about the ghosts that still appear in the rooms at night, but the truth is rather more prosaic. People falling ill with the plague often voluntarily quarantined themselves in their own houses to avoid passing the disease on, indicating their status by placing white flags in the windows. Friends and neighbours passed food and supplies to them until they either got better (unlikely) or died (much more likely). There were even special places set up outside the city where plague victims could go to be segregated from everyone else.

Interestingly (or perhaps not) Arthur Conan Doyle was born in Edinburgh in 1859 and studied medicine there from 1876 to 1881. One of his teachers was a man named Joseph Bell, and it is widely accepted that Doyle based the character of Sherlock Holmes on Bell (who, it was said, could diagnose not only a patient's illness but also their occupation merely by looking at them). I did briefly consider including an appearance by Joseph Bell in this book, but I quickly decided not to. It would have been too much like an in-joke, and there was no real reason for him to be there.

It would be wrong of me not to mention, by the way, the Sherlock Holmes novel written by American author Caleb Carr entitled *The Italian Secretary: A Further Adventure of Sherlock Holmes* (Little, Brown, 2005). It takes place largely around Edinburgh. Carr is an excellent writer, and his version of Sherlock Holmes is perhaps as close to Arthur Conan Doyle's as anyone has managed since Doyle's death in 1931.

The story that Amyus Crowe tells about Colonel John Chivington and the appalling attack he mounted on the Native American tribe led by Chief Black Kettle is, tragically, true. I grew up watching Western movies in which the Native Americans (or Red Indians as they were known then) were the bad guys and the noble white soldiers were the good guys. Those movies were lies, and I still feel a sense of betrayal that Hollywood convinced so many people otherwise. There is, of course, no record of Chivington having a second in command named Bryce Scobell, but there is no record that he didn't either.

The bizarre fact that rabbits are immune to the poisons contained in the stalk and leaves of the foxglove is something I first discovered in *The Wordsworth Guide to Poisons and Antidotes* by Carol Turkington (Wordsworth Editions, 1997). Having done some checking around I have since found that opinion is divided on the subject. Maybe they are; maybe they aren't. At any rate, Sherlock Holmes believes it to be true.

Bear-baiting was a well-known 'sport' in England for hundreds of years, until it was made illegal in 1835. It usually took the form of a bear being tied to a stake and dogs set on it. Either the bear would kill the dogs or the dogs would kill the bear. It was rare that a bear and a man were set to fight, although not unknown. For some reason (possibly a surplus of bears) Russia was better known for its bear-versus-man contests. I had originally intended to have Amyus Crowe face off against a bear in *Black Ice*, but I couldn't find a place where it made sense to slot that scene in. For some reason it made more sense in this one – probably because Crowe didn't have a lot to do in *Black Ice*, but in *Fire Storm* he pretty much finds himself pushed to the limit.

The material concerning the Mormon Church's belief that the word of God was handed down to their prophet Joseph Smith Jr in 1823 on golden plates is also true (by which I mean that the story as I describe it is more or less what the Mormon Church claim – not that the story is actually *true*. That's not for me to say).

So, Sherlock has finally confronted the evil Mrs Eglantine and had her banished from the Holmes household. He has also grown up now to the point where he can stand on his own two feet and rescue his brother and his surrogate fathers (Amyus Crowe and Rufus Stone) from trouble, rather than rely on them to rescue *him*. What next for Sherlock? Well, according to Arthur Conan Doyle, who wrote the original fifty-six short stories and four novels about a grown-up Sherlock Holmes, his character was an expert at martial arts. Where, I wondered, would he *learn* those martial arts? China perhaps, or Japan. Time, and the prevailing winds and currents, will tell.

ABOUT THE AUTHOR

Andrew Lane is the author of some twenty previous books. Some are original novels set in the same universes as the BBC TV programmes *Doctor Who*, *Torchwood* and *Randall and Hopkirk (Deceased)*, some are contemporary novels written under a pseudonym, and some are non-fiction books concerning specific film and TV programme characters (notably James Bond, and Wallace & Gromit). He has also written for the *Radio Times* and its US equivalent, *TV Guide*. Andrew lives in Dorset with his wife, his son and a vast collection of Sherlock Holmes books, the purchase of which over the past twenty years is now a justifiably tax-deductible expense.

ANDREW LANE

SNAKE BITE

Sherlock Holmes has been kidnapped! Stuck on a boat
that's heading for China, he's getting further and further
away from his family, from his friends and from safety.
But when he gets to the port of Shanghai, Sherlock finds
a mystery waiting for him. How can three men be bitten
by the same poisonous snake in different parts of the
town? Who – or what – exactly seems to be following him
around? Can he decode the message that's hidden in a
diagram like a spider's web? And what has all this got to do
with a plot to blow up an American warship?

Soon Sherlock will be braving terrors greater than any he
has faced in his life . . .

Turn the page to read an exciting extract from the fifth
Young Sherlock Holmes adventure!

PROLOGUE

The Diogenes Club is, perhaps, the quietest place in the whole of London. Nobody who enters is allowed to speak – except within the Strangers Room, and only then when the door is closed. The servants who work there – the footmen and the waiters – have padded cloths attached to their shoes so that they can move silently about their duties, and the newspapers which the club members read are printed specially for the Diogenes, every day, on a paper that does not rustle when it is folded.

The Diogenes Club was set up as a refuge from the bustle of the city – a place where very important men could go to get away from the noise of conversation and the clatter of passing carriages. Coughs and sneezes are reported to the club secretary, and a member who clears his throat or clears his nose more than three times in a month is given a written warning. Three written warnings lead to expulsion from the club.

The members of the Diogenes Club value their silence.

When Amyus Crowe pushed past the footman in the lobby and strode through the club's maze of corridors and reading rooms to where Mycroft Holmes waited for him, he didn't say a word, but there was something about him that made everyone look at him in disapproval, and then look away suddenly when he met their gaze. Although he was silent, although his clothes barely whispered as they brushed against one another, although the leather soles of his boots made little more than a scuffing noise against the floor tiles, he seemed to radiate an energy that crackled fiercely and loudly. He seemed to be broadcasting fury from every pore in his body.

He slammed the door of the Strangers Room behind him so hard that even the special pneumatic hinges failed to stop the *bang*!

'What have you heard?' he demanded.

Mycroft Holmes was standing to one side of the main table. He winced, although it wasn't clear whether it was the sound of the door slamming or the raw anger in Crowe's voice that disturbed him.

'My agents have confirmed that Sherlock was kidnapped in Farnham and transported in a drugged state to London. There, in Rotherhithe, he was loaded on to a boat named the *Matilda Briggs*.'

'Ship,' Crowe corrected.

Mycroft raised an eyebrow. 'There is a difference?' he asked.

'A ship leans outwards when it turns, whereas a boat

leans inwards when it turns. It's to do with whether the centre of gravity is above or below the waterline. Another way to look at it is that you can carry a boat on a ship – like a lifeboat – but you can't carry a ship on a boat.'

Mycroft nodded. 'I will file that away for later reference,' he said.

'You are trying to distract me from mah anger,' Crowe pointed out, his accent becoming more noticeable. 'Ah will not be distracted. Ah want to know what you are doin' about rescuin' your brother an' my student.'

'I am doing all I can,' Mycroft said. 'Which is not very much, I am afraid. The boat – my apologies, the *ship* – has sailed, bound for China with a cargo of Sheffield steel cutlery and Nottingham lace. I am attempting to track down a ship's manifest so that I can anticipate when and where the ship will dock for supplies along the way, but that is proving problematic. The ship's voyages are organized at the behest of its captain, who is notoriously eccentric, according to my agents. His starting and finishing points are fixed – London and Shanghai – but he might stop anywhere in between. His purpose, by the way, is to exchange the cutlery and the lace for silk and tea, bring them back and sell them for a profit.'

'And –' Crowe paused – 'and you are sure that Sherlock is *alive?*'

'Why drug and kidnap him if the intention is to kill

him? Why go to the trouble of transporting him to a ship when he could just be buried in the woods somewhere? No, logic tells me that he *is* still alive.'

'Then what is the point of takin' him?'

Mycroft paused for a moment. His face grew, if anything, more serious. 'The answer to that question depends on who it was that took him.'

'Ah think we both know the answer to that,' Crowe growled.

Mycroft nodded. 'Reluctant as I am to come to conclusions in the absence of evidence, I cannot think of any other possibility. The Paradol Chamber has him.'

'There is some evidence,' Crowe pointed out. 'On his way up to Edinburgh he swore he saw that man Kyte, who turned out to be an agent of the Paradol Chamber. He mentioned it to Rufus Stone, and Stone mentioned it to me. We both suspected that the Paradol Chamber was keepin' an eye on him, but we didn't think they'd actually take any *action*.'

Mycroft nodded. 'And that explains your anger, which is not directed at me but at yourself. You are angry that you did not anticipate the danger that Sherlock was in.'

Crowe glanced away from Mycroft, his eyes glaring from beneath bushy white eyebrows. 'You said that if we knew who'd taken him then we'd know why he was taken. So – we know it's the Paradol Chamber. What do they *want*?'

'The Paradol Chamber is – forgive me, would you care for a small dry sherry? No? Well, you don't mind if I help myself then? Yes, the Paradol Chamber is a group of politically motivated agitators who wish to change Governments in order to achieve their own ends, which I presume are to make a great deal of money from dealing in stocks and shares and from armament sales, among other things. I have heard them described as being like a small nation without boundaries, territory or a capital city, which seems as good a description as any. In my limited experience they rarely have one reason for doing anything. Any action of theirs is predicated on that action helping them to progress on a series of fronts. If I were to venture a guess –' he broke off, and shook his large head – 'a past-time I find most abhorrent, by the way. But yes, if I were to venture a guess then I would suggest that their reasons for abducting Sherlock are, firstly to punish him for his involvement in stopping several of their plots, secondly to prevent him from stopping any *more* of their plots and thirdly to throw you and I into a state of confusion which would hamper our efforts to find out what their other plots actually *are*.'

'But they didn't kill him,' Crowe pointed out. 'Why not?'

'Killing Sherlock would have punished him for a few seconds, after which he would not care one way or the other what they did. Being stuck on a dirty, leaky ship in the middle of tropical storms, separated from his friends, his family and any possibility of a decent meal – no, that kind of torture lasts for a long while, at no cost to them. And rather than hampering our efforts in discovering their plots, they must know enough about you and me to understand that if Sherlock were to die then we would spend every waking moment and every guinea we could lay our hands on in tracking them down and bringing them to justice.'

'Or metin' out some justice of our own,' Crowe rumbled. 'The kind of justice that comes out of the barrel of a gun.'

'For once,' Mycroft conceded, 'I might just agree with you on that one.'

'Can't you send a Royal Navy ship to intercept this *Matilda Briggs*?'

Mycroft shook his head. 'I do not have the authority to dispatch a vessel for one boy, even if that boy is my brother. And even if I did I would not. Those ships have more important duties, guarding our coasts against attack and enforcing the will of the Queen abroad. Against that, the life of one child weighs as nothing.' He sighed, and clenched a fist helplessly. 'All of this discussion leaves us better informed but no better off. We cannot *help* Sherlock. He is on his own.'

'Sherlock on his own has better resources at his command than most people surrounded by friends an' family.' Crowe's tone was calmer now, and the fierce energy that had appeared to radiate from his body had abated somewhat. 'He's brave, he's strong an' he knows his own mind. Oh, an' he's handy with his fists as well. Ah think he'll think through his situation an' work out that he's got to make the best of it. He knows that the ship is comin' back to London, eventually, an' that gives him a guarantee of returnin' that he doesn't get if he tries to jump ship in mid-voyage an' find a ship comin' in the opposite direction. The captain will be short-handed, because captains always are, an' so he'll set the youngster to work. It'll be hard work, but he'll come through it. An' he'll probably come through it stronger an' more self-reliant as well.'

'Hardly the kind of torture that the Paradol Chamber was thinking of,' Mycroft pointed out dryly.

Crowe smiled. 'The people in charge of the Paradol Chamber, as far as ah can tell, live comfortable lives with servants tendin' to their every whim. For them, splicin' a main brace or haulin' anchor *would* be torture. For young Sherlock it'll be an adventure — if he chooses to make it so.'

'I hope so. I really do hope so.'

'Ah think ah'll take advantage of that dry sherry now,' Crowe said. 'God knows ah can't see the appeal of it mahself, but ah do feel in need of some strong liquor.'

Mycroft busied himself with pouring a glass for Crowe from the decanter on the sideboard.

'I will write letters,' he said as he handed the glass across. It was almost lost in Crowe's enormous and weather-beaten hand. 'They can be transmitted by telegraph to various ports along his route. I can ensure that diplomatic staffs are on the lookout for the *Matilda Briggs*. They can pass on our messages and report back on how he is. And he can write to us. There will be ships at every port he stops at which are heading back to England. They can bring letters back to us.'

'He'll only be gone for a year or so,' Crowe pointed out. 'Maybe less, wind an' weather permittin'. You'll see him again.'

Mycroft nodded. 'I know. I just . . . I feel so *responsible*. And so helpless.' He took a deep breath, steadying himself against some sudden storm of emotion. 'I shall not tell mother, of course. Her health would not stand it. And I will not write to father until I have more news – and perhaps not even then. I will send a note to our aunt and uncle in Farnham telling them that everything is all right. They do worry about him.'

'And ah'll find some way of tellin' Virginia 'bout what's happened,' Crowe said. 'An', frankly, that conversation scares me more than anythin'. She's really taken a fancy to that brother of yours.'

'And he to her,' Mycroft mused. 'Let's hope that the memories they have of each other are enough to keep them going . . .'

ANDREW LANE

BEDLAM

THINK YOU KNOW HIM? THINK AGAIN.

**Sherlock Holmes is insane.
He must be – he's in Bedlam.**

Sherlock has been incarcerated in the Bethlehem
Hospital – Bedlam – where Victorian London's most
unfortunate citizens are locked away in squalor, cruelty and
hopelessness. Sherlock tells them he's not mad –
but who'd believe a lunatic? There's only one option:
he has to escape – and then use all his rational powers to
work out who put him there in the first place . . .

An original short story – available exclusively as an eBook!

To find out more visit
www.panmacmillan.com/author/andrewlane

Find out more about

at

www.youngsherlock.com

**YOUNG SHERLOCK HOLMES –
THINK YOU KNOW HIM?
THINK AGAIN**